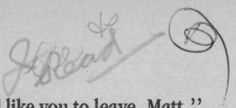

"I'd like you to leave, Matt."

She sat up and moved away from him.

A muscle in his cheek jumped. "I'm sorry if I offended you," he said. "Perhaps I didn't say it the way I meant it. Colorado can be a difficult place for a woman alone, especially a woman with a child. You need someone to—"

"I don't need anyone," she snapped. "I can take care of myself, and I can take care of Sarah." She glared at him. "I'm tired. I'd appreciate it if you'd leave."

Matt got up and started toward the door. "Think about what I've said, Carrie. If you change your mind..."

"I won't change my mind."

"I still want to help you," he said. "If I can do anything..."

"You can't."

He hesitated at the door. "It could be good between us." His voice was low. "I'd give you everything you've ever wanted..."

Dear Reader,

Welcome to Harlequin Historicals, where the new year could be any year—from the turn of the twentieth century to one as far back as our talented authors can take us. From medieval castles to the wide-open prairies, come join our brave heroines and dashing heroes as they battle the odds and discover romance.

In Barbara Faith's first historical, *Gamblin' Man,* Carrie McClennon's simple life is turned upside down by a notorious saloon owner.

Jasmine and Silk, from Sandra Chastain, is set on a Georgian plantation soon after the American Revolution.

Louisa Rawlings's *Wicked Stranger* is the sequel to her *Stranger in My Arms,* and tells the story of the second Bouchard brother.

A luckless Southern belle finds herself stranded in Panama in Kristie Knight's *No Man's Fortune.*

Four new adventures from Harlequin Historicals. We hope you enjoy them all.

Sincerely,

Tracy Farrell
Senior Editor

Gamblin' Man

Barbara Faith

Harlequin Books

TORONTO • NEW YORK • LONDON
AMSTERDAM • PARIS • SYDNEY • HAMBURG
STOCKHOLM • ATHENS • TOKYO • MILAN
MADRID • WARSAW • BUDAPEST • AUCKLAND

Harlequin Historicals first edition January 1993

ISBN 0-373-28755-0

GAMBLIN' MAN

BARBARA FAITH

After years of big-city life in places like Miami and San Diego, Barbara Faith now resides in a small Spanish colonial town in Central Mexico, where instead of the familiar sounds of cars starting and horns blowing, she wakens to church bells ringing, roosters crowing and burros braying.

Married to a Mexican matador who continues to be the inspiration for every book she writes, Barbara is happily content with life in Mexico.

To supportive writing friends
in my new home of San Miguel de Allende:
Berle Buchanan, Marne Martin, Celia Wakefield,
Charlie Magee, Marty Fraser, and last,
but never least, Sharon Steeber Orozco.

Chapter One

Denver, Colorado, 1895

It had never been this cold back in Ohio. And surely there'd never been this much snow. Powdery white, it drifted down in big fat flakes that covered everything in sight. Earlier in the day, clouds had almost hidden the mountains, and except for jagged snowcapped peaks, there had been little to see from the train window except for a vast wilderness of pines and endless stretches of snow.

A little after nine the train chugged into the Denver station and a kindly porter helped Carrie out with her luggage.

"The train for Cripple Creek will be along in a little while, ma'am," he said. Touching his fingers to his cap, he swung aboard, and Carrie stood there, watching the train disappear into the night, feeling more alone than she'd ever felt in her life.

With a shiver she pulled her gray serge cloak closer, picked up the portmanteau, her smaller carpetbag and hatbox, and headed for the dimly lit station.

A swish of wind propelled her inside when she opened the door. She hesitated there, confused by the startled stares of a dozen or so men. An elderly black man looked around. "Be right with you, ma'am," he said. Then he added a few pieces of wood to the potbellied stove in the middle of the room, slammed the door closed and hurried toward her.

"Let me take these for you," he said and, picking up her bags, motioned her to one of the straight-backed benches.

"Th-thank you." Carrie sat down. Keeping her eyes lowered, she tried to brush the snow off the cloak and the bottom of her skirt. Painfully aware of the men watching her, it was all she could do not to retreat outside. If it hadn't been for the wind, she would have.

Most of the men were rough looking and unshaven. Chins sunk low in the turned-up collars of their mackinaws, they silently appraised her. Two of them were chewing tobacco, and every now and then one of them would get up, open the door of the stove, and spit a splat of tobacco juice into the smoldering flames.

"Mighty cold evening."

Carrie looked up, and the word *dapper* came to mind as she took in the bowler hat, spats and pointy-toed shoes of the man standing in front of her.

"You on your way to Cripple Creek?"

She frowned, not at all sure she wanted to speak to this stranger.

"That's where I'm headed," he went on. "The way it's snowing though, we'll be lucky if we get there by morning." He took off the hat. "Mind if I sit down?" he asked, and then did, without waiting for her response. "Name's Nathan LaRue. Anything a'tall I can do for you, all you got to do is ask."

"How soon will the train be in?"

"Hard to say. Winter storm like this, no telling how long it'll take going through the mountains." The man carefully surveyed Carrie's gray feathered hat, the cloak and the high-buttoned shoes. "You got a place to stay in Cripple Creek?"

"I'm not sure. I..." Carrie hesitated. Her father, the Reverend Horacio McClennon, had warned her from the time she was a child about speaking to strangers, yet it seemed unfriendly to ignore this man when he was trying to be helpful. On the other hand, she didn't want to give him the wrong idea. "Yes," she said firmly. "I have a place to stay." And hoped that it was true.

Two months had passed since she'd had the letter from her sister, postmarked Cripple Creek. Carrie had written back, addressing the envelope to "Rosalinda McClennon, Cripple Creek, Colorado," but there hadn't been an answer. Which could have been, Carrie knew, because of the uncertain mail service or simply because she hadn't had a sufficient address for her sister.

Rosalinda had given up her acting career, she'd said in the letter. Though things had not been going too well for a while, they were better now. Her sister had made good friends...she hoped to find a job soon...and she had a darling little girl, Sarah, named after their mother. "She'll be three next month, Carrie, and she looks just like you," Rosalinda had written.

A child? Rosalinda had a child? Carrie had smiled, then her smile had faded because Rosalinda had not mentioned anything about a husband. Had he died? Had they separated, or... or what?

Her brows wrinkled in a frown, Carrie had read on.

Rosalinda spoke in glowing terms of Cripple Creek. It was a boomtown, she'd said, a prosperous gold min-

ing town of endless possibilities. A wonderful place to
start anew.

She had ended the letter by saying that she hoped
their mother and father were well, and that they had
forgiven her for running away.

But both their parents were dead. Their father had
drowned in a storm on the way to a tent meeting three
years before. Their mother, after a lingering illness, had
died a year ago. Carrie was alone; there had been nothing to keep her in Ohio. And though Josiah Wilkinson,
the preacher who had taken over as minister of the
church when her father died, warned her of the dan-
gers that lay in wait for a young lady traveling alone,
Carrie had refused to be dissuaded.

"You will not survive the ways of the Wild West,"
he'd said. "Sin is rampant there, temptation awaits the
unwary. Saloons on every street, drunken men, loose
women. It's no place for a decently raised Christian girl.

"Stay here," he'd said. "I have need of a wife."

Even now the thought of Josiah Wilkinson's slicked-
down thinning hair, pallid complexion and too-moist
mouth made Carrie shudder.

In spite of what he had said, or perhaps because of it,
Carrie had sold the small house where she had grown
up, paid off the bills that had accrued in the last months
of her mother's illness, and with what was left, set out
for Colorado.

Nathan LaRue kept up a steady stream of talk,
mostly about himself. There was a coarseness about him
that Carrie didn't like, and she was sorry that she had
let him sit next to her. Once on the train, she decided,
she would choose a seat by herself, and would explain
to him that she preferred to be alone—using the excuse
that she was tired.

Bored by all his talk but not wanting to be rude, Carrie glanced about the room.

That was when she saw him watching her.

Tall and well dressed, with a fur-lined greatcoat over his dark suit, he met her gaze, then looked from her to Nathan LaRue with narrowed eyes. He took a cheroot out of a pocket of his brocade vest, bit the end off and lit it. As the smoke drifted about his face, Carrie could discern the hard angles and planes, the no-nonsense nose, the square, thrusting jaw. There was something about him, something in the dark eyes closely scrutinizing the man sitting next to her, that sent a shiver through Carrie. But Nathan LaRue, absorbed in telling Carrie all about himself, seemed unaware of the man watching him.

Almost an hour passed before the train chugged into the station and the black man called out, "Train for Cripple Creek."

Men shuffled to their feet and gathered their gear together. LaRue picked up her portmanteau and led the way out of the station. As a gust of wind and whirling snow hit them, he put an arm around Carrie's waist. She stepped away.

The other men were behind them when LaRue lifted her portmanteau up into the train, along with the two small bags. "Allow me, ma'am," he said, and once again his arm encircled her waist.

"Please," she started to say as she placed her foot on the step, but before she could move away from him up into the train, he cried out, "What the hell?" When she turned, she saw that the man who had been watching LaRue had grabbed his shoulder, yanked him away from her, and sent him skidding and sliding across the snow-covered platform onto his backside.

Arms flailing in the air, LaRue's obscenities were all but drowned out by the cheers of the men who had followed them from the waiting room.

Before Carrie could react, the conductor shouted, "'Board!" and she was picked up and lifted into the train.

"Wait!" she gasped. "That poor man…what do you think you're doing?"

Mad as a peahen, she tore herself free and delivered a blow square on the shoulder of the man who was holding her.

He grinned, and, lifting her off her feet, headed into the coach and along the aisle to a maroon upholstered seat, where he unceremoniously plunked her down.

Carrie leaped up, but just as she did, the train, with a huff and a jerk, started forward, throwing her off balance and once again into his arms. He steadied her, his hands on her shoulders. Ready to fight, she looked up at him. And stopped. He was tall, well over six feet, and broad of shoulder. His black hair was damp from the snow. Heavy black eyebrows jutted over his dark green eyes. Black Irish, she decided, and dangerous.

He sat her down again and took the seat facing her as the train began its slow chug out of the station. Furious, Carrie turned away toward the window, just in time to see Nathan LaRue, his face contorted with anger, running alongside, frantically trying to catch up with them.

Turning on the man opposite her, Carrie said, "How could you? Heaven only knows when another train will be along. That poor man!"

Matt Craddock looked Carrie straight in the eye. "The poor man is a pimp," he said.

"I beg your pardon?"

"A pimp. A panderer. He recruits girls for some of Cripple Creek's cheaper parlor houses."

"Parlor houses?"

Matt raised one eyebrow. Either the young woman was putting on an act or she was the greenest greenhorn he'd met in a long time.

"A whor—a house of ill repute," he said. "Where men go to pay for the enjoyment of a young lady's companionship."

"Her companionship? I don't understand. What . . . ?" Color flooded Carrie's face. "Oh! Oh, you mean . . . and that man wanted me to . . . ? He thought that I—"

"He'd have gained your confidence, maybe said he'd help you find a place to stay once you got to Cripple Creek. He'd have taken you to one of our seedier hotels, would probably have drugged you by slipping something into your coffee, and you'd have come to in one of the houses he works for."

Carrie looked unbelievingly at the man sitting across from her. This had all seemed like a fine adventure when she'd set out, for though she had never been away from home before, she'd felt no trepidation about making the trip. In spite of what Josiah Wilkinson had said, she hadn't been afraid because, she'd known that when she reached her final destination, she would be reunited with her sister.

"You have very little money," Josiah had said.

"I have enough to keep me until I find a teaching job," she had answered, confident that with her teaching credentials from Ohio Northern University in Ada, and a letter from the principal of the Norwalk High School where she had taught for the past five years, she would have no trouble finding a position.

It had all seemed so simple in the early planning stages, but now, for the first time since she had left Ohio, Carrie felt a tremor of fear. She had known from Rosalinda's letter, and what little information she could find at the library, and in the local Norwalk newspaper, that mining towns had sprung up all over Colorado. Cripple Creek and the neighboring Victor had turned into actual boomtowns. There were hotels, grocery stores, churches, even an opera house. She had pictured it as a prosperous, cozy little town, a place to begin anew, as Rosalinda had said in her letter.

But now this man was telling her that there were actually houses of ill repute in Cripple Creek.

"I suppose there are saloons and gambling halls as well," she said with tightened lips.

"Enough to keep most men happy for a long, long time," Matt answered with a grin.

He was curious about her. He'd started up out of his own seat to help her with her bags when she'd first come into the station, but Albert had taken care of her, and then LaRue had made his move. He'd watched, waiting for her reaction.

She gave the appearance of being as prim and proper as a Sunday school teacher, but you could never tell about appearances. A lot of woman had been coming West these past few years, many of them looking for a husband who'd struck it rich. Some came as mail-order brides, others looking to get a job in one of the saloons, serving drinks, smiles or sometimes a song to the miners. A lot of them ended up in one of the parlor houses. This young woman didn't look the type to be singing in a saloon, so maybe she'd come West looking for a husband.

"Are you coming out here to get married?" he asked abruptly.

"Married?" Delicate eyebrows arched in question.

"I thought you might be one of those mail-order brides."

"Heavens no!" Carrie turned away from him and stared out into the night. What was wrong with Western men? she thought angrily. LaRue, if what the man opposite her had said was true, had wanted to recruit her for one of those sinful places. And this man assumed she was traveling to Cripple Creek to find a husband. Was that the choice of women coming West, the choice of becoming either a prostitute or a wife? She felt angry enough to spit.

"I didn't mean to offend you before when I hustled you up into the train, but Nathan LaRue is a bad character." He smiled. "Perhaps we could start over. My name is Matthew Craddock. And you are...?"

She hesitated, but some of her anger eased. If what he'd said about LaRue was true, he had done her a service in leaving the man behind.

"I'm Carrie McClennon," she said.

"McClennon?"

Carrie nodded. "I'm going to Cripple Creek to be with my sister."

Matt, who had leaned forward on his seat, now moved back, a quizzical expression on his face. "Does your sister know you're coming?" he asked.

"I'm not sure. She said that she was staying with friends, but she forgot to put a return address on the envelope. When I answered her letter, I simply addressed it to her at Cripple Creek, hoping it would reach her." A smile played at the corners of Carrie's lips. "If she didn't receive my letter, my arrival will be quite a surprise."

"Yes, I imagine it will be."

"We haven't seen each other in four years. She left home when she was sixteen." Then, as though defending Rosalinda, Carrie said, "Our father was a minister. I'm sure he meant well, and that he wanted only the best for us, but he didn't understand Rosalinda. Things were . . . were difficult for her at home."

The shadow of a smile crossed Carrie's face. "She was so different than I was. To begin with, she was the pretty one. She loved to sing. Sometimes she'd just burst into a song for no reason at all, a popular song, not a hymn, and Papa didn't like that. He was…he was awfully hard on her."

Tears stung Carrie's eyes and she turned away to stare out of the dark window into the night. When she spoke again, it was more to herself than to the man sitting across from her. "A theatrical group came to town. Rosie wanted to go, but Papa wouldn't allow it because he said it was sinful. But Rosie went anyway and when she came home Papa was waiting for her with the razor strap." She turned away from the window and looked at the man across from her. "She ran away from home that night. I never blamed her, but I wish she hadn't left without telling me. And now I want to tell her that I understand, that no matter what happened we're still sisters and that I love her."

Matt didn't say anything. He looked at Carrie, his dark eyebrows drawn together in a frown. He seemed about to speak, but before he could, Carrie said, "I'm sorry. I shouldn't have bored you with these personal things. I haven't really talked to anybody in over a week and I'm afraid I got carried away."

"You haven't bored me," he said. Again he hesitated, as though debating with himself. And finally said, "I know your sister."

"You know Rosalinda?"

Matt nodded.

"And her little girl?"

"Yes, I know Sarah."

Carrie stared at him. "Then you know where she is."

"I know where she was, Miss McClennon, but I've been in New York for a month. Your sister may have moved since I've been away."

"But you know her!" Excited now, anxious to know all about her sister and her little niece, Carrie said, "How is she? Is she all right? Who are the friends she was staying with? Do you know them?"

A smile twitched the corners of Matt's mouth. "Yes," he said. "I know them."

"Well, my goodness!" Smiling, Carrie sat back against the plush seat, hands in her lap, and looked expectantly at Matt Craddock. "What do you do in Cripple Creek, Mr. Craddock?"

"I own some saloons and a couple of gambling houses."

Carrie's eyes widened. "You're a gambling man?"

"That's right." He stretched his long legs out in front of him and grinned at her. "I reckon your daddy thought gambling was a sin and gamblers were sinners just like show people."

Lips pursed in a frown, Carrie said, "Yes, I suppose he did." She turned her attention to the window and stared out into the darkness. After a little while, she said, "I'm really quite tired, Mr. Craddock. I believe I'll try to sleep." She drew her gray cloak about her and closed her eyes. A gambler! She gave an inward shudder and resolved that as soon as they got to Cripple Creek she'd have nothing further to do with Matthew Craddock.

When Carrie woke she was shivering with cold. The lantern lights had been dimmed and the narrow-gauge train had begun to climb. She rubbed a hand against the frosty window and peered out into the night. Snow was coming down in thick heavy flakes and the wind was blowing so hard it rocked the coach.

She looked toward the small stove and saw that the fire that had kindled there had gone out. Huddling inside the gray cloak, she closed her eyes, but sleep was impossible. It was freezing cold, so cold that try as she might, she couldn't keep her teeth from chattering.

The train slowed and chugged to a stop. Carrie opened her eyes and looked out of the window.

"It's the storm," Matt Craddock said. "I don't think we're going to be able to get through."

"Not get through?"

"The mountain pass." He looked up as the conductor came down the aisle toward them, lighting his way with a lantern. When the man was abreast of him, Matt asked, "What's going on?"

"Tracks blocked up ahead, Mr. Craddock. We won't be able to move on until they've been cleared."

"When will that be?" Carrie asked.

"Not till morning, ma'am. It's going to be a long night. You'd best try to get some sleep."

"Sleep!" She sneezed. "I'm freezing to death."

"Sorry about that, but I'm afraid we've run out of wood. Don't you worry though, the tracks'll be cleared when the sun comes up."

"When the sun comes up!" Carrie muttered as the man made his way down the aisle. She glared at Matt as though this whole thing were his fault, gathered her cloak about her and determinedly closed her eyes. They snapped open when Matt Craddock sat down next to her.

"What are you doing?" she sputtered. "You can't—"

"If I don't, we're both going to freeze to death." He took his fur-lined greatcoat off, and, before Carrie could protest, he put his arm around her, drew her close, then covered both of them with his coat.

"You're so cold your teeth are chattering," he said when she tried to struggle out of his grasp.

"Let me go at once or I'll call the conductor!"

"Stop being childish. I'm just as cold as you are, and this way we'll both be warm."

"I demand that you . . ." She hesitated. The coat was still warm from his body. In spite of herself she snuggled lower so that the fur covered her chin. It was the first time she'd been warm since she'd gotten off the train in Denver.

"Isn't this better?" he asked.

"It's warmer," she murmured.

A smile curved at the corners of his mouth. "Think you can get to sleep now?"

Carrie tilted her face up and gave him a look that warned what would happen if he so much as laid one hand on her. Their faces were close, their lips only a fraction of an inch apart. She quickly bobbed her head down against the collar of his coat.

"Good night," she said.

And though she had promised herself that she wouldn't sleep lest he take advantage of her, little by little her eyes drifted closed and her breathing evened.

When he knew that she slept, Matt pulled her closer so that her head rested against his shoulder. She sighed and snuggled against him.

With a smile he tightened his arms around her and closed his eyes. His last conscious thought was that this was the first time he'd ever slept with a woman without making love to her. And that maybe one of these fine days he just might do something about that.

Chapter Two

The softness of fur brushed her cheek and Carrie snuggled down into it, closer to the warmth of the body next to hers. He...*he?* Her eyes snapped open.

"Good morning, Miss McClennon," Matthew Craddock said.

Carrie sat up and moved away from him, taken aback by the glint of humor in his eyes. The gray feathered hat had come off in the night, and her hair was undone from the pins that held it.

"Good morning," she murmured, and tried to brush the curly strands back from her face into a semblance of order.

"They cleared the tracks earlier this morning. We're on our way to Cripple Creek." Knowing she was uncomfortable, Matt stood and moved into the aisle. "The conductor made some coffee a few minutes ago," he said. "Would you like some?"

"Yes, thank you."

Still half-asleep, Carrie watched Matthew Craddock make his way toward the front of the car. The fine fabric of his suit coat stretched over his broad back. His legs were long, the trousers just the right length over his boots. He looked to be a powerful man, and the idea that she had actually slept with him all night brought hot color to her cheeks, along with the barest suggestion of a smile, because now if anyone ever asked if she'd slept with a man she could say that she had. That made her feel somehow more worldly than she had been the day before.

When he returned with a large mug of black coffee, she accepted it gratefully. Still wrapped in his coat, Carrie turned toward the window to gaze out at the passing countryside. The snow had stopped during the night, but the land was covered with it. The whole world seemed white and clean—the mountains, the tall straight pines, everything for as far as her eye could see.

"It's lovely," she said, sensing a silence in the land, and a beauty unlike anything she had ever known before.

"Yes, it is." But Matt wasn't looking out of the window. He was looking at her.

He really hadn't observed her closely last night, but he looked at her now. Her hair was a lustrous shade of auburn, her eyes were more gray than blue. She was not classically beautiful, but there was an endearing innocence and gentility about her that somehow touched him. Her gray suit, softened by a white shirtwaist pinned at the collar by a silver filigree brooch, seemed too severe, too old for her. And he found himself wondering how she would look in softer fabrics and lighter, more vibrant colors.

He also wondered how she would fare out here in this part of the country that seemed too wild for a woman of her obviously sheltered background. Her shock in learning about the parlor houses had been genuine, as had her dismay when she learned that he owned saloons and gambling houses.

Cripple Creek had come a long way since gold had been discovered back in 1891 over in Poverty Gulch, Matt thought as he sipped the mug of steaming coffee. When word of the discovery got around, people had rushed to Cripple Creek and in five years what had been little more than a mining camp had grown into a thriving town of almost twenty-five thousand people.

But in many ways Cripple Creek was still a gold camp, for along with the respected townspeople, the churches, the general stores and the schools, there were gambling halls, saloons, and, yes, parlor houses.

It wasn't the place for a woman like Carrie McClennon. He should have told her that last night when he learned that she was Rosalinda's sister. If her sister hadn't received the letter telling her that Carrie was on her way to Cripple Creek, it would be quite a surprise, for both of them.

Knowing that he should tell her what the situation was, Matt took a deep breath and said, "Miss McClennon?"

She turned. The fur from the collar of his coat brushed her face, and the sun streaming in through the window turned her skin to a shade of ivory touched with rose. He knew in that minute that he had been wrong, that she was, after all, quite beautiful.

Something quickened in Matt's body, seeing her that way, something he couldn't quite define. And he didn't say the words that might have made her turn around and go back to the life she knew.

Though Carrie argued that she would leave her bags at the station, Matt remained firm. It would be best, he told her, to check into a hotel before she found her sister. He gave her no opportunity to argue, he simply took her bags, put them into one of the rigs waiting at the station and, once he had helped her in, said, "The Palace Hotel."

The countryside on the approach to the town had been beautiful, and Carrie had gazed entranced at the distant Sangre de Cristo peaks that rimmed the far west edge of the bowl that encircled Cripple Creek. Her excitement had grown when the train chugged into the station. She knew she had been right to come. Soon she would see Rosalinda, and together with Rosie's little girl, she and her sister would make a whole new start.

But Carrie's excitement faded as the rig they were riding in made its way down the main street of the town. Flimsy pine shacks housed bakery shops, restaurants, a grocery and a meat market, a hardware store. Farther on they passed a One Price Shoes and Clothing House, a livery stable, the stage line, and *The Crusher,* that was, Matt told her, Cripple Creek's first newspaper.

She didn't see any saloons or what might have been gambling houses, and she didn't think the signs that read Furnished Rooms, were what Matt had called "parlor houses."

Horse-drawn wagons clattered up and down the street, the horses' breaths making puffs of white steam in the cold morning air. A few men and women, bundled in heavy coats and woolen caps, hurried in and out of the shops.

As their rig approached the Palace Hotel on Bennett Avenue, Carrie heard what sounded to her like a brass band. And just as they pulled up in front of the hotel, the band, all twenty-some pieces of it, rounded the corner at the far end of the street. Behind it, on a horse-drawn wagon, was a hearse, and behind that, several carriages filled with women.

As the cortege grew closer, Carrie gave an audible gasp. The women weren't like any she'd ever seen before. Their faces were painted. Even bundled in winter clothing they looked flashy. She stared at them open-mouthed and knew they were what her father would have called "fallen women."

Walking behind them came what looked like half the men in Cripple Creek.

So curious she could hardly take her eyes off the scene passing by the hotel, Carrie let Matt help her down from the rig.

"I've never seen anything like it," she said. "Look at all the people, and those women!"

Just then, two of the carriages with the painted ladies passed and one of the women called out, "Hey Matt! When'd you get back?"

"Just got in," he said.

"Come on over to the house tonight," said a big blonde wearing a purple velvet cape.

"We missed you," another girl shouted.

"Sure as hell did," someone else yelled, and all of the women waved their gloved hands or their muffs, calling out, "See you later, Matt. See you later."

He grinned and waved back.

"Those…those women are…are *loose* women, aren't they?" Carrie sputtered.

"Yes, ma'am, they surely are," Matt said with a grin.

"And you know them. You actually know them."

"I certainly do."

"Well!" Face averted, chin up, Carrie watched the procession pass on down the street. When Matt went to take her arm to lead her into the hotel, she jerked away, but since he had her bags, she had no choice but to follow him into the hotel.

He stopped in front of the desk. "A single room for the lady, Harry," he said to the man behind the desk. "Something in the back on the second floor, away from the noise."

"Sure thing, Matt." The man Matt had spoken to reached around behind him and selected a key. In his middle sixties, with a fringe of dusty hair around his otherwise bald head, he wore trousers that were held up by bright red suspenders, a startling contrast to his green-and-yellow-plaid shirt.

"We saw the funeral procession," Matt said. "Who died?"

"One of them women over at Charmaine's place. Rosalinda, the little red-haired gal."

"Rosa..." Carrie stared at the man, then at Matt.

There was a moment of total silence. Matt took a step forward. "Miss McClennon," he said. "Carrie."

Her face went white. "That's not my sister," she managed to say. "It can't be Rosalinda. She isn't dead."

"Carrie—"

"I...I know that Rosalinda isn't all that common a name, but it certainly isn't unusual. I mean a lot of women have the same name. They—"

Matt gripped her arms. "Take it easy," he said.

Her eyes had gone wide with shock, her face was ashen. She tried to struggle out of his grasp. "It isn't Rosalinda," she said again. "It can't be."

Matt tightened his grip on her arms. He was as sorry as death, but she had to know. "I think it is," he said. "For the last couple of months your sister was living at The Chateau, that's Charmaine's place. It's a parlor house, Carrie, but your sister wasn't—"

She pulled away from him. Tears of disbelief and anguish streamed down her face. Her little sister was dead and Matthew Craddock was trying to tell her that she had lived in a parlor house.

She gripped the edge of the desk. To the man behind it she said, as calmly as she could, "Would you be so kind as to have someone take my bags up to my room?"

He looked uncertainly at Matt. "Well, I..." he started to say, then cleared his throat and finished. "I'll attend to it right away, Miss McClennon."

"Thank you." She started out of the hotel.

"Wait," Matt said, and put a hand on her arm. "Where are you going?"

"To my sister's funeral."

"I'll take you."

She hesitated. The funeral cortege had already passed, she didn't know where the cemetery was. "Very well," she said. "Thank you. If you don't mind I'd like to freshen up first. It will only take a moment."

"Lavatory's at the end of the hall, ma'am," Harry Hotchkiss said.

"Thank you." Back straight, chin up, Carrie went down the dimly lighted hallway to the door marked Ladies. Once inside, she leaned against the door and closed her eyes, her shock and disbelief slowly replaced by shattering grief. Rosie was dead. Her sister was dead.

"Carrie fix... Carrie fix..." The words, like an almost forgotten song, echoed in her brain. It seemed to her as she stood there in that small, not-too-clean bathroom, that she could see the child her sister had been, holding her chubby arms out, crying, "Carrie, fix."

A broken doll, a scraped knee, a hard spanking from their father... whatever it was, Rosalinda had always come running to her.

But Carrie hadn't been able to fix whatever it was that had gone wrong in Rosalinda's life once she had left home. She'd been all alone and now she was dead and there wasn't anything Carrie could do about it. She hadn't been here when Rosie needed her, she'd come too late.

She splashed cold water on her face. Removing the gray hat, she combed her hair and straightened the bun at the back of her head. Then she brushed the specks of dirt off her long skirt and, gathering her cloak about her, left the bathroom.

She did not cry, because there was no time for tears. Later, when she was alone, there would be time.

Snow crunched beneath their shoes as Carrie passed through the wooden fence that encircled the cemetery. Matthew Craddock was by her side. The landscape was cold and harsh for as far as she could see. The mountains that before she had thought so majestic now looked only threatening.

Mourners circled the grave site. Matt took her arm and led her through the crowd so that she stood in front, closer to the minister and the rough pine box.

There was a faint stir of murmuring from the people gathered about. The minister paused in what he had been saying, then went on. "Rosalinda McClennon is in the hands of our Lord now," he said. "She..."

Carrie stared down at the cold hard earth. It's only a dream, she told herself. I'm going to awaken in a moment and this will all be over. But as the words went on, she knew that this wasn't a dream. Her sweet and loving little sister, who had been so filled with the bright joy of life that no one, not even their father, had been able to extinguish, was dead.

The service drew to a close. One by one the women, many of them weeping, stepped forward to drop a dried flower or a pine branch down onto the coffin. One of them handed Carrie a flower. She took it and laid it on the coffin. For a brief moment she rested her hand there, then she stepped back.

The brass band began to play an old familiar hymn. Matt Craddock tightened his arm around her shoulders and Carrie closed her eyes. When she opened them again, the casket had been lowered. People were leaving the cemetery, but some of the women remained there, huddled in small groups, wiping their eyes, comforting one another. Then one of them, a tall, handsome woman in her early forties, dressed in a wool suit with a fur collar and cuffs and a fur-lined cloak, stepped away from the others and came toward them.

"It's a sad day, Matt," she said, wiping her eyes. "We've lost Rosalinda." She looked inquiringly at Carrie. "Did you know her?" she asked.

"She was my sister," Carrie said.

The woman's dark eyes widened with shock. "Your sister?"

"This is Carrie McClennon, Charmaine," Matt said. "Carrie, this is Charmaine Duval. She's the owner of The Chateau."

The Chateau? "One of them women over at Charmaine's place," the man at the hotel had said.

Charmaine owned The Chateau. She was a madam. Rosalinda had worked for her.

Later, Carrie told herself. I'll think about this later.

She wet her lips. "I'd like to know..." She took a deep breath to steady herself. "I'd like to know how my sister died, Miss Duval. Was she alone when it happened? Was she..." She couldn't go on.

"Why no, honey, Rosie wasn't alone. I was with her and so were the others—Effie and Lorelei and Miss

Binty. We were right there with her, holding her hand. We did everything we could, and Doc Taylor did everything he could to try to save her."

"What did she . . . ?" Carrie swallowed hard. "What did Rosalinda die of? What was the cause of her death?"

"Pneumonia, Miss Carrie. She'd caught a cold last fall and it just kept hanging on and hanging on till it went to pneumonia."

"When did she die, Miss Duval?"

"Yesterday."

Yesterday. If the train hadn't been delayed because of the snow she might have arrived in time to "fix" things as she had so often. Maybe she could have . . . Carrie's knees buckled. She knew she was falling but it didn't matter, nothing mattered, for the blackness of the grave had closed in about her, too.

Carrie remembered little of the carriage ride back to the Palace Hotel. She opened her eyes once and tried to tell Matt Craddock that she was all right, but that seemed like too much of an effort. The next time she opened her eyes, she was in bed and Matt and a man she had never seen before were looking down at her.

"How're you feeling?" the strange man asked.

"I . . . I don't know." She pushed herself up on the pillows. "Who are you?"

"Dr. Elsworth Taylor, at your service, ma'am."

"Where am I?"

"At the Palace Hotel. Matt and Miss Charmaine brought you here. She loosened your clothes and sent somebody running for me. Don't appear to me that there's anything bad wrong with you 'cept maybe the beginnings of a cold. Mostly I think you're tuckered out. Good-night's sleep and you ought to be just fine.''

He reached for the black bag on the nightstand beside the bed and snapped it shut. "Anything you want, you tell Matt or old Harry downstairs.''

"I will. Thank you.''

"Then I'll be running along.'' He nodded to Matt and with an "I'll see you later,'' went out of the room.

"I fainted.'' Carrie pushed herself further up in the bed. "I've never done that before.''

"You had a bad shock.''

"Yes.'' She looked away from him. "You knew that Rosalinda was living at that place, didn't you? You knew she was a...was a..'' Tears filled Carrie's eyes and she couldn't go on.

"Rosalinda was living at The Chateau because she was down on her luck and had nowhere else to go,'' Matt said. "Charmaine took her and Sarah in.''

"Charmaine, the...the madam?''

"Yes.''

"And my sister...my sister lived in that place with her child?''

"Yes, she did.'' Matt took a cheroot out of his vest pocket, hesitated, then put it back. "I know what you're thinking,'' he said, "but you're wrong. Your sister wasn't working at The Chateau. She was a guest there.''

"A guest?'' Carrie shook her head. "I find that hard to believe, Mr. Craddock.'' Her lips tightened. "Is Rosalinda's little girl still at The Chateau?''

"I imagine so.''

Carrie sat up. "I have to take her away from there. It's no place for a child, there with those...those women. I have to take her out of there.''

"You're going back to Ohio?"

"On the first train I can get. I..." Carrie stopped and a look of utter dismay came over her face. She couldn't leave! She didn't have enough money to leave! She had enough for the train fare, but that was all. Most of the money she'd got for selling the house had gone to pay off the debts she had incurred during her mother's last illness. She'd bought some new clothes: a traveling suit, a few new shirtwaists, a pair of boots, the cloak and the hat, assuming she would move into her sister's house until she found work.

But there wasn't a house, at least not the kind of a house Carrie had thought Rosalinda lived in. Her sister was dead; she had Rosalinda's child to take care of.

She had no choice, she would have to stay in Cripple Creek until she had enough money to take both of them back to Ohio.

She thought then that the Reverend Josiah Wilkinson had said he had need of a wife. She could...no! She could not! Whatever might happen, she could never become Josiah Wilkinson's wife.

"I won't be going back to Ohio, at least not for a while," she told Matt.

"What are you going to do?"

"I was a teacher back home," Carrie said. "I'm sure I can find work here." She smoothed a wrinkle out of the patchwork quilt. "I want to thank you for helping me, Mr. Craddock. But I'm all right now and it really isn't proper, your being here I mean."

"Then by all means I will absent myself," he said in a voice as formal as hers had been. "I've sent down to the restaurant for some dinner for you. I'll leave as soon as it arrives."

A knock sounded at the door, and when he opened it, a boy handed him a tray. Matt paid him, and when he'd closed the door, he brought the tray back and set it across Carrie's lap.

"I hope it's all right," he said.

"I'm sure it will be. If you'll hand me my bag, Mr. Craddock, I'll reimburse you."

"The dinner's on me." He gathered up his coat from the chair. "And my name is Matt, Carrie."

She nodded. "Thank you . . . Matt. I'm sorry to have been such a bother."

"No bother, Miss Carrie." He started toward the door, then hesitating, turned back. "I'm very sorry about your sister," he said. "If there's anything I can do for you, please don't hesitate to call on me."

"I'd like to go to that place, to The Chateau, tomorrow. I don't know where it is or how to get there, and I'd appreciate it, if it wouldn't be too much trouble, if you would take me there." Her gray eyes darkened. "I simply cannot let Rosalinda's little girl stay in a place like that any longer than necessary."

"No, I don't suppose you can." Matt looked at her, one eyebrow raised. "I have some business to attend to in the morning, but I should be finished by noon. I'll come by for you then." He put the fur-lined coat over his shoulders and started toward the door. But there he hesitated once more. Taking a cheroot out of his pocket, he snapped the end off with his teeth.

"You really should go back to Ohio, Miss Carrie," he said. "You don't belong here."

And before she could answer, he went out and closed the door behind him.

Carrie stared at the closed door, then at the tray of food on her lap. Tears ran down her face and splashed into the bowl of vegetable soup. She knuckled them away. I won't cry, she told herself. I absolutely will not cry.

Nor would she think about Rosalinda, because if she did, she would not be able to stand the pain of having lost the one person in the world she had loved above all others. She would think instead about her niece. Sarah was her responsibility now. With the money she had left, she would find a small house to rent and she would get a job. She would care for and love Rosalinda's child. She would . .

The tears kept coming and she could not stop them. She wept for the sister she had lost, and for her own desperate situation. And because she didn't want to be here in this godforsaken place with fallen women and gambling men. She wanted to be home. She wanted to be safe.

Chapter Three

Carrie spent an almost sleepless night going over the events of the previous day that seemed like a terrible dream.

Rosalinda was dead.

She had lived in a house of prostitution.

Matt Craddock had told her that Rosalinda had only been a guest in the house, that she had lived there because she had nowhere else to go. With all her heart, Carrie wanted to believe that, but she did not.

She wished that she had never left home, but she had, and now she had to stay in Cripple Creek until she made enough money to take Rosalinda's little girl back to Ohio. Thinking of the child, who was still in that dreadful place where Rosalinda had died, Carrie started to get up. But the moment she did, the room began to spin.

She lay still for a moment and closed her eyes until the room stopped spinning. Her head throbbed, her throat was sore, and every bone in her body ached. It was an effort to move, but finally, clinging to the bedpost to keep her balance, she managed to stand. No matter how she felt, she had to get up and get dressed.

She had to retrieve her sister's child from that terrible place, and those dreadful women.

Last night Matt had returned to see if there was anything he could do for her. "I'll be here as soon after my appointment as I can manage," he'd promised before he left. "At any rate, Charmaine and the other girls rarely get up before noon."

"Noon!" Carrie had been shocked. "But by then half the day is gone. Why...?" And she'd blushed to the roots of her auburn hair because she'd suddenly realized that the ladies would be sleeping late because they'd have been plying their trade until the wee hours of the morning.

In as controlled a voice as she could manage, she had said, "Very well, Mr. Craddock. I'll be ready whenever you arrive." Then, in spite of the fact that she felt uncomfortable with him, that he was a stranger, a gambler, and that he obviously had more than a nodding acquaintance with the painted ladies who had gone to Rosalinda's funeral, she had offered her hand and said, "Thank you for all the help you've given me. You've been very kind. I'm most grateful."

"I'm glad I was there to help," he'd answered. "I know your sister's death must have been a terrible shock."

Unable to answer, Carrie had only nodded.

Now, shivering with cold, she got up and went to the dresser. The water in the pitcher had frozen during the night and she stood for a moment, holding her robe around her, moaning in frustration before she picked up her hairbrush and proceeded to whack through the top layer of ice with the handle. Pouring the freezing cold water into the white porcelain basin, she bathed as quickly as she could. And when she had finished she began to dress. First came the plain cotton chemise, then her corset, a cotton camisole, bloomers of white muslin over her corset, and a flannel petticoat. At last she slipped a black worsted dress over her head, smoothed the skirt and put on her shoes.

Still dizzy, she had to sit down to brush and pin up her long auburn hair. When that was done, she lay back against the headboard of the bed and closed her eyes. At eleven-thirty, knowing that although she wasn't hungry she had to eat something, she put on her gray hat and, with her cloak over her arm, went downstairs to the dining room.

She had hot tea and forced herself to eat a piece of toast. When she had finished, she went into the lobby to wait for Matthew Craddock. He arrived a little after twelve-thirty, looking rich and warm in his fur-lined greatcoat. He was, Carrie reluctantly admitted to herself, a devilishly handsome man. And certainly *devil* was the right word. There was a glint of wickedness in his green eyes and something about the curve of his mouth that made him look dangerous.

"Ready?" he asked.

"Yes, I..." Carrie got up from the chair in the lobby where she'd been waiting. When she did, she was overcome by another wave of dizziness and had to put a hand on the back of the chair to steady herself.

"Are you all right?" Matt asked.

"Yes, I'm...I'm fine. Just a little tired, that's all. Shall we go?"

He put a hand under her elbow and led her out through the lobby. "It's only a few blocks to Myers Avenue," he said, "but the temperature is below zero this morning. I've brought my rig."

"Myers Avenue?"

"That's where most of the gambling halls and the saloons are." Matt glanced down at her. "The houses are there, too."

"The houses?"

"Like The Chateau."

"Oh." Holding herself erect, mentally and physically bracing herself, Carrie allowed Matt to help her into the rig and place a fur-lined robe over her knees.

She looked straight ahead when they started off, as though, like Lot's wife, she'd be turned into a pillar of salt if she so much as looked at the scene around her.

Matt repressed a smile when he saw the rigid expression on her face. This was still the better part of town.

He could only imagine what kind of a shock it had been to discover that her sister was dead and that she had been living in a place like The Chateau. But though Carrie McClennon was in an atmosphere that was completely foreign to her, her jaw was firm and her back was straight. He knew she couldn't wait to get out of Cripple Creek, that all she wanted to do was to get her sister's child and take the first train back to Ohio, as well she should. Cripple Creek wasn't her kind of town; the sooner she left, the better it would be for her.

When he turned onto Myers Avenue and passed the pine shacks that were the cribs along Poverty Gulch, he saw her eyes go wide with shock. In spite of the cold, some of the doors were half-open, and the girls, bundled in coats or shawls, stood in their doorways looking for early customers.

"Are they..." Carrie looked at him, then quickly away. "Are they... you know?"

"Yes."

"Is The Chateau..." It was hard to get the words out. "Is that the kind of place The Chateau is?"

"Of course not. These poor girls are at the bottom of the ladder. The Chateau isn't anything like that."

A little farther on they heard music and laughter coming from the saloons. And Carrie spied drunks loitering on the street. At the end of the block two disreputable-looking miners were slugging it out. Blood ran down the face of one of them, and the carriage passed so close that Carrie could hear their grunts and the impact of fists on flesh.

Suddenly, almost in front of them, a man shot out of the swinging doors of one of the saloons and landed on his backside. He picked himself up, dusted himself off and staggered back through the doors.

Carrie clutched the side of the rig. She'd been right, the town really was a Sodom and Gomorrah.

A little farther along they came to the better houses: Laura Bell's, The Harem, Nellie Grady's, The Pleasure Palace, the Manor House, and finally The Chateau, a plain two-story house at the end of the block. There were lace curtains at the windows, and an American flag flying from the roof.

When Matt brought the rig to a halt, Carrie clutched the side of her seat. She had to go in, but the thought of stepping over the threshold of such a place filled her with horror. Nevertheless, when Matt offered his hand to help her down, she took it.

They went up the two steps to the front door. He knocked and, when the door was opened by an elderly gray-haired woman, he said, "Good afternoon, Miss Binty. May we come in?"

"Course, Mr. Matt." She opened the door and offered Carrie a tentative smile. "You must be Miz McClennon," she said. "We're all mighty sorry about your sister, ma'am. Every one of us is going to miss her. You surely do have my condolences."

"Thank you." Carrie took another step into the room.

She wasn't sure what she had expected—satin-covered beds in the parlor probably, semi-naked women, and a hoard of drunken, sex-crazed men. Instead, what she found was a fairly ordinary front parlor. There were two love seats in the room, a wooden rocker and several straight-backed chairs. A pigeon-blood glass lamp graced one of the carved tables, an Edison phonograph sat atop another. The floor was covered with an Oriental rug, and red velvet drapes framed the lace curtains.

"Could I get you a cup of coffee or maybe a nice cup of tea?" Miss Binty asked.

"No, thank you. I..." Carrie looked up to see Charmaine Duval coming down the stairs toward her. Behind Charmaine came five young women. While Charmaine and two of her girls were conservatively dressed in long dark skirts and white shirtwaists, most of the others were not. One of the girls, who looked to be no more than fifteen or sixteen, with carrot-red hair and a freckled face, wore a cotton housedress and an old gray sweater that hung halfway to her knees.

A slightly plump girl, with the brightest yellow hair Carrie had ever seen, wore a flowered silk kimono. Another, a dark-skinned girl with a wild untamed mane of black hair, wore a blue flannel bathrobe.

"These are my girls," Charmaine said, her face solemn, her dark eyes serious. Motioning them forward, she introduced them one by one.

"This is Babette."

A small girl with soft brown eyes curtsied and said, "How do, ma'am."

"And Dorrie O'Keefe."

The girl with the yellow hair stepped forward.

Next came the red-haired, freckled-faced girl. "Effie Davis," Charmaine said, and the girl offered a tentative smile.

"And Conchita Sanchez."

The dark-skinned woman with the wild mane of black hair said, "*Mucho gusto*, Señorita McClennon, *a sus ordenes*, I am at your service." She looked up at Matt and with a wink added, "And at yours, Señor Craddock."

"Behave yourself, Conchita," Charmaine snapped. And motioning the last girl forward, she said, "This is Lorelei, Miss McClennon. She and Effie are the ones who's mostly been tending to Rosalinda's little girl."

"How do you do," Carrie said, stiffly polite. She tried not to stare, but she couldn't help herself. The girls were all younger than she was. And they didn't look like what she knew they were.

"I know you'd like to see Sarah," Charmaine said. "She's sleeping right now, but we can wake her up. I've told her her auntie's coming and she's excited as she can be. Let's go on upstairs."

Upstairs? Carrie glanced nervously upward, then looked at Matt. He raised his dark eyebrows and she found herself wondering how many times he had trod those stairs, and with whom.

She didn't want to go up, but she had no choice. With a nod she followed Charmaine. When they reached the top of the stairs, she stared straight ahead, not even daring to look inside any of the rooms for fear of what she might see.

"This is my room." Charmaine stood aside and motioned Carrie in.

It was a room not unlike her bedroom back in Ohio. There was a double four-poster with a colorful patchwork quilt, a marble-top dresser on which rested a curling iron, a silver-backed hairbrush and a pearl-covered box for hairpins. There was a spittoon in the corner and a chamber pot under the bed. Off to one side, there was a smaller bed where Rosalinda's little girl lay sleeping.

Carrie looked down at the child. Sarah lay on her stomach, one small fist up to her mouth. Her hair was tousled, her cheeks were apple red.

Tears flooded Carrie's eyes. She tried to stem them, but it seemed to her, as she looked down at the child, that she was looking at the little girl Rosalinda had once been. She touched one rosy cheek, then covering her eyes with her hands, turned away, silently weeping for the sister she had lost, for the child who was now her responsibility, and for her own desperate situation.

Far away from the only home she had ever known, she had barely a hundred dollars to her name. It would have been enough for a train ticket and to last her until she found another teaching job if she'd had a home to go back to. But she'd sold the house and now she couldn't afford to take the chance of going back, not with a child to support. She had no choice, she had to stay in this dreadful town until she could find a job and save enough money to get them back to Ohio.

"Now, now," Charmaine soothed as she led Carrie to the bed. "Go on and cry if you want to, honey. Get it all out, you'll feel better if you do."

"I'm . . . I'm all right," Carrie managed to say.

Charmaine patted Carrie's shoulder and handed her a white lace handkerchief. "I reckon this has been a terrible shock, you coming all this way only to find your sister dead. Best thing you can do, soon's you're rested some, is to go on back home to Ohio."

"I can't go back," Carrie wept. "I spent almost all the money I had getting here. I thought Rosalinda and I would live together. I thought we would..." The tears started again. "I can't go back," she said again, "not until I get a job and make enough money to take Sarah back home with me."

"You could stay here for a while, Miss Carrie," Charmaine offered. "You could have the little room downstairs that was Rosie's. You could—"

"No!" Carrie swiped away the tears with the back of her hand and quickly stood. But when she did, a wave of dizziness overcame her and she saw dark spots before her eyes. As she grasped the bedpost, from a great distance she heard the other woman asking, "What is it? Are you all right?"

Carrie tried to speak, but the words wouldn't come. She fell back onto the bed just as the dark spots converged into one great darkness.

Carrie opened her eyes to see the doctor who had attended her the day before standing over her.

"How you feeling, missy?" he asked.

"Head aches," she managed to croak.

"Throat sore?"

Carrie nodded.

"She's got the grippe all right," he said to someone in the room. When Carrie turned her head, she saw Matt Craddock at the foot of the bed, standing next to the Duval woman.

"Can't risk taking her out in the cold," the doctor went on. "She gets one blast of the wind and we'll be worrying about pneumonia."

"She can stay here," Charmaine said.

Here! Carrie tried to sit up, but the effort was too much for her. "Hotel," she tried to say. "I want to go back to the hotel." But the words were little more than a whisper that no one heard.

"That's real nice of you, Charmaine." Doc Taylor closed his black bag. "You give her a spoonful of this medicine every four hours, day and night. I'll check back in the morning. If she gets any worse before then, you send someone to get me."

"I will, Doc. Thank..."

The voices faded and Carrie's last thought as she drifted off was that she was going to have to spend the night in a house of ill repute. What would Papa have had to say about that?

"Papa," she whispered. "I'm sorry, Papa."

Sorry, sorry, sorry. How many times over how many years had she said those words to the father whose credo had been Spare The Rod And Spoil The Child? How many times had she watched the bushy black brows furrow, the cold eyes darken, and heard his voice thunder?

She moaned, caught in that half world of sleep and wakefulness, trying to fight the memory of those childhood years when through painful experience she had learned to be submissive. Learned not to speak unless she was spoken to, especially at mealtime, and learned never to speak back to her parents.

Once, when she was seven, she had rushed to defend her four-year-old sister. Rosalinda, determined she would not eat the mashed yellow squash that had been placed in front of her, had defiantly pushed the plate off the table onto the floor.

Their father's black brows had come together, his eyes had darkened. Their mother, in a voice quivering with fear, begged, "Horacio, please," as he yanked Rosalinda up out of her high chair, and snatching the strap that hung on the back of the kitchen door, had commenced to beat the child.

Carrie had flown at him. She'd pounded her small ineffectual fists against his legs, crying, "Let my sister go! Let my sister go!"

He had. And then he had whipped Carrie so badly that she hadn't been able to go to school the next day.

Carrie had learned, and, though in the years that followed she had done her best to protect her sister, she had never again openly defied their father.

When she grew older she had sung in the church choir and taught Sunday School, and when she had found herself mouthing the same words her father had spoken—"Never talk back to your parents.... Children must be seen and not heard.... Playing cards is a sin.... Dancing is a sin..."—she sometimes stopped in mid-sentence.

And when she cringed at her father's hell, fire and brimstone Sunday sermons, she tried to tell herself he was only trying to save the souls of his parishioners. The Sunday he pointed his finger at sixteen-year-old Maybelle Hunnicut and said, "I know all about you, Maybelle. I know you went buggy riding after last Wednesday night's prayer meeting with the oldest Carvell boy."

Arms folded over the pulpit, his face mottled with righteous indignation, he had roared, "Methodists! The Carvells are Methodists! And you..." He'd shaken a bony finger down at the weeping girl. "Ridin' around back country roads. Spoonin', fornicatin'..."

Carrie had wanted to leap to her feet and defend the hapless girl. She'd wanted to cry out, "You have no right to say those things." But she hadn't. And when, beside her, Rosalinda had whispered, "I hate him. I hate him," she had squeezed her sister's hand, silencing her.

But Rosalinda, in the years that followed, had not remained silent. Too many times she had spoken out against their father, defying him, even in the face of punishment, until at last she had run away.

Memories of that fateful night came into Carrie's dreams, the night she had tried to defend her sister against their father, and later had held the weeping girl in her arms.

"Rosie," she whispered. "Oh, Rosie."

"Shush now, Miss Carrie," someone said. A wet cloth was laid on her brow, a cool hand soothed hers.

She floated in and out of consciousness, and whenever she woke, someone spooned medicine into her mouth.

"Awful, ain't it?" a voice said one morning when Carrie made a face. "But I reckon medicine has to taste bad 'fore it does you any good, leastwise that's what my mama always said."

She smoothed Carrie's pillows and eased her back down. "You just rest now and don't worry about anything. You're getting better every day."

"Thank you," Carrie whispered. Wanting to say more but feeling too weak to speak, she simply closed her eyes.

There were times when she became aware of either Effie or Charmaine hovering over her, and of the doctor who came and went. And once she opened her eyes to see Matt Craddock at the foot of her bed, holding little Sarah.

"This is your Aunt Carrie," Matt told the child. "She's been sick but she's getting better."

"Hello," Carrie said. "How are you, Sarah?"

"Fine." Thumb in her mouth, the little girl looked down at her. "My mommy went away," she said.

"I know, honey. But I'm your auntie and I'm going to take care of you."

"Aunt Carrie has to rest now, Sarah," Matt told the child. "You can come back tomorrow."

"Will you put me to bed, Uncle Matt?"

He kissed her cheek. "Of course I will, honey. You're my favorite girl, aren't you?"

The child hugged his neck. "Rest now," he said to Carrie.

The next time Carrie woke it was morning. Sunshine streamed across the counterpane, and for the first time since she had fallen ill her head was clear. She looked around as Charmaine, dressed in a navy blue wool skirt and a white shirtwaist with leg-of-mutton sleeves, came in with a tray.

"Good morning," she said. "I do believe you're feeling better."

"Yes, I am." Carrie sat up. "How long have I been here?"

"A little over a week."

"A week!"

Charmaine nodded. "You been real sick, honey. Doc was doing his best, but when you didn't seem to be getting any better Matt sent to Denver for another doctor. He came two days ago. Whatever he gave you must've helped because your fever broke last night. Now all you got to do is rest and get well.''

Matt Craddock had sent to Denver for a different doctor? Carrie groaned inwardly. She would have to repay him, of course, as well as paying the local doctor. Bit by bit her last hundred dollars was dwindling.

"I'm sorry that I've been so much trouble," she said. "I'm better now and I'm sure that by tomorrow I'll be able to go back to the hotel."

Charmaine shook her head. "That high-priced Denver doctor said you were to stay in bed for at least another four or five days and that's what you're going to do." As though to emphasize her words, she plumped Carrie's pillows and said, "Rosie was your sister, Miss Carrie. That means you're practically one of the family."

"But I'm inconveniencing you," Carrie protested. "This is your room."

"I'm doubling up with Dorrie and we're managing. Sometimes she sleeps downstairs on the sofa. Sometimes I do. We work it out."

When there were special customers? Carrie wondered. She looked at Charmaine, then away. This was such a puzzle. She had been brought up to believe there were bad women and good women. Her father would have said that Charmaine and the women who worked for her were bad. Yet they had cared for her sister and her child, and now her. She couldn't get it straight in her mind.

Charmaine helped her to sit up, then placed the tray across her lap. "Soon's you're done eating I'll have Miss Binty bring up hot water so you can wash," she said.

"I'm awfully sorry to be so much trouble."

"You aren't any trouble at all. We all thought a lot of Rosalinda. We felt real bad when she died and when you came it was a little like having her back with us."

"Matt...Mr. Craddock said that she didn't..." Carrie hesitated, not sure how to phrase the question she wanted to ask but needing to know. "Mr. Craddock said that Rosalinda wasn't...employed here. He said that she was more like a guest, but I'm afraid I find that hard to believe. I'd like to know the truth."

Charmaine's face went suddenly still. In a cold, expressionless voice, she said, "Your sister wasn't a whore, if that's what you're asking. She and Sarah had a little room off the kitchen and she didn't hardly come upstairs unless it was to visit one of the girls."

Her blue eyes bright with anger, Charmaine looked down at Carrie. "Your sister told me about her family and I was the one who told her to write you. Right now I wish I hadn't. She loved you and she loved your ma. She didn't say too much about your father, but from what little she did say it sounded to me like he was as mean a son of a bitch as ever lived."

Hands on her hips, Charmaine glared down at Carrie. "She told me how you used to stand up for her when you were little girls, and without even knowing you, I liked you because of that. I even thought maybe you'd be like her. But you aren't. Rosie treated everybody alike, nice proper folks and folks like me and the girls. She didn't judge anybody. But you do. You're just as much of a self-righteous so-and-so as your daddy was."

With that, Charmaine went out and slammed the door.

Carrie swallowed hard. No one had ever talked to her the way Charmaine had. No one had ever made her feel so small that she wanted to retreat under the covers and pull the blankets over her head.

But she didn't slink down under the blankets. Instead, placing the slightly heavy tray to one side, she threw them back and stood up. Or tried to.

"Charmaine?" she called out, and started toward the door. "Charmaine, wait!"

Charmaine opened the door. "What in blazes do you think you're doing getting out of bed?" she snapped.

"I wanted to..." Carrie swayed and would have fallen if Charmaine hadn't run to put an arm around her waist. She held her up and steered her back toward the bed.

"I wanted to tell you..." Carrie took a deep gulping breath. "I'm sorry. I didn't mean to hurt your feelings. I apologize. I—"

"Get back in bed. You're white as a sheet."

"Miss Duval... Charmaine... please. I'm more grateful than I can say for your taking care of Rosalinda and Sarah. I don't mean to be judgmental. It was the way I was raised, I guess. I... I can't seem to help it."

Charmaine eased her back into the bed. "Maybe you can't," she said. "It don't bother me none, you thinking you're better than me and the girls, or the fact that you don't like me, which is all right with me because I don't reckon I like you, either." She yanked the blankets up over Carrie's shoulders. "But I catch you being uppity with my girls or looking down on them, I'll throw you out in the snow on your ass, no matter what that fancy Denver doctor says."

Carrie stared up at the other woman, her eyes wide with shock. "I'd never do that," she whispered. "I'd never—"

But Charmaine had already gone out and slammed the door behind her.

Chapter Four

Not strong enough to get up and out, but well enough to be restless and aware of what was going on around her, Carrie fretted away the next few days.

"Be another week before you can be up and around," Doc Taylor said. "It's cold as a buzzard's nose outside and the snow's dern near up to your armpits. You just stay on here at Miss Charmaine's till you get your strength back."

And though Carrie argued, the doctor stuck to his guns. She wasn't to leave The Chateau until he said so.

Ever since her altercation with Charmaine, Carrie had felt even more uncomfortable about being there at The Chateau. One morning, determined to leave, she had gotten up and bathed. But by that time she was so weak, she lay back on the bed, half-dressed.

"You can't go nowhere yet, Miss Carrie," Effie said when she found her there. "You just gotta do what Doc Taylor says. You gotta get your strength back 'fore you start traipsin' around." She patted Carrie's hand, then helped her undress and get into bed. "I reckon you're bored stiff having to lay around," she said. "How'd it be if we moved Sarah's bed back in so's the two of you can start getting acquainted? Would you like that?"

That afternoon Effie and a man Carrie had never seen before, brought the smaller bed in and put it next to Carrie's.

"This here's Noah Pierce," Effie said. "He plays the piano downstairs and keeps things orderly, just in case any of the gentlemen get out of hand. They don't hardly never though, because Miss Charmaine is mighty particular about the kind of...of..." She struggled for the word and the man said, "Clientele."

Tall and lanky, with sandy hair and a plain and honest face, Noah Pierce appeared to be in his late twenties. His striped pants were just a little too short and his shirtsleeves were just a little too long. But his brown eyes were as warm as his smile as he took Carrie's hand and said, "How do, Miss Carrie. We sure are glad you're feeling better. And won't it be nice having Sarah in here with you. She's as good as she is pretty and I don't hardly believe she'll be any trouble at all."

The little girl wasn't any trouble. Though shy at first, Sarah soon warmed to Carrie. During the day, she played on the floor beside Carrie's bed or sat on the bed next to Carrie while Carrie told her stories about her mother and how it had been when she and Rosalinda were young.

Carrie had expected to love this niece of hers, but she had not expected the love to come so quickly or so deeply. Nor had she expected the almost overwhelming emotion she experienced when she watched Sarah at play, or felt the small hand resting on her arm when she read her a story. Sarah was her own special self, and yet there was so much of Rosalinda in her that when Carrie kissed her good-night, it seemed to her as though she were looking at Rosalinda at that age.

"Good night, darling," she said each night.

"Night, Auntie Carrie."

"Sleep tight, baby."

"You, too." And when Sarah held her arms up for that last hug, something wonderful clutched at Carrie's heart, for Sarah was her child now and she would love her as she had loved Rosalinda.

The only thing that bothered her was Sarah's constant references to her "Uncle Matt."

"Uncle Matt took me and Mama for rides in his buggy before she went away," she'd tell Carrie. "Sometimes he brought me and Mama candy. He still brings me candy, but he says I can't eat it unless I eat all of my dinner. How come, Auntie Carrie? How come?"

"Because sweets are for after dinner," Carrie said. "First come vegetables and bread and meat. If there's still room in your tummy after that then you can have a piece of candy."

Sarah also spoke in glowing terms about her Auntie Charmaine, as well as her other "aunties." She loved them all, especially Effie.

Effie Davis appeared even younger than her fifteen years. She looked, Carrie thought, like a scrawny sparrow who'd been out in the rain too long. She was small, no more than five one or two, and probably didn't weigh more than ninety pounds. Her bright red hair was straight as a stick and her milk-white face was sprinkled with freckles.

Every afternoon when it was time for the gentlemen to come calling, Charmaine and the other girls did their best to dress Effie up, but to Carrie's way of thinking, they only made matters worse. The curling iron frizzled the baby-fine hair, and the rouge blotched over the freckles on her too-white skin giving her a sad-clown look.

The fancy dresses didn't help, either. They hung on her skinny frame, emphasizing the smallness of her budding breasts and her almost nonexistent bottom.

She looked more like a lost orphan of the storm than a fallen woman.

"She's my bestest friend," Sarah told Carrie. "She tells me stories and she makes dresses for Mary Agnes."

Mary Agnes, a china doll with long dark curls, had been a gift from Uncle Matt. She was Sarah's prized possession and the little girl carried the doll with her everywhere she went.

"Uncle Matt got her in Chicago," Sarah said.

The fact that Uncle Matt, Aunt Charmaine and all the other aunties were taking the place of Sarah's playmates concerned Carrie. For though the women of The Chateau were unfailingly sweet to both her and Sarah, they were not her kind of people. She was determined to take Sarah out of this environment just as soon as she was able.

But no matter how she felt about the women who worked here, Carrie did her best to be pleasant to them when they came to visit. Dressed in silk kimonos or flannel robes, their hair loose about their shoulders, they lounged on her bed, chatting, as curious about Carrie as she was about them.

She soon discovered that Babette had a little boy about Sarah's age who lived with her folks in Arkansas.

"Miss Charmaine gave me some time off just before Christmas last year," Babette told Carrie. "And Mr. Matt got me a ticket on the train. It was a real nice trip. I was glad to see my little boy and my folks and all, but I was so sad when it came time to say goodbye that I don't hardly think I'll be going back. Timmie calls my own mama "Mama," and maybe it's better that he does. I can't do for him like she can, so it's best he just keeps on thinking she's his mama and Papa is his papa. Mr. Matt offered to pay my way back to Arkansas this Christmas, but I told him I'd better stay here. He's a real nice man, Miss Carrie. He's different than any man I've ever known, and I guess I've known my share."

Like Babette, the other girls also spoke in glowing terms of Matt Craddock.

"He's the richest man in Cripple Creek," Dorrie told Carrie.

"It all started when he won the High Stakes Saloon in a poker game five years ago," Lorelei said. "After that he bought the Dirty Shame, the Silver Dollar and that fancy gambling place of his."

"Old Dewlap Drummond took me there once," Conchita said. "You should see the place, *muchachas.* There are real honest-to-God crystal chandeliers and red velvet drapes. There are girls there, too, but mostly they just circulate among the customers. They wear expensive gowns... *Chihuahua!* You should see the gowns! And all they do is drink champagne and dance with the men. And the men that go there! *Carumba,* they look almost as rich as Señor Matt."

"That's where Sally LeBeau sings," Lorelei said. "She's the belle of the tenderloin district."

"The tenderloin?" Carrie asked.

"The place where all the action is," Dorrie explained.

"Matt has a gold mine, too," Lorelei said. "The Lucky Lady. A fella from Chicago bought it a few years back but it never did pay off. Mr. Matt won it from him in a poker game and six months later he struck gold."

Lorelei smiled. "Never did see a luckier man than Matt. He's got the golden touch."

"In more ways than one," Conchita said with a laugh.

"That ain't nice." Effie frowned at the other girl. "You just hush up with such talk around Miss Carrie."

The golden touch in more ways than one. Carrie's mouth tightened. That certainly confirmed her suspicion about Matt Craddock. He was a gambler, a rogue, and worst of all he was a client of The Chateau. He'd probably done wicked things with every female resident in the house, these very same females that sat chatting on her bed like schoolgirls.

But they weren't schoolgirls. They were fallen women, bad women.

In late afternoon Miss Binty always came to close the door of Carrie's room. Soon after that the brass knocker on the front door would sound again and again, and Carrie would hear, over the lively music of Noah Pierce's piano, the high-pitched voices of the women mingled with the laughter of men. It all sounded like any normal party, and for a little while, lying there, that's what Carrie pretended that it was.

But as the afternoon wore on into evening, the pretending stopped, for that was when she would hear the footsteps on the stairs, the smothered giggles, the hushed whispers, the male voices.

And often as she lay there, she wondered if Matt Craddock was one of the men, and which of the women he was with.

She wondered about what they did. More than kissing, she knew. She didn't know *exactly* what men and women did when they were alone in a bed, but whatever it was, she knew it wasn't nice.

* * *

One afternoon when Sarah was taking her nap, Noah
Pierce knocked on the open door of Carrie's room.

"Howdy, ma'am," he said. "I hope I'm not bothering you." He handed her a box tied with a red ribbon.
"It's fudge," he said. "I thought that after a steady diet
of Miss Binty's chicken soup you might like a taste of
something sweet. I bought it at the Bon Ton this morning."

"Why, thank you, Mr. Pierce." Carrie took the box
and, removing the lid, offered it to him. "Won't you
have some?"

"Thank you, ma'am. Don't mind if I do."

She bit into a piece. "It's delicious, Mr. Pierce."

He blushed and looked down at his feet. "I been
wanting to tell you how sorry I was about everything,
Miss Carrie. About poor Rosalinda dying and about
your being sick and all. Your sister was nice as could be
and I reckon Sarah's just about the sweetest little girl I
ever saw." He looked over at the sleeping child. "She's
lucky to have you."

"And I'm lucky to have her, Mr. Pierce."

"She's become mighty attached to Effie."

"Yes, so it seems."

"And Effie's mighty attached to her."

Carrie nodded. "Yes, I know."

"Effie's a real nice girl, Miss Carrie. She came here
last winter. Knocked at the door looking half-frozen
and asked Miss Charmaine for work. She looks better
now, but back then she was so skinny and run-down she
could barely stand. Miss Charmaine took her in and
took care of her. Made her eat and got her some halfway decent clothes.

"A week or two later her daddy came looking for her,
wanting to take her back home. Effie took one look at

him and started to cry. Said she'd never go back, and
Miss Charmaine said if Mr. Davis didn't leave she was
going to call the sheriff. She called him words I didn't
know any lady knew and shoved him right off the front
porch.''

Noah shoved his big bony hands into his pockets.
''For a while Miss Charmaine wouldn't let Effie work,
but Effie kept insisting that she do her share to pay for
her board and room or she was going to leave, and finally Miss Charmaine said all right.''

He looked at Carrie. ''She doesn't belong here,'' he
said. ''I was thinking...'' He cleared his throat before
he went on. ''I was thinking that when you leave here
you might need help with Sarah and keeping house and
all. And that maybe...well maybe Effie could help
you.''

Carrie looked at Noah, then away. He wanted her to
take Effie Davis with her when she left. She couldn't do
that. She could not possibly take on the responsibility
of another person, especially a person who made her
living as a prostitute.

''I really don't think—'' she started to say.

But Noah stopped her. ''She doesn't belong here,
ma'am,'' he said again. ''I wish you'd at least think
about it.''

''I can't...'' She shook her head, then, stopped by the
appeal in his eyes, said, ''All right. I'll think about it.''

Toward the end of the week Matt Craddock came to
see Carrie. It was evening, and from below she could
hear the voices and the music of the piano.

''You're looking much better,'' he said from the
doorway. ''May I come in?''

Before Carrie could answer, Sarah launched herself at him, squealing, "Uncle Matt! Uncle Matt!"

"Hello, princess." He swung Sarah up into his arms. "How's my best girl?"

"Fine, Uncle Matt." He put her down, and when he did she tugged at his hand to bring him into the bedroom. "Aunt Carrie was just telling a story about when Mama was a little girl back in Ohio. We're going there sometime, aren't we, Aunt Carrie?"

"Is that what you've decided?" Matt pulled a chair closer to the bed and asked, "May I?" When Carrie nodded, he sat down and took Sarah up onto his lap.

"Yes, we'll go back," Carrie said, "but I'm afraid it won't be for a while yet, a year or two at least."

One black eyebrow raised in question. "I thought you didn't like Cripple Creek."

"I don't. But I don't have any choice. I have to stay until I get a teaching job and can save enough money to get Sarah and myself back home." She reached for her purse. "Speaking of money, I owe you for the doctor you had come from Denver. How much did he charge?"

"Not much."

"How much?"

Matt shook his head. "We can talk about it later."

Carrie firmed her chin. "How much?" she insisted.

"Twenty-five dollars. But you don't have to—"

Twenty-five dollars! She swallowed hard, but trying not to show her chagrin, counted the money out and gave it to Matt. Her entire savings at this point was a little over sixty dollars.

"I don't want it," he said. "But if you insist on paying me then why don't you wait until you have a job?"

"I don't believe in owing money," she said stiffly. "My father always paid his bills on time and so do I."

"I don't want your money. I—"

"I insist," she said.

She was the damnedest woman he'd ever met, Matt decided as he took the money. Stiff-necked and rigid as a straight-backed chair. No wonder she was an old maid. If a man ever tried to put his arm around her she'd probably scream bloody murder. Besides, no man in his right mind would ever want to. Making love to her would be like making love to an icicle.

It was too bad, because she wasn't half-bad to look at. The other times he'd seen her she'd been wearing a flannel nightshirt, but tonight she had on some kind of blue gown with frilly white lace around her throat. In the light of the bedside lamp, and with her auburn hair loose about her shoulders, she looked very pretty. Her eyes were more gray than blue and her eyelashes were long and silky. She'd be a damned good-looking woman, if she ever loosened up. Not a woman he'd ever be interested in of course, but still...

"There is a school here, isn't there?" she asked, interrupting his thoughts.

"One here and another one over in Victor."

"Do you think I'd have any trouble finding a teaching position?"

Matt shook his head. "The school board's always looking for good teachers. A woman by the name of Elvira Primrose is head of the board. She's the one you'd want to talk to." Sarah moved in his arms, and when he saw that she was sleeping, he said, "Is it all right if I put her to bed?"

"Yes, if you don't mind."

"I never mind doing anything for Sarah." He lay the child down on her bed, pulled the blankets up to her chin, then stooped to kiss her cheek. "She's a sweet baby," he said. "She looks like Rosalinda, but there's a little of you in her, too. Your eyes I think." He turned and looked at Carrie. "You have very beautiful eyes," he said.

Carrie looked up at him, and suddenly the silence in the room was almost palpable. From below came the music and the sound of laughter, but here it was quiet.

Matt moved closer to the bed and stood looking down at Carrie. Her eyes were wide, her lips were parted.

He sat on the edge of the bed beside her.

"What are you doing?" she whispered.

He curled a strand of her auburn hair around his finger.

She didn't move.

Nor for a moment did he. Then suddenly, Matt put his arms under her shoulders and lifted her closer. She started to speak, but before she could, he covered her mouth with his.

Carrie stiffened and gasped. With her hands flat against his chest, she tried to push him away, but he held her there and kissed her, gently at first. Then with a growing need to make her respond his mouth moved over hers, demanding, willing her to answer his kiss. She tightened her lips and tried to draw away. But Matt held her there, held her and kissed her until her lips parted and softened under his.

"Carrie," he whispered, and tightened his arms around her.

He could feel the press of her breasts through the thin material of the gown. Her body felt womanly soft, her skin scented with roses.

"Please," she whispered, and this time when she struggled, Matt let her go and gently laid her back upon the pillows.

"I'm sorry." He took a steadying breath. "I shouldn't have done that."

"No. You...you shouldn't have." Her voice was shaking. She was shaking. She'd never been kissed before. She didn't know...hadn't known that a kiss could affect anyone the way it had affected her. She looked at his mouth and a shiver ran through her. Her hand went to the top of the blue gown and she held it closer about her throat. "I think you'd better leave," she said.

Matt stood and started for the door. "That won't happen again," he said. "Good night, Carrie. Sleep well."

Sleep well! When her mind was a jumble of mixed-up thoughts and her body so strangely weak and warm?

She touched the lips his lips had touched and pulled the blankets up under her chin. Matt Craddock had kissed her, and in a way she could not explain, she didn't think she would ever be the same again.

Chapter Five

Matthew Artemius Craddock was thirty-six years old. Born and raised in Chicago, he had attended school there, and one week after his graduation from the University of Illinois, he set his sights West.

For as long as Matt could remember, his father had talked about quitting his job on the Erie Canal and going to California. He'd never made it, mostly because Matt's mother had a fainting spell every time he'd mentioned leaving Chicago. When he told his father his plan, Henry Craddock had said, "You're right to go, son. I just wish to God I was young enough to be going with you."

Matt worked his way down through Missouri, taking whatever job he could find to keep himself going. In Springfield he worked in a livery stable during the day, and started spending some of his nights playing faro in a local saloon. Six months later, convinced that there was more money to be made in games of chance than there was in shoveling manure, he quit his job and devoted all of his time and energy to gambling.

He knew early on that he had a knack for it. He could sense what the other players were going to do before they did it. He watched their faces, that slight movement of eye, the tightening of mouth, the thin film of sweat on the upper lip, the small, almost imperceptible twitch of hand. He never dealt a dishonest game, but he soon learned to spot the men who did.

By the time he was twenty-five, he'd been in a couple of gunfights, had gotten himself engaged and unengaged to several of the city's most eligible young ladies, and owned half interest in a saloon. But he never lost sight of the fact that Springfield was only a temporary stopover on his way to California. When one of the young ladies he'd gotten himself engaged to threatened to sue unless he married her, he sold his half of the saloon and left Springfield.

Wichita was his next stop. He stayed for a year, and it was there he began to hear talk about Colorado.

Like California, gold had been discovered in Colorado, and while Matt had little or no interest in prospecting for gold, he knew that wherever there were gold mines, there were men mining them, and wherever there were men, there was gambling. He decided to have a look at Colorado before he went on to California, especially when a man he'd played faro with started talking about a place called Cripple Creek.

"Darnedest thing anybody ever saw," the man said. "Fella by the name of Bob Womack had been prospecting there for almost fifteen years without any luck when one day damned if he didn't strike it rich. Discovered gold in a place called Poverty Gulch. Word got around and pretty soon a bunch of other prospectors headed for Cripple Creek. Whole danged town is booming. Ore's being assayed at more than two hundred dollars a ton and everybody and their twin brother's going to Cripple Creek faster 'n a mule can spit. There's hotels there now, dance halls, variety theaters, saloons, and enough whorehouses and gambling places to keep every one of them miners happy till he's ninety.''

A week later Matt was on his way to Cripple Creek. He won the High Stakes Saloon in a poker game and a year later, bought his second saloon, and then his third. Three years after that he won the Lucky Lady mine in a game of chance, and hit a vein of gold that made him richer than he'd ever dreamed of being.

A millionaire several times over, he could have gone back to Chicago or even to New York and just let the money come in. But Matt liked Cripple Creek and the people who lived there. He liked owning and operating his saloons and the gambling palace. Most important, Matt liked his life just the way it was; he didn't need or want any complications. But somehow he knew, the way he always knew when the man across the gaming table from him was bluffing, that if he wasn't careful, Miss Carrie McClennon could become a complication.

She was different from the other women he'd known, and he'd known quite a few. She was narrow-minded and prim, proper as a church deacon and twice as straitlaced. He wasn't sure why he'd kissed her the other night, curiosity maybe. Or maybe it had been that she looked so feminine and pretty in that blue gown with the white lace curled up around her throat. Lord knows it had shocked the socks off her, and truth to tell, he'd been a little taken aback himself.

She'd jumped like a scared rabbit when he kissed her, but just for a minute her lips had parted and softened under his. When they did, he had felt a surge of excitement unlike anything he'd ever experienced before. The press of her breasts against him had set Matt so hot on fire that he'd thought he'd explode if he didn't touch them. He hadn't, but it had taken every bit of his will-power not to.

He had a pretty good idea from the way she'd re-acted that she'd probably never been kissed before, at least not the way he'd kissed her. That intimidated as well as excited Matt, and that night after he'd left her, he thought what it would be like to awaken Miss Carrie McClennon, to teach her the many ways of love, to have her respond as she had for that one brief moment.

During the next few days, Matt did his damnedest to shrug off all thoughts of Carrie. She was dangerous. Her innocence was more appealing than he wanted to admit. But try as he might to put her out of his mind, Matt found himself thinking about her at the oddest moments—in the middle of a high-stakes game; when he went to bed at night or awakened in the morning. He even dreamed about her, about the tumble of her au-burn hair, the sweet fullness of her lips.

He told himself he'd only helped her because she was Rosalinda's sister and Sarah's aunt, but there was a part of him that had known he'd been attracted to her from the night on the snowbound train when he'd held her close to keep her warm. Her innocence and vulnerabil-ity had stirred something deep within him. Lord knows she wasn't the kind of a woman he wanted to become involved with, and yet each time he was with her he felt an overwhelming need to take her in his arms, to hold and cuddle her, to kiss her until she was warm and pli-ant, and his.

He told himself that maybe he would have felt the same about anybody who'd gone through what Carrie had. Not only had she lost the sister she had come so far to see, she had discovered that her sister had spent the last few months of her life in a whorehouse. And no

matter what anybody said, he knew she believed that
Rosalinda had been more than just a guest there. Now
Carrie herself was staying in that same house, and while
the thought amused Matt, it also made him sympathize
with how she must feel about that. She was a straitlaced preacher's daughter, reduced to living among
women who made their way by selling their bodies.

Soon she'd be able to leave The Chateau, and the
sooner she left, the better it would be for her and everybody else, especially for Sarah. Until she did, he'd
stay away.

But three days later Matt once again found himself
climbing the stairs to Carrie's room, just to see Sarah,
he told himself.

The bedroom door was open and Carrie was sitting
in a rocking chair by the window, singing to Sarah. The
song was "Jeanie With the Light Brown Hair," but
each time the word *Jeanie* was used she substituted
Sarah.

Her voice was sweet and clear and so beautiful it
made the breath catch in his throat. And she was beautiful. In a long cotton nightgown with a blue shawl over
her shoulders, and the afternoon sun slanting in
through the window, setting her auburn hair afire, she
was just about the prettiest thing he'd ever seen.

As he watched, she feathered a kiss on the sleeping
child's forehead.

Something he could not give name to stirred deep
within Matt. Silently he closed the door and took a step
into the room. "I dream of Sarah..." she sang.

A floorboard creaked. The song stopped. Carrie
looked up and saw him.

"You have a lovely voice," he said.

A pale hand fluttered to her throat. "I...I didn't hear you come in."

"Sarah's asleep?"

"Yes."

"Let me take her." He crossed the room and gently lifted the sleeping child out of Carrie's arms. When she stirred, he said, "Hush, baby. Hush, my little girl. Everything's all right. Uncle Matt is going to put you to bed for your nap now."

Holding her cradled in one arm, he laid back the blanket and placed her on the bed, covered her and stood for a moment looking down at her.

"She's such a sweet thing," he said so low that Carrie could barely hear him. But she did hear, and smiled.

"You're very good to her," she said when he came back to where she was sitting.

"She's easy to be good to." He looked down at Carrie. "It's getting colder," he said. "You should get back into bed."

"Yes, I suppose I should." She stood and rested for a moment with one hand on the back of the rocker. "It's going to snow. The wind's getting colder."

"Yes." He came closer and placed his hands on her shoulders. "Let me help you back to bed," he said, and before Carrie could stop him, he picked her up in his arms.

"Put me down," she protested. "I..." She stopped and drew in her breath because he was looking at her the way he had the other night just before he had kissed her. "Mr. Craddock," she said. "Matt—"

"Say my name again."

"Put me down!"

"Say my name."

Carrie felt the flutter of a pulse beat in her throat. "Matt," she said.

He kissed her, there by the window in the sunlight. Kissed her with lips that were full and firm and surprisingly gentle against hers. And though she struggled, he held her there, cradled against his chest.

His face felt clean and cold against hers. His mouth was warm and demanding and she tasted the good pungent odor of a cigar he'd smoked earlier, and smelled the good man scent of him, and knew that this was wicked. That she mustn't let him kiss her like this. But oh, it was nice. He made her feel warm and alive, more alive than she'd ever felt before.

He pulled at her lower lip, and she moaned low in her throat. He glided his tongue into her mouth, seeking her tongue, and when he touched it, it was as though she had been touched by a flame, and she cried aloud. The hands that had flattened against his chest to push him away crept up around the back of his neck. She touched the warm skin there and curled her fingers through the thickness of his velvet black hair.

Carrie knew she had to stop. She couldn't let him kiss her like this. She had to... With a cry, she turned her face from his. "No," she whispered. "This isn't..."

"It isn't nice?" Matt chuckled low in his throat. "It's just about the nicest thing that's ever happened to me, Miss Carrie." His eyes, green as new spring grass looked down into hers. "Isn't it nice for you?" he said. "Isn't it, Carrie?"

He took her mouth again and kissed her deep and hard and good. She clung to him, but when he cupped her breast she startled like a frightened bird, jerking her arms from the back of his neck to clamp down on his wrist. "No," she said. "No—"

He silenced her words with his mouth, and though she struggled against him, he would not move his hand.

His fingers burned through the thin fabric of her nightgown, and as he brushed his thumb against her nipple, he kissed her with a force that left her breathless.

"Carrie," he whispered against her lips. "Carrie." Resting his face against the top of her head, he held her there until she quieted.

"I didn't mean to do that." He took a deep and shaking breath. "I only meant to carry you to your bed."

She hid her face in the fabric of his coat, too ashamed to look at him.

He took her to her bed, laid her down there and pulled the blankets around her. He sat beside her, and he took her chin between his thumb and first finger and turned her face toward his.

"You think that I shouldn't have kissed you that way," he said. "That I shouldn't have touched you."

"No." Her breath felt ragged. "No, you shouldn't have."

"I didn't mean to, but when you looked at me the way you did. . ." Matt shook his head. "There's something between us, Carrie. I'm not sure what it is, I only know that it exists."

It was true. There was something about her, something that heated his blood and hardened his body with a desire unlike anything he had ever known. He wanted her more than he had ever wanted a woman before. He gazed down into her gray-blue eyes, eyes still smoky with a desire she didn't even understand, and began to stroke the auburn hair back from her face. "You need someone to take care of you," he said. "I want to be that someone, Carrie."

"Take care of me? I . . . I don't understand."

"I have a house in town. You and Sarah could live there."

"With you?"

Matt smiled. "Of course with me, Carrie. You won't have to teach school, you can stay home and take care of Sarah." He caressed her cheek. "And me," he said.

Before she could move away, he put his arms around her and brought her closer. "It could be good between us, Carrie. It could be so good."

"I . . . I'm not sure I understand, Matt. Are you asking me to marry you?"

Frowning, Matt shook his head. "I'm not a man who would be comfortable with marriage," he said. "But I care about you and I'll be good to you. When the time comes and you'd like to go back to Ohio, I'll make sure that you and Sarah have enough money to make you both comfortable for a very long time."

Carrie stared at him, shock showing in her eyes. Matt Craddock wasn't asking her to marry him, he was asking her to live in sin.

"Let go of me," she said in a steely, quiet voice.

The hand on her cheek stilled. "Carrie," he started to say. "Let me explain, my dear. I—"

"No." She sat up and moved away from him. "I'd like you to leave, Matt."

A muscle in his cheek jumped. "I'm sorry if I offended you," he said. "Perhaps I didn't say it the way I meant it. Colorado can be a difficult place for a woman alone, especially a woman with a child. You need someone to—"

"I don't need anyone," she snapped. "I can take care of myself and I can take care of Sarah." She glared at him. "I'm tired. I'd appreciate it if you'd leave."

Matt got up and started toward the door. "Think about what I've said, Carrie. If you change your mind—"

"I won't change my mind."

"I still want to help you," he said. "If I can do any-thing—"

"You can't."

He hesitated at the door. "It could be good between us," he said in a low voice. "I'd give you everything you've ever wanted. I'd dress you in silk and furs. I'd—"

She picked up the clock from the bedside table and hurled it at him. He ducked and it clanged hard against the door.

"Get out!" she cried. "Get out!"

The suggestion of a grin curved Matt's mouth as he bowed from the waist. With exaggerated politeness, he said, "I'll bid you good afternoon, ma'am," and closed the door just as she reached under the bed for the chamber pot.

Hot tears ran down Carrie's cheeks. She'd never been angrier in her life, as angry with herself as she was with Matt Craddock. Angry because she'd behaved like a hussy and allowed Matt Craddock to take liberties with her. Angry at him because he'd taken advantage of her.

She threw herself down on the bed and covered her head. Oh Lord, what had she done? For all she knew she might even be pregnant.

"You can get in a family way through kissing," her friend Margaret Louise Fairbanks had told her. "My cousin Hildy warned me never to kiss a man lest I end up with a baby. No decent girl ever lets a man kiss her until she says, 'I do.' It's all right to let him to kiss your forehead or your cheek, but never on the lips until the preacher says you're married."

Married. She had assumed Matt was asking her to marry him! She'd never live down the shame of asking him if that's what he meant.

Someone knocked. Had he come back! She couldn't face him. Couldn't...

Charmaine opened the door. "Are you all right?" she asked. "I heard a crash and..." She looked at the clock and raised her eyebrows.

Carrie knuckled away her tears. "I'm...I'm fine," she managed to say. "I'm sorry I broke your clock."

"That's all right." Charmaine picked up the pieces and put them on the bureau. "Matt ran out of the house looking like old Nick himself was after him and you're up here crying. What happened? Do you want to talk about it?"

"No."

Charmaine sat on the edge of the bed. "Maybe you'll feel better if you do."

"No, I won't." Carrie looked at Charmaine, then away. The fear that she might be pregnant scared her to death. If a girl really could get that way by kissing a man then she surely was. Charmaine was a woman of the world, she'd probably know whether what Margaret Louise had said was true or not. It would embarrass her to ask, but...

She took a deep breath. "I'd like to ask you a question," she said.

"All right, shoot."

"If a girl..." Carrie took a deep breath. "If a girl kisses a man will she get...you know?"

"Will she get what?"

Carrie swallowed hard. "With child," she whispered.

The corners of Charmaine's mouth turned up in a smile that she tried to hide. "Wherever did you get an idea like that?"

"My friend Margaret Louise told me."

"Well, Margaret Louise was wrong. It takes a hell of a lot more than that to make a girl pregnant."

What? Carrie wanted to ask but didn't.

"Matt kissed you?" Charmaine asked.

Carrie, too ashamed to say yes, merely nodded.

"Is that why you're so upset?"

"Yes, and because . . . ?"

"Because?" Charmaine prompted.

"Because he asked me to . . . to live in sin with him."

"To live with him?" Charmaine's blue eyes widened. "Matt asked you to live with him?"

"He said he'd take care of Sarah and me."

"I'll be damned!" For a moment Charmaine was too surprised to say anything. "And you refused him?" she said at last.

"Of course I refused him!"

"I'll be damned." Charmaine shook her head. "I've never known Matt Craddock to ask any other woman that question. If he had, you can bet your Aunt Tilly they'd have said yes."

"Well, I'm not any other woman."

"No, I don't guess you are." Charmaine gazed out of the window for a moment or two. "Matt's as fine a man as I ever knew," she said. "There isn't a woman in this town would turn him down if he asked them what he asked you."

"Then let him ask one of them."

Charmaine shook her head. "He doesn't want any of them, he wants you." And almost to herself, she added, "It beats the hell out of me why he does though."

Carrie frowned, but before she could say anything, Charmaine continued. "There's not another man like Matt in all Colorado, Carrie. Anybody down on their luck and he's right there helping, just like the way he helped Rosie."

"What do you mean?"

"He'd met her a few years ago in Kansas City. She came here with some no-good varmint who'd made all sorts of promises about getting her a job singing. But a job wasn't what he had in mind. She was sick and scared and trying to take care of Sarah and finally she sent word to Matt. He went to see the man who'd brought her here, and from what I heard, he knocked the tar out of him. After a while he brought Rosie here and asked me to take her and Sarah in. He paid me rent for the room I gave her."

"He paid you to take care of her?"

Charmaine smiled. "He surely did, Miss Carrie, and he was mighty nice to your sister the whole time she was here. He brought Sarah presents, and now and then he'd bring something special for Rosie. I think it was almost as much of a shock for him as it was for you when she died. When he found out I was paying the funeral expenses he wouldn't let me do it. He paid for everything. He's even having a nice tombstone made for her grave."

"I see." And suddenly Carrie did see. Matt had known Rosalinda before. He had helped her when she was in trouble and he'd brought her presents. He called Sarah "my little girl."

Lorelei's words, "He couldn't be nicer to Sarah if she were his own little girl," echoed in Carrie's ears. His own little girl.

She put a hand over her eyes.

"You feeling all right?" Charmaine asked.

"Yes, I . . . I'm just a little tired."

"I'll let you rest a while then." She patted Carrie's hand. "You sure you're all right."

"Yes, thank you."

But she wasn't all right.

Charmaine had told her Matt had known Rosalinda a couple of years before she'd come here. A couple of years? Three or four?

She felt ill, filled with shame, sick with a truth she didn't want to face but knew that she had to. Matt and her sister had done what married people do; as a result, she had become pregnant with Sarah. Sarah was Matt's daughter.

Snow and sleet beat hard against the window, and wind shook the house. But Carrie didn't hear it. She cried for a long time, and when the tears ended, she got out of bed and began to pack.

Chapter Six

"If you're bound and determined to go gallivanting all over Cripple Creek, then at least take Effie with you," Charmaine said.

Carrie was bound and determined all right, and she had been ever since yesterday afternoon. Bitterly ashamed for having allowed Matt Craddock to take liberties, and humiliated because she had assumed, when he asked her to live with him, that he was talking about marriage, the final blow had come with the realization that he had been Rosalinda's lover. And Sarah's father. Why else would he have paid Charmaine to take Rosalinda and her child in? Why else would he have brought gifts for Sarah and called her his little girl?

"I'm not going gallivanting," Carrie told Charmaine. "I'm going to look for a house." She put on her gray hat and fastened it with a three-inch-long pin. "It was kind of you to take me in the way you did, Miss Duval, but—"

"Charmaine! For Lord's sake, call me Charmaine."

"All right. Charmaine."

"I don't know why you're in such an all-fired hurry

to leave. It's cold out there and you're still peaked looking. If you were to catch another chill—''

"I won't." Carrie put the gray cloak over her shoulders. "I'm fine, really, but it's time I left. I have to find a place to live and a job. The sooner I start looking the better."

"If you're determined to leave, then go on over to the general store and see Mr. Davenport. He knows everything that's going on around town. If there're places to rent he'll know about them." Charmaine went to the door of Carrie's room and called out, "Effie? You ready?"

"I'm coming, Miss Charmaine." And before Carrie could say that she didn't need anybody to go with her, Effie had hurried out into the hallway. She wore a shabby, threadbare coat that came almost down to her ankles and a red wool cap pulled down over her carrot-red hair. She looked as excited as though she were going to a party instead of house hunting.

"I don't get out much," she confided as she took Carrie's arm to help her down the front steps. More animated than Carrie had ever seen her, the younger girl's cheeks were flushed with pleasure. "The nice folks in town don't much like us girls traipsing around over in their part of Cripple Creek," she confided. "But you're respectable. Won't nobody say nothing to me long's I'm with you." She took a deep breath of the clear morning air. "Isn't this the nicest day?" she said. "I love it when it's snowed. It makes everything look so clean and pretty, don't it?"

Effie stepped around a snowdrift. Glancing down, Carrie saw how worn the girl's shoes were, and knew that her feet must already be wet.

Pointing to a single-story frame house, Effie said, "That's Hazel McMurphy's place. I tried to go to work there, too, but Miz McMurphy said I looked like a plucked chicken and that I wasn't strong enough or pretty enough for the kind of gents that came there." She shook her head. "I'm stronger now, but I don't guess nothing's ever going to make me any prettier."

Carrie stopped. "Of course you're pretty," she said. "Whoever told you that you weren't?"

"My pa." Effie buried her chin in the collar of her coat and, in a voice so low Carrie could barely hear her, said, "Course that didn't keep him from trying to put his hands on me every chance he got." She shot a glance at Carrie. "He's a real mean man, Miss Carrie. I don't much like what I have to do at Miss Charmaine's, but I'd a sight rather be there than living with Pa."

"Have you ever thought of doing any other kind of work?"

"No, ma'am. My pa said I was too dumb for anything except laying on my back."

"You're not dumb," Carrie said emphatically. "It's just that nobody's ever given you a chance. Look how good you are with Sarah. She loves you, Effie."

"I love her, too, Miss Carrie, and I'm purely going to hate it when you and her leave The Chateau. I'm going to miss both of you more'n I even want to think about."

"And I'll miss you, Effie," Carrie said as they turned onto Bennett Avenue. Strangely enough, she knew that it was true. There was something about the girl that touched her, for even when she was all decked out in her "working" clothes, the silk gowns that all of Charmaine's girls wore for the benefit of the customers, Effie still looked like a lost soul.

Life was hard, particularly here in this western boomtown, Carrie realized. It was particularly hard on young women like Effie who had no one to protect them. If they had no family, no education, no talent or hope of a decent job, there were two choices left to them: they could marry if they could find a man who wanted them, or prostitute themselves. Effie hadn't had any choice in the path she chose. And neither, perhaps, had Rosalinda when she allowed Matt to take care of her.

Lord, how that hurt and galled, hurt like a knife going into her deep, galled because for a few moments yesterday she had allowed Matt to hold and kiss her, as he had once held and kissed Rosalinda.

But she wouldn't think about that now. She would find a place to rent, and she would never have to see Matt Craddock again.

Though the snow had stopped during the night, it was banked in three-foot drifts all along the street. Because of the cold there weren't many people out, but those that were were bundled in heavy coats and caps that pulled down over their ears.

Carrie and Effie made their way down Bennett Avenue, past the Boston Café, the bake shop, the drugstore, the millinery shop, a hotel and a meat market. Across the street there was another meat market, the shoe and clothing store, a pawnshop, a sign that read Dancing School, a Chinese laundry, and the general store. Farther down on the other side of the street was the livery stable and the blacksmith.

When they reached the store, Effie hesitated. "Maybe I'd better wait outside," she murmured.

"You'll do no such thing." Carrie took her arm and together they went into the store.

A potbellied stove warmed the room. Cans and jars and bottles lined the shelves, cooking utensils hung from every nail. There was a crock of dill pickles near the door, and to one side, a covered glass display of licorice sticks and hard candy balls. The man behind the counter had a white apron tied around his waist. His cheeks were as red as the apples he had displayed in a basket at one side of the counter. His hair was salt-and-pepper gray and his eyes were a fine deep blue.

"Help you, ladies?" he asked.

"I'm looking for a house to rent," Carrie said. "Someone told me you might know of something."

Mr. Davenport ran a hand across his face. "Believe I do, ma'am. Believe I do. Old Miz Bisbee went bad last month and she had to move in with her daughter over in Victor. Her house is for rent furnished and it might just be what you're looking for."

"How much is she asking for it?" Carrie said.

"Twenty dollars a month, ma'am."

Twenty dollars. Carrie gripped the edge of the counter. She hadn't figured on paying that much. She might be able to manage two months' rent, with a little left over for food and someone to stay with Sarah while she was at school, but if she didn't find a teaching position right away she'd be in serious trouble.

"Is there anything else?" she asked. "Anything a little cheaper?"

"I'm afraid not. Miz Bisbee's is a nice little house and if I was you I'd snap it up before somebody else gets it. There're families coming to Cripple Creek every day and houses are hard to find. When would you figure on moving in?"

"Tomorrow, if I can."

Mr. Davenport reached behind the counter and handed Carrie a key. "It's on Second Street," he said. "Gray house at the end of the block. You look it over. If you like it and you've got twenty dollars you can move in tomorrow."

Carrie hesitated for a moment, then she picked up the key and, with Effie in tow, walked the three blocks to Second Street.

A white picket fence enclosed the front yard of the small Victorian house. Icicles hung from the roof gutters and the elaborately carved trim of the arches over the porch. The steps were piled high with snow that creaked under their feet. The house looked bleak and unlived in, and it was with a heavy heart that Carrie put the key in the lock.

It was as cold inside as it was outside, but the living room looked pleasant enough. Well-worn Oriental rugs covered the polished wooden floor; heavy gold and tasseled drapes hung on either side of the big bay window. A brocade love seat and a matching hassock were arranged in front of the fireplace, and a curio cabinet filled with all sorts of bric-a-brac stood against a wall. There was a piano in one corner, a gold-covered sofa, satin-covered chairs, carved end tables and lamps, an ornately framed gilded mirror. With a fire, and the lamps lighted, the room would be cozy and warm.

There was a dining room with a big round table and six chairs, a breakfront lined with dishes, and a serving table against one wall. The kitchen was big and the shelves of the pantry were lined with canned fruit and vegetables.

Upstairs there were three bedrooms, each one furnished with a four-poster, dresser and wardrobe.

It was a nice house, a comfortable house. She and Sarah would be happy here until she had made enough money to take them both back to Ohio. But she had to get a job right away. If she didn't . . . no, she wasn't going to worry about it. She had her teaching credentials: she'd get a job. She knew she would.

"I like it," she told Effie. "Let's go back and tell Mr. Davenport I'm going to take it. I can bring Sarah's and my things over in the morning."

"I don't guess I'll be seeing you once you and Sarah move in here." Effie ran her hand over the back of one of the chairs. "It's a real pretty house, Miss Carrie. I reckon you and Sarah are going to be happy here, but I sure am going to miss you."

"I'll miss you, too, Effie." And though Carrie was tempted to say, "But of course you can visit," she didn't. She liked Effie and she was sorry for her, but the facts remained that the girl worked at The Chateau and that this was a respectable neighborhood.

Back at the general store, she gave Mr. Davenport twenty dollars and told him she would move in the following day. He in turn said that he'd have one of his helpers go over to the house early in the morning and light a fire so that it wouldn't be so cold when Carrie moved in. Then he gave each of them an apple and bid them good day.

Carrie was packed and ready by ten the next morning. She bundled Sarah in her coat and hat, leggings and little fur-lined boots that had been, Sarah told her, a present from Uncle Matt.

And though excited about all the hustle and bustle of packing, the child was confused about the move. "But why are we leaving?" she asked Carrie again and again. "I like it here."

"We're going to have our own house now," Carrie told her.

"But I like this house," Sarah protested.

"I know, dear. But don't you think it will be nice having a room of your own and a whole house that you can play in?"

"But what about Auntie Charmaine and Effie? Why can't they come with us?"

"Auntie Charmaine has to stay here and take care of her own house and of...of the other girls who live here."

"Will Uncle Matt come to visit us when we move?"

"I don't think so, Sarah."

"Why not?" Her lower lip came out in a pout. "Why not, Aunt Carrie?"

"Well, he..." Carrie hesitated, trying to find the right words. "We're going to be living in a different part of town," she said at last. "Your Uncle Matt is so busy he probably won't have the time to visit." She knelt down to fasten the buttons of Sarah's coat. "You'll make new friends, honey. I'm sure there are a lot of children near where we're going to live." She gave Sarah a hug. "It's going to be fine, Sarah. Just you wait and see."

But Sarah's lower lip still pouted and her face was solemn when Noah, who had volunteered to help Carrie move, knocked on the door. "Are you ready, Miss Carrie? I've got a carriage waiting out front." He patted Sarah's head. "I bet you're all excited, aren't you, honey?"

"No!" Sarah stamped her foot. "I don't want to go!"

"Well, now..." Noah looked at Carrie. "You'll love your new house," he told Sarah. "Why, I bet you've even got your own room."

"Don't want my own room. Don't want to go away from here." And to emphasize what she was saying, Sarah stamped her foot again.

"That's enough!" Carrie took her niece's hand and led her from the room. Charmaine and all of the girls waited at the bottom of the stairs to say goodbye.

"I guess you're ready," Charmaine said.

"Yes, I am." Carrie let go of Sarah's hand. "I can't thank you enough for all you've done for us," she said. "And for what you did for Rosalinda. I'll never forget you, Charmaine."

"You sound like you're moving back to Ohio." Charmaine raised an eyebrow. "But I suppose you might as well be, seeing as how you're going to be living on the other side of town."

"Well, I..." Carrie felt hot color creep into her cheeks. "I guess I'd better be going."

"Yes, maybe you had." Charmaine knelt down and picked Sarah up in her arms. "Bye bye, honey babe," she said, and kissed Sarah's cheek.

"Bye, Auntie Charmaine." Sarah's lower lip began to tremble. "I love you, Auntie Charmaine."

"And I love you, sweetheart." Charmaine hugged her close for a moment then set her down.

Dorrie and Lorelei kissed Sarah. Babette gave her a rag doll with button eyes and a painted mouth. Conchita took the pair of yellow beads she was wearing and put them in Sarah's hand. "To remember me by, *muchachita*," she said.

Effie handed her a tissue-wrapped package. "I made some new clothes for Mary Agnes," she whispered. Then her lower lip trembled and she started to cry.

"Oh, for the Lord's sweet sake," Charmaine said. "Stop your crying."

"I can't hardly stand it," Effie wept. "Sarah's just like the little sister I always wanted. I don't want her to go away. I'll never see her again. I—"

"Hush up!" Charmaine looked almost as heartbroken as the weeping girl. "You're upsetting Sarah."

"I can't help it," Effie sobbed. "I don't want her and Miss Carrie to go."

"Effie...Effie, dear..." Carrie put her arms around the girl's shoulders. "Please don't cry," she said. "You can come and see us sometime. You can..." She looked at Effie, and at Sarah who had taken Effie's hand as though to console her. She took a deep breath. "Effie," she said quickly, before she could change her mind, "How would you like to come with us, Effie?"

"What?" Effie's eyes went big with surprise. "Come with you?"

"I'll need somebody to stay with Sarah while I'm teaching school. We'd both like it if you moved in with us and..." She looked over Effie's shoulder to Charmaine. "I know Effie works for you and I know I-haven't any right to ask, but if you could—"

"Sure." Charmaine grinned. "What the hell, Miss Carrie, she'll be happier with you than she's ever been here working for me. Go ahead, take her along with you and Sarah." And to Effie, she said, "Now stop your crying and go on up and bundle your things together."

Effie looked from Charmaine to Carrie. Still sniffing, unable to believe this sudden turn of fortune, she knuckled her tears away. "You'll wait for me?" she asked Carrie.

"Of course we will." She patted Effie's shoulder.

She wasn't sure she'd done the right thing, or even why she'd done it. Perhaps it was because, in a way she could not define, Effie reminded her of Rosalinda. She hadn't been here when Rosalinda needed her, but maybe she could be here for Effie.

Carrie saw the look of gratitude in Effie's eyes before the girl turned and ran up the stairs. Now there would be another mouth to feed, another person to be responsible for. But she could do it. All she had to do was get a job.

The Cripple Creek schoolhouse was on the edge of town surrounded by a stand of tall ponderosa pines. As Carrie approached the white clapboard building, the front door opened and what seemed like dozens of children ran out in a confusion of unfastened coats and galoshes. Snowballs were made and thrown, girls squealed, boys shouted, yipped and yelled. It was the usual after-school exuberance and Carrie smiled as she approached the steps.

A harried-looking middle-aged woman stood in the doorway. "Those children!" she muttered. "Regular little hellions. They're going to be the death of me yet. I'm glad to be leaving."

"You're leaving?"

"Yes, I..." The woman looked at Carrie. "Oh, dear," she said. "You must be one of the new mothers."

Carrie smiled reassuringly. "Actually, Miss...?"

"Eberhart," the teacher said.

"Actually, Miss Eberhart, I'm a teacher, too. I've just come from Ohio and I'm looking for a teaching position."

"Well now, doesn't that beat all. I'm leaving at the end of the month and the school board has been trying to find a replacement. If you've got a teaching certificate they're certainly going to be glad to see you."

Relief flooded through Carrie. She'd been sure she could get a job, but she hadn't expected it to be this easy. "I have my teaching credentials from Ohio Northern University," she said. "And a letter from the principal of the school where I taught for the last five years."

"That ought to satisfy everybody, even Mrs. Primrose, the head of the school board. I shouldn't say anything, but there've been a couple of applicants. One of them had been teaching over at Elkton. He wasn't as well qualified as you are, but to my way of thinking he would have been all right. But Mrs. Primrose..." The teacher shook her head. "I don't like to say anything, but she's a mighty hard woman to please. There's a meeting of the board tomorrow night here in the schoolhouse at eight o'clock. I'm going to be there and I'll tell them about you. Why don't you come about eight-fifteen? The sooner you're hired the sooner I can leave."

So it was arranged, and on the following night at eight, Carrie made her way to the schoolhouse. She had dressed modestly in a black wool suit, her gray cloak and gray feathered hat, and her spirits were high.

Effie and Sarah had helped her settle into the cozy little house and she was glad now that she had asked the girl to come with them. Effie had smiled and sung while she helped with the housework, but most important of all, she was wonderful with Sarah. And she certainly solved the problem of someone staying with Sarah while Carrie was away.

Things were working out. She had a home, a live-in nursemaid for Sarah, and if things went well tonight, she'd have a job. Pausing on the steps of the school-house to stamp the snow off her feet, Carrie took a deep breath and opened the door.

At the front of the room six men sat in a row of chairs near the teacher's desk. A woman sat at the desk and Miss Eberhart in one of the chairs in the first row.

There seemed to be a discussion going on, but it stopped abruptly when Carrie entered. They all looked at her. "I hope I'm not too early," she said.

"Please come up to the front." The woman at the desk motioned her forward. "I am Mrs. Elvira Primrose. These gentlemen are Mr. Lorenz, Mr. Gardner, Mr. Knudson, Mr. Neilson, and Mr. Satterwhite. You already know Miss Eberhart."

"Yes." Carrie cleared her throat. She hadn't been nervous when she'd come in, but she was nervous now. Mrs. Primrose's voice was as frosty as the weather, and her slate-gray eyes, as she looked Carrie up and down, were disapproving. She didn't ask Carrie to sit down.

"I've brought my credentials with me." Carrie took them out of her bag. "If you'd like to see them."

"I hardly think that will be necessary," Mrs. Primrose said.

Carrie shifted nervously. She looked at Miss Eberhart. Miss Eberhart looked at her, then quickly away.

"I have a few questions." Mrs. Primrose looked down at a paper in front of her. "I believe you came to

Cripple Creek to see your sister," she said. "A Miss Rosalinda McClennon."

"Yes, that's right."

"An unmarried woman with a child?"

One of the men seated in the row of chairs facing Carrie coughed.

"Yes," Carrie said. "My sister had a child."

"But no husband?"

Carrie's chin lifted. "I'm afraid I can't really answer that. You see I hadn't seen my sister for several years. She—"

"I believe she was living in The Chateau at the time of her death."

Carrie tightened her hands around her bag.

"The Chateau is a house of prostitution," Mrs. Primrose said.

"But she wasn't..." Carrie took a deep breath. "My sister wasn't a prostitute, Mrs. Primrose. She had been ill and Miss Duval—"

"The madam?" one of the men asked.

Carrie nodded. "Miss Duval took her in," she finished.

"You yourself live there, don't you?"

"No, Mrs. Primrose. I've rented a house for myself and my niece on Second Street."

"With one of the girls from The Chateau, I believe." The slate-gray eyes narrowed. "A known prostitute."

"The girl is only fifteen," Carrie said. "She—"

"I hardly think her age is relevant. What is, is that both you and your sister lived, and I presume worked, at The Chateau. We cannot have your type of woman teaching our children. We—"

"*My* type of woman?" Carrie took a step forward. "You presume wrong. My sister was not a prostitute, Mrs. Primrose. Neither am I. Miss Duval was kind enough to take me in when I was ill. I left as soon as I was able to—"

"I don't think we need to discuss this any longer. I believe the board has already decided." Miss Primrose started up out of her chair.

"We ought to vote on it," one of the men said.

Miss Eberhart stood. "I wonder if I might say something," she murmured. "It seems to me—"

"You're not a member of the board," one of the men said disapprovingly.

"But Miss McClennon's credentials are excellent," Miss Eberhart said. "She graduated from Ohio Northern University. She's had five years of teaching experience, and she—"

"That will be all!" Mrs. Primrose banged a wooden gavel on the desk. "I don't believe we need your presence now, Miss Eberhart. You may be excused."

"But..." The teacher reached down on the seat for her bag. She looked at the panel of board members, then at Carrie. "I'm sorry," she said, and fastening her coat, she hurried out of the schoolhouse.

"Well, now," Mrs. Primrose said. "I don't believe there's anything more to say, is there gentlemen?"

"I don't believe so," one of the men said.

"I for one go along with your decision, Mrs. Primrose," a bearded man said. "We can't have a woman of questionable character teaching our youngsters."

Questionable character? Hot blood rushed to Carrie's cheeks. Never before had her character been questioned, she couldn't believe that it was being questioned now. And while she wanted to defend herself, she knew as she looked at the men in front of her and at Mrs. Primrose's set and angry face, that it would do her no good. They had made up their minds before she had come in tonight.

There was nothing to say, and yet . . . "You're wrong about me," she said with as much dignity as she could muster. "My moral standards are as high as any of yours, probably higher. And I am good with children, as Mrs. Hargreaves, the principal back in Norwalk, Ohio, would be happy to attest to."

Mrs. Primrose rose and fastened her fur-trimmed coat about her. "We are not interested in what someone from Norwalk, Ohio, has to say," she said.

"No, I don't suppose you are."

"That will be all, Miss McClennon. You are dismissed."

Dismissed? Like a naughty child? Carrie drew herself up to her full five foot four, turned and hurried out of the building.

She didn't cry until she was outside, and when she did, her tears were tears of anger and outrage. How dare these people sit in judgment of her? How dare they treat her as though she were a common prostitute? How could you prove to people like that that you weren't what they said you were? That you were what Papa would have called "A decent Christian girl." If she were back in Ohio where people knew her . . .

But she wasn't back in Ohio, she was in Cripple Creek, Colorado.

She was alone. Her only friends, if she could call them that, were a madam and five prostitutes. And a man who wanted to live in sin with her.

Carrie dried her face and straightened her shoulders. She wasn't beaten yet, not by a long shot. She would persevere. Someway, somehow, she would find a job. She would save her money and in a year, or possibly two, she would have enough to take herself and her niece away from this godforsaken town.

She *would* get a job. She had to.

Chapter Seven

The next morning Carrie took the narrow-gauge train to Victor. There was no heat in the car, and as the train wound its way around the mountains and climbed to over ten thousand feet, gusts of wind blew the snow flurries in through cracks and the air was stinging cold.

She thought how difficult this ride would be if she had to travel back and forth every day. But difficult or not, she prayed that there would be an opening for her in Victor.

The snow was coming down heavier when Carrie got off the train. She stopped at the general store to ask the way to the schoolhouse and was told that it was at the other end of town. Bundling her muffler up around her throat, and wishing she had worn boots instead of thin-soled, high-top shoes, she walked the several blocks to the Victor schoolhouse, thinking how nice it would be to be inside where it was warm. Carrie pressed on, saying a silent prayer that there would be an opening for her here.

She had slept little the night before. Sick with disappointment at not getting the teaching position in Cripple Creek, and angry because of the reason why, she had paced the floor in her small bedroom.

Elvira Primrose had been her judge and her jury; Carrie had been found guilty before she'd set foot in the schoolhouse. And they needed a schoolteacher! That's what galled her the most. They needed her, but because her sister had lived at The Chateau, because she herself had stayed there, she had been judged a fallen woman.

The wind blew harder. Snow whipped about her face and her feet were freezing. When she saw the wooden-frame schoolhouse just ahead, she breathed a sigh of relief and tried to stop her teeth from chattering.

Once inside, she brushed the snow from her cloak, then turned to look into the schoolroom.

The teacher was a heavy-set, middle-aged man. Steel-rimmed half glasses rested low on his nose. He held a book in one hand, a long pointy stick in the other, and each time he asked a child a question, he smacked the stick hard against the desk of that child. Even from where she stood, Carrie could see each child flinch when he thwacked the stick.

Carrie cleared her throat. The children swiveled on their seats and stared her way. The teacher looked at her over his glasses and pursed his thin lips. He barked at the children, "Eyes forward!" and started down the aisle toward Carrie.

"How do you do," she said. "I—"

"I'm trying to conduct a class. What do you want?"

"My name is Carrie McClennon. I'm a teacher. I have all my credentials and I—"

"McClennon?" His heavy black eyebrows met in a disapproving frown. "I've heard about you, Miss McClennon, and I can tell you right off that we don't want your kind teaching our children."

"My kind?" Carrie drew herself up and glared at him. "I'm a schoolteacher. I—"

"I know what you are. If you want a job here in Victor I suggest you try one of the parlor houses. I hear they're looking for girls over at Lizzie Muldoone's place—"

Carrie hit him. She didn't mean to, she didn't even know that she had until she heard the slap of her hand across his face and saw the red outline there.

The children turned, wide-eyed, their mouths agape. The man's face went white except for the growing red of Carrie's handprint. "Get out!" he roared. "Get out of here before I call for the sheriff!"

She glared at him, fists clenched at her sides, then turned and ran outside.

Snow blinded her, but she didn't feel the cold. She wanted to throttle both Mrs. Primrose and the sorry excuse for a teacher she had just encountered. But more than anything she wanted to get out of Colorado, away from the snow and the wind. Back home to Norwalk, Ohio, and the house on Chestnut Street. That was where she belonged, not here in this godforsaken country.

There were two extremes of society here. On one side were the Elvira Primroses, the "good" people of the town. On the other side were the people who ran the tenderloin district, the houses of ill repute, the saloons and gambling parlors, men like Matt Craddock. And though Carrie knew that Matt Craddock had nothing to do with her present situation, the thought of him added fuel to her rage.

She had never been so angry in her life, but her anger faded while she waited for the train. Into its place crept a feeling of desperation. She had to find work, if not in her own profession then whatever kind of job she could find. There was a millinery shop in Cripple Creek, a dry goods store, and two general stores. Surely she could get work in one of those places.

She worried all the way back to Cripple Creek, and by the time she got off the train and walked half the length of the town to the house on Second Street, she was shaking with cold. Stamping the snow off her feet and trying to brush the snow from her cloak, she opened the front door.

"Auntie Carrie! Auntie Carrie!" Sarah called, and rushed to greet her. "Where you been? It's snowing outside. Can I go out and play? Can I?"

"No, sweetheart. It's much too frigid." Carrie took her cloak off and stooped to kiss the little girl. "Let's go inside by the fire. I'm a little cold."

"A little cold!" Matt Craddock said from the doorway of the living room. "You look half-frozen. Where have you been? Why in the hell did you go out on a day like this? Dammit, woman, you've only just recovered from pneumonia."

"Miss Carrie went over to Victor to see about a job teaching school." Effie, wiping her hands on a big white apron, stepped into the entry hall. "Did you get the job, Miss Carrie? Is everything all right?"

"You took the train to Victor on a day like this?" Matt took Carrie's arm. "Come in by the fire," he ordered. "You're freezing."

"I'm not freezing." She tried to pull out of his grasp, but Matt held on to her and led her in toward the hearth.

"You can't teach school in Victor," he said. "It's too far to go all the way over there every day in the winter. You'd have to leave before sunup to get there and get things going before the students arrive and—"

"I'm not going to teach in Victor!" Carrie turned on him, her face burning with anger. "I'm not going to teach in Cripple Creek, either. And do you know why? Because a narrow-minded biddy by the name of Elvira Primrose and a terrible man who teaches school with a stick in his hand think I'm unfit."

"Unfit?" Matt stared at her. "What are you talking about?"

"Unfit!" Carrie shouted, all of her pent-up anger breaking loose. "Because Rosalinda was my sister and she lived at The Chateau. Because I stayed there. Because they think I'm a . . ." She looked at Effie and bit her lip. "They think I worked there," she said.

"I see." Matt scowled and shook his head. "Everybody knows that Elvira Primrose is the town busybody. But surely the school board—"

"Wanted nothing to do with me," Carrie said.

"Uncle Matt?" Sarah tugged on his trouser leg. "Why is Aunt Carrie mad, Uncle Matt?"

He picked her up. "She's not really mad, Sarah. She's just a little upset." He handed the child to Effie. "Take her upstairs, Effie," he said. "I'd like to talk to Carrie for a few minutes."

"Sure thing, Mr. Matt. Let's you'n me go upstairs and play with your dollies, Sarah."

Carrie kissed Sarah's cheek. "I'm not mad, baby. You go along with Effie. I'll be up in a few minutes."

When they left the room, she moved closer to the fireplace and, turning her back to Matt, began to warm her hands. She wasn't aware that he had moved closer to her until he said, "Why did you leave The Chateau without telling me?"

"I wasn't aware that I had to report my movements to you."

"What's wrong? Why are you angry?"

"I'm not angry. It's just..." She shook her head.

"Just what?"

"I really prefer that you not come here again." She tightened her hands together behind her back. "I'm grateful to you for helping me, but under the circumstances—"

"What circumstances?"

"I know," she said in a low voice. "I know about you and Rosalinda."

"Rosalinda?" His face went still. "What are you talking about?"

She met his angry gaze, then quickly lowered her eyes. "Charmaine told me you knew Rosalinda before she came to Cripple Creek. You bought her presents. You took her buggy riding. You and she were..." She shook her head, unable to say the word.

"Lovers? You think your sister and I were lovers?"

"You knew her before Sarah was born. You were together there, and here, and now that she's dead you thought that I...that I could take her place. You said—"

"I said that I wanted to take care of you. But not because you're anything like Rosalinda." His mouth tightened into a cruel, hard line. "You're not like her, Carrie. Rosalinda was a sweet and loving woman who saw good in everybody. She did the best she could, for herself and for Sarah. She—"

"You're her father."

"What?" Matt's fingers bit hard into Carrie's shoulders. "What did you say?"

"You're Sarah's father." She looked up at him, her face set and angry. "I know it's true so don't try to deny it. You bring her presents, you—"

"And that makes me her father?"

"Doesn't it?"

He stared down into her face, his eyes burning with anger. "My God," he said, "what kind of woman are you?"

"Let me go!"

He released her, breathing hard, his hands curled into fists.

"Do you deny it?" she said.

Matt didn't answer.

She gripped the edge of the mantel. "Can you tell me that you and Rosalinda weren't lovers? That you're not Sarah's father?"

"I won't tell you a damn thing!" He grabbed his coat up off the chair by the fireplace and headed for the door.

"Don't come here again," she said.

He stopped. "A few minutes ago you talked about Mrs. Primrose being a narrow-minded biddy. Well, maybe you'd better take a look at yourself, Carrie. A good long look."

He turned and left, slamming the door behind him.

Carrie stood there for a moment, then with a cry, she covered her face with her hands and sank down onto the sofa.

"Matt," she whispered into the stillness of the room.

A chill crept through her body that had nothing to do with the cold or the wind that howled outside the small house. "Matt," she said again. And began to weep.

The blizzard began before dawn the next day. It snowed hard for three days, crippling the town, forcing the people who lived there to stay in their homes. Coal and firewood ran low, and so did food. Though Carrie managed to keep the downstairs of the house on Second Street warm, the upstairs was freezing cold. She and Effie brought a mattress downstairs and the three of them slept in front of the fire.

As she lay there at night with Rosalinda's little girl in her arms, Carrie experienced a rush of feeling she hadn't thought possible, for she had grown to love Rosalinda's daughter, her daughter now. As she kissed the top of Sarah's head, she tried not to think that this was Matt's child. She did not know why it hurt so much, but it did.

On the evening of the third night, with the snow still falling, Sarah developed a fever. By midnight she had a cough and her throat was so swollen she could barely speak. Her face was red and her eyes were weepy.

"I don't feel good," she managed to say. "My throat hurts."

"I know, baby." Carrie kissed the feverish forehead. "I've got to go for the doctor, Effie."

"I'll go, Miss Carrie," Effie protested. "It's best you stay here with Sarah."

But Carrie insisted that she should be the one to go. She tied a muffler over her head, and with the gray cloak closed around her, opened the door and stepped outside. Four-foot drifts lined the street, and still the snow came down. The wind-blown flakes blinded her and took her breath away.

The streets were dark, everything was closed. Because of the hour, and the cold, no one was out. A few blocks down, a lone horse-drawn rig passed her. White steam rolled from the horse's nostrils and the animal snorted with cold.

The rig slowed and stopped.

"Carrie?" Matt looked down at her. "Is that you? What's wrong? What are you doing out this time of night?"

"It's Sarah. She's ill. I'm on my way to Dr. Taylor's."

He reached his hand down to her. "Get in."

"No, I—"

"Dammit, get in!" he roared. When Carrie climbed up, he covered her with the lap rug and flicked the whip across the horse's back. "Ya! Giddap!"

Five minutes later he pulled to a stop in front of Elsworth Taylor's office. "Wait here," he told Carrie, and jumped down off the rig.

He returned quickly, Dr. Taylor in tow.

The older man got in beside Carrie. "What's the matter with the little girl?" he asked as Matt took his seat and called out to the horse.

"She has a fever and a cough. Her throat is so sore she can hardly speak," Carrie said.

"Croup most likely." Dr. Taylor pulled his muffler up to cover his ears. "Lots of it going around. No wonder. Terrible weather. Not fit fer man ner mule." He patted Carrie's hand. "Don't look so scared, Miss Carrie. We're going to fix her up just fine."

But Carrie was scared. By the time they reached the house, Sarah's breathing was labored, and, in spite of the cold, her hair was damp and she was burning with fever. She lay on the sofa near the fireplace with Effie beside her. A steam kettle simmered over the fire, puffing out hot moist air that smelled of liniment and eucalyptus oil.

"Good girl, Effie," Dr. Taylor said. "That'll help her chest and make it easier for her to breathe." He pulled a chair up close to the sofa. "Now then, let's have a look at her."

Sarah opened her eyes when he touched her, but it was Matt she saw, not the doctor. "Uncle Matt," she whispered, and holding her arms up to be held, she began to cry.

Matt knelt beside the sofa and put his arms around her. "It's all right, baby," he said. "I'm here and so is Dr. Taylor. He's going to make you better." He soothed the tangled hair back and kissed her forehead. "Don't cry, little love. Don't cry, little Sarah."

"Will you stay with me, Uncle Matt?"

He looked up at Carrie. Her expression was unreadable. Before he could answer, Carrie spoke up, "Of course he will, Sarah."

The doctor took a bottle of cough syrup out of his black bag. "Let's get some of this into her." He shook the bottle. "Get a spoon, will you, Effie? And Matt, you raise Sarah up some."

Effie hurried back with the spoon. The doctor poured the cough syrup into it. "Open your mouth, Sarah," he coaxed.

She shook her head.

"Come on, baby," Matt said. "Do it for me."

The corners of her mouth turned down, but she opened her mouth and took the syrup.

"That's my girl," Matt said.

My girl. Carrie clenched her hands to her sides. "What can I do?" she asked Dr. Taylor.

He reached into his bag and took out several packets of what appeared to be herbs. "Boil these up for the poultice, Miss Carrie. One of 'ems asafetida. Smells pure awful but it'll help."

Things seemed to move quickly after that. The poultice was made and applied to Sarah's chest, and a warm cloth containing some of the evil-smelling asafetida was placed around her throat. Dr. Taylor tried to give her another spoonful of cough syrup, but she refused to take it unless Matt held her. Finally, cradled in Matt's arms, her breathing easier, the child went to sleep.

"Do beat all how that young'un takes to you, Matt," Dr. Taylor said, closing his bag. "I'll be back in the morning, but I'm pretty sure she's going to be all right now. You keep her good and warm, Miss Carrie, and give her another spoonful of the medicine when she wakes up. Tomorrow you fix her a nice bowl of chicken soup, that'll help, too."

Chicken soup? The farmers who sold chickens lived on the other side of town. She didn't know if they were open in this weather. She hadn't even been able to get milk for three days because of the storm. But she nodded and said, "I will, Doctor," vowing that somehow she would find a chicken.

Dr. Taylor nodded to Matt. "If you want to stay here with the little girl, I'll just borrow your rig and bring it back when I come in the morning." He rested a hand on Carrie's shoulder. "I'm sure Miss Carrie would feel a whole lot better if you did, seeing as how the little girl dotes on you."

Carrie looked at Matt and at Sarah. The child's head rested against his shoulder, and her chubby little fingers were curled around his hand. Matt looked up at Carrie, something unreadable in his eyes, waiting.

"It would be..." She swallowed hard. "It would be nice if you would stay, Matt, for Sarah's sake."

"Then I will," Matt said. "For Sarah's sake."

After the doctor left, Carrie sent Effie to try to get some sleep. "It's not as cold as it was," Carrie said. "Go upstairs so you can rest."

But the girl shook her head. "Won't be no sleeping for me till I know Sarah's all right. I'll fix you and Mr. Matt some coffee and then I'll just sit here in the rocker by the fire, case you need something."

Effie went into the kitchen, and the only sound in the room was the crackle of the fire in the fireplace. Because she needed to be close to Sarah, Carrie moved to the other end of the sofa so that she could touch the child. Sarah's cheeks were flushed, her breathing was labored.

"She's so small," Carrie whispered, almost to herself. She laid a finger on Sarah's cheek. "Children are so vulnerable, Matt. So helpless, so dependent on the adults in their lives. I remember Rosalinda at this age. I was older and I tried to..." She shook her head and a look of intense pain crossed her face.

"What, Carrie? You tried to what?"

"To protect her," she said. "But I couldn't. He was so big. He was always so angry."

"Your father?"

A shudder ran through Carrie and he saw that her hands were shaking.

"Sarah looks like Rosie." Carrie smiled. "And sometimes she's as feisty as Rosie was." She stroked Sarah's cheek. "Even when Rosie was Sarah's age she tried to defy Father." She looked at Matt, then away, ashamed at having told him, yet somehow needing to. "She was so little and he was so big and mean...to Rosie mostly. Our mother didn't try to stop him. Maybe she should have." Carrie shook her head. "I don't know. I suppose she was afraid. I tried, but when I did..." She stopped, unable to go on.

"He beat you, too?" Matt said.

"Yes." The word trembled from her lips. "Yes, he beat me, too." She swiped at her tearstained cheeks with the back of her hand. "I never blamed Rosie for running away, Matt, but I wish she had told me she was leaving."

Matt wanted to touch her, to hold her as he held Sarah, but knew that he couldn't, that she didn't want him to. He thought of the child she had been, small and defenseless, trying to protect her younger sister.

The other night, he'd been so angry he'd wanted to throttle her. She was opinionated, strongly independent, and because of the way she had been raised, set in her ideas of right and wrong. She thought Charmaine and the girls who had tried to help her were sinners headed straight for hell. Yet she had taken young Effie in.

With the firelight on her tearstained face, she looked young and vulnerable. He thought of what she must have been like when she was a child, and the thought of her being abused tightened his stomach with a visceral pain that made him wince. He looked down at the child he was holding and he thought of her mother, and of Carrie, and of how it had been for them when they were her age.

Again he was overwhelmed by the need to hold Carrie, and he watched with lowered eyes when she eased the blanket closer about the sleeping child. He knew he still wanted her, straitlaced and opinionated though she was. But now with a wanting came a new emotion. He wanted to make up to Carrie for all the bad times she had ever suffered. He wanted to spoil her, to pet her, to buy pretty things for her. He wanted . . . God help him, he wasn't sure what he wanted.

Effie came back with the coffee. They drank it and when they'd finished, Effie took the cups out to the kitchen, then settled herself in the rocking chair by the fire. Within minutes her head nodded and soon she was asleep.

Carrie smiled. "Poor little thing. She loves Sarah as much as I do. She was as frightened tonight as I was." She looked at Matt. "And I was frightened," she said. "I still am."

Again Matt felt an overwhelming urge to touch her, but knew that if he did, the closeness they shared would vanish.

Besides which, he was aware that their love for Sarah was the only reason they were together tonight. "She's going to be all right," he said. "Her breathing is easier."

"Yes." Carrie smoothed the damp hair back from Sarah's forehead. When she did, her fingers brushed against Matt's. She stopped what she was doing and looked up at him.

"Carrie," he said.

Inhaling deeply, Carrie removed her hand. "She's sleeping now," she whispered in a shaky voice. "You can put her down."

But Matt shook his head. "No, I like to hold her."

Because she's yours. A sigh whispered through Carrie. Sarah was Matt's child and he loved her. His tenderness showed in the way he held her, the gentleness in his voice when he spoke to her.

Carrie thought then of the father who had never touched either her or Rosalinda with tenderness or with love, and she said, "The other night I told you that I didn't want you to come here again. It was wrong of me. You're Sarah's father, you have a right to see her."

"Carrie—"

"No, it's all right," she said. "I understand. I won't stop you from trying to see her."

"Dammit, woman, will you listen to me? I..." Just then, Sarah stirred in his arms.

"Hush, baby," he said caressingly.

Matt reached for Carrie's hand. "There's something I want to tell you. I should have before, but I—"

"Wait." Carrie put her hand on Sarah's forehead. "She's sweating," she said. "The fever's breaking. I've got to dry her off and change her nightshirt. I'll get a clean one."

"Carrie, listen—"

"I'll be right back," she said.

And the moment was lost.

When Carrie came downstairs with a towel and a fresh flannel nightshirt, Matt held Sarah so that Carrie could take the damp garment off and dry her. Then, with Matt still holding Sarah, she slipped the clean nightshirt over the little girl's head. "She'll be all right now, Matt. You don't have to stay."

"What about you, Carrie? Will you be all right?"

"Yes, now that Sarah is." She moved to stand in front of the fire. "Thank you for coming, Matt. For helping."

He took a step toward her. "Carrie, I—"

"No." She put her hands in front of her as though to defend herself. "No," she said again. "You can come to visit Sarah. Not me."

His nostrils flared. "I see."

"I'm sorry, but under the circumstances..." She shook her head, unable to go on.

"Because you believe that Rosalinda and I were lovers?"

"Yes." She waited for him to deny it, but he said nothing.

He picked up his hat and coat. "When Doc Taylor comes, tell him I'm walking home. It's almost light and the snow has stopped." He hesitated. "If you don't mind I'd like to stop by in the morning to check on Sarah."

"Of course I don't mind." She went with him to the door. "Thank you for bringing the doctor. Thank you for everything, Matt."

"You're welcome." He looked down at her and it was all he could do not to gather her in his arms. He wanted to hold her. He wanted to kiss her until her lips parted, until her body went soft against his the way it once had. He wanted to touch her until it was too much for them both. He wanted . . .

He turned away. "Sleep if you can," he said. And before Carrie could answer, he went out, closing the door behind him.

The next morning Matt returned at eight-thirty while Sarah and Effie were still asleep. He came with three chickens, plucked and cleaned, a gallon of milk, and a bag of oranges.

"Oranges!" Carrie looked at them, dumbfounded. "Where did you get them?"

"Mr. Davenport got them in all the way from California just before the storm started. The juice will be good for Sarah."

"She'll love it. Just let me get my purse and I'll—"

"Dammit," Matt snapped. "Dammit to hell, Carrie. I don't want your money."

"You have to let me pay you."

"No!"

"I insist."

"You insist and I'll take these things back where I got them." He glared at her. "You're the most exasperating woman I've ever met," he said. "You make me so mad I want to..." He growled low in his throat. "Dammit," he said, and before she could back away, he grabbed her and pulled her into his arms.

He kissed her the way he'd wanted to kiss her the night before. He kissed her with all the anger and the passion he'd been holding in check since that day in the bedroom at Charmaine's. Opinionated and narrow-minded she might be, but by God, she set his blood on fire as no woman had ever before.

Her lips were tightly compressed under his, and that made him even angrier. He ground his mouth against hers. When she gasped in protest, he slid his tongue past her lips. Her mouth was sweet and warm and tasted of her. She tried to get away, but he held her there, held her while a fire raged through his veins, constricting every muscle in his body. When she tried to squirm free, he put one hand against the small of her back and pressed her to him.

She felt his hardness and brought her hands up against his chest. Twisting her face from his, she whispered, "No! Let me go! Effie might—"

"Effie won't." He captured her mouth again and pulled her body tighter to his. "Kiss me, Carrie," he said against her lips. "Kiss me, sweetheart."

She didn't want to kiss him, didn't want her body to yearn toward his. But suddenly her lips parted and, with a sob, she was answering his kiss and pressing her body close to his. Somewhere within her a flame kindled and grew. She moaned into his mouth and knew that this was wrong.

"Oh, please," she said against his lips. "Oh, please. Let me go."

A sigh shuddered through Matt, but he did as she asked.

"Carrie," he murmured, wearing a look she had never seen on a man's face before. A look of such hunger, of such need that for a moment she almost relented.

Cupping her face in his hands, he bent to kiss her again.

"No," she whispered. "No, it's . . . it's wicked. What we feel is wicked."

Matt's scowling expression looked almost frightening.

She stepped away from him. "I'm not like this. I'm not the kind of woman who does things like this."

He looked down at her. "What kind of woman are you, Carrie?" he asked in a voice so soft she could barely hear him.

"I'm not like the women you know. Women like Charmaine and Lorelei and—"

"Women like Rosalinda?"

She flinched as though he had struck her. "Please," she whispered. "Please go."

His nostrils flared. She thought for a moment he was going to speak. Instead he looked at her, one long look that seemed to touch her very soul.

"Goodbye," he said. Then he turned and went out the door.

Chapter Eight

By the end of the week Sarah was almost well. Matt came to see her on Saturday evening with a bag of lemon drops and a box of building blocks. Carrie was upstairs when he came, and that was where she stayed until he left. When she heard the door close, she went to the window and looked at the street below.

In the lamplight she saw the snow drifting down over the shoulders of his overcoat, dusting his thick black hair with flakes of white.

He was so tall, so powerfully built. For a moment, watching him, Carrie felt the same flutter of excitement, the same fear she had experienced the first time she had seen him.

He was so overwhelmingly male, a man in every sense of the word. She had felt the strength and the comfort of his arms around her, the hardness of his body when he drew her close to him. God help her, she had felt the heated response of her own body, the flame that had flared and crept down to the private part of her. Even now, watching him this way, knowing that what she felt was wicked, she could not help the fire that burned with the memory of their embrace.

Matt turned back to wave to Sarah, and when he did, he looked up, and when he saw Carrie, his expression changed. It seemed to her that even from this distance he could see, and know, the shameful secret of her desire.

Carrie let the curtain fall back into place and stood there by the window, feeling the agitated rise and fall of her breathing. With a strangled cry, she went to the pitcher and bowl on her dressing table to splash cold water on her face. And wash her hands.

These strange desires were bad. Nice women weren't supposed to feel this way. Desires of the flesh were shameful. She knew, because she had heard her father preach it almost every Sunday for twenty years. She had learned well that pleasures of the flesh were the work of the devil.

Once, when Rosalinda had been two or three years old, their mother had put her down on the old worn sofa in the parlor for a nap. She had been waking up when their father came home. Half-asleep, Rosalinda had been touching herself. And their father had seen her.

With a roar he had yanked her up off the sofa and whipped the offending hand until blisters rose. Then he had locked Rosalinda in the hall closet.

There were other memories; so many of them dealt with sin and shame. Carrie remembered when she was eight. On her way home from school she had come upon two dogs locked together. She had stared at them wide-eyed, wondering how in the world they had gotten that way. She had puzzled about it all the way home and she'd burst into the house saying, "Mama, guess what? I saw two dogs all hitched up together and the one dog was crying and the other dog was sort of moving and looking real funny and—"

"Enough!" Her father jumped up out of his chair and started toward her. "I won't have this kind of wicked talk in my house." And he had slapped her, hard across her face.

After that Carrie had learned to keep her thoughts and her wonderings to herself. As the years passed the difference between good and evil, between nice girls and bad girls, had been firmly implanted into her mind. Marilla Buehler, who had a baby seven months after she married, was bad. So was sixteen-year-old Jessie Adkins who was caught kissing freckle-faced Carlisle Collier behind the book stands in the library.

Carrie never saw her father kiss or show any affection toward her mother, but once a month, always on a Saturday night after he had told her and her sister to go to bed, he would say, "Get on in the bedroom, Sarah."

And once when Carrie was older, she had awakened to hear her mother's muffled cry, "Horacio...stop, please. You're hurting me."

And her father's grunting sound, his muffled reply, "It's your duty, woman."

The next morning his sermon would be on the sins of the flesh.

The sins of the flesh. Carrie washed her hands again.

On Monday morning Sarah was well enough to be left with Effie. At nine o'clock Carrie kissed her niece goodbye, donned her hat and cloak and set out to find a job.

There was a sign in the millinery shop that read Help Wanted.

Thank God, she thought, and with a smile, opened the door and went in. A bell over the door tinkled and a nice-looking, silver-haired woman hurried in from the back room.

"Good morning," she said. "May I help you?"

"I saw your sign in the window," Carrie said. "I'd like to apply for the job."

"Well, my goodness, isn't this my lucky day." The woman beamed. "Have you had any experience in a shop like this?"

"No, I haven't. I'm a schoolteacher and I—"

"A teacher? You're the teacher Mrs. Primrose...?" The woman's cheeks turned pink. "Miss...?"

"McClennon," Carrie said with a sinking feeling.

"Yes, well...I really am sorry, Miss McClennon, but I'm afraid the position has already been filled."

"But the sign is still in the window."

"Is it?" The woman's hands fluttered over her ample chest. "Oh, dear me, I should have taken it out." She stepped over to the window and removed it. "I...I'm really very sorry. I hope you understand."

"I understand," Carrie said.

She went to the dry goods store next. The woman behind the counter smiled until Carrie introduced herself. Then, with a sniff of her pudgy nose, said there was no opening for the likes of such as Carrie.

Nor was there an opening at the shoe and clothing store, the drugstore, the hardware store or the café. There wasn't an opening at the bakeshop, either, but as she was leaving, the owner touched her arm and said, "I'm sorry. Believe me, if I could I'd give you a job."

By the time Carrie reached Mr. Davenport's general store, she was tired and discouraged. He was her last hope in Cripple Creek.

"I'm sorry," he said with a shake of his head when she asked if he needed any help. "I'd hire you if I could, but the only help I really need is old Homer Teasdale." His blue eyes were kind. "I heard the gossip that old hellcat Elvira Primrose has been spreading all over town and how she acted when you went to the schoolhouse. Time somebody shut her up. It's her husband's job, but I reckon she's had poor Thaddeus buffaloed from the day he said 'I do.'" Mr. Davenport scratched his whiskered chin, then changing the subject, said, "I heard your sister's little girl has been poorly. How's she doing?"

"She's better now, thank you." Carrie drew her cloak closer about her.

"Why don't you take her some of these apples?" Mr. Davenport reached behind him, took a brown paper bag and began to fill it with the apples from the barrel near the counter. "You give her these," he said. "They're real tasty."

Carrie opened her purse. "How much are they, Mr. Davenport?"

"They're a gift ma'am. From me to the little girl."

"But I . . ." She felt the sting of tears behind her eyelids. The hurts and the insults she had suffered all this long morning hadn't made her cry, but this sudden kindness did. Lowering her eyes, she took a big shaky breath. "You're very kind," she managed to say. "I know Sarah will love them."

The snow had stopped when at last she started home, but the air was bitterly cold and she was glad when she climbed the steps of the house on Second Street.

"Hey, there!"

Carrie turned just as a man rounded the corner of the street and started toward her.

"Well, if this don't beat all," he said. "I been looking all over town for you ever since I got back from Cheyenne." He grinned and came up onto the porch. "You're just as pert and pretty as I remember. Carrie, isn't it? Carrie McClennon?"

"Yes, but I'm afraid I don't remember you, Mr....?"

"LaRue," he said. "Nathan LaRue. We met in the Denver railroad station." His face darkened. "I was helping you aboard when that highfalutin Matt Craddock stopped me. Near broke my jaw." His voice took on a whining tone. "And for no reason a'tall. All I was trying to do was help a lady in distress. Here he is, a no-count gamblin' man who just because he struck it rich with a gold mine thinks he's better than us common folks. I surely do hope you haven't been having anything to do with him."

Nathan LaRue. The last time she'd seen him he'd been running alongside the train trying to catch up with it. Matt had said he was a procurer, a man who recruited girls for the cribs and parlor houses. Girls like Effie.

Carrie stepped closer to the door. "I'm very cold, Mr. LaRue," she said. "I really must go in now."

He winked and sidled closer. "I'm a little cold myself, Miss McClennon. Could use a nice cup of coffee or maybe even something stronger if you was to offer it."

"I'm sorry, Mr. LaRue, but I'm afraid not."

"I'm just trying to be friendly." He stepped around in front of Carrie, blocking her way to the door. "How've things been going for you?"

"Well enough."

"You're looking a little peaked, if you don't mind my saying so."

"I'm very tired. I've been out today trying to find work. So if you'll excuse me—"

"If it's work you want then you're mighty lucky I happened along." He grinned. "I can put you to work tomorrow."

"To work?" Carrie asked with a frown.

"A girl like you, Miss McClennon, why I could make you the toast of the tenderloin. Set you up real nice in one of the houses and I bet in a week you'd have more money than you'd know what to do with."

"What?" Carrie's voice rose. "What?"

LaRue's grin widened. "You know what."

"Get off my porch," she said.

"Ain't no call to get all riled up. You need a job, I need an extra girl. With your looks—"

She shoved him in the chest with the flat of her hand. "Get away from me!" she cried.

"Now you just wait a minute."

But Carrie wasn't waiting for anything. All her frustration and anger over being rejected by everybody in town boiled to the surface. How dare this man think that she would sell herself? How dare he?

She pushed with all her might, catching him by surprise as he backed away. With one hard final push, she shoved him right off the front porch into a snowbank.

"Get out of here!" she screamed. "And don't ever come back!"

She yanked open the front door just as Effie, armed with a black iron skillet, started to open it from the other side.

"Lord, Miss Carrie, what's going on? I heard…" She saw LaRue picking himself up out of the snow and raised the skillet above her head. "Is that no-good var-

mint bothering you? Let me get a whack at him.
I'll—"

"No, it's all right." Carrie put a restraining hand on
Effie's. "He's leaving. He won't be back."

Hoping to God it was true, Carrie led the girl inside
and closed the door.

That night after Carrie had put Sarah to bed, she
came back downstairs to the kitchen. There was a fire
in the fireplace and Effie had the kettle on.

"You look real done in," she told Carrie. "I thought
maybe a nice cup of tea would perk you up."

"Yes, it would, Effie. Thanks."

"I don't guess you had any luck finding a job today,
did you?"

"No, I didn't, Effie. I went into every store in Cripple Creek, but nobody would hire me." Carrie looked
down at her hands. "Mrs. Primrose got to them before
I did."

She watched Effie pour a cup of hot tea into one of
the china cups and put it on a saucer, and though Carrie was depressed, it cheered her to see how much better the girl looked than when she had first seen her. Effie
had gained a little weight and her face didn't look as
worried and pinched as it had when she'd been at The
Chateau. At Carrie's suggestion, she now wore her hair
in a softer style around her face. In one of the shirtwaists and the long dark blue skirt that Carrie had given
her, she looked less waiflike and prettier.

"I know you're real worried about money," Effie
said, breaking in on her thoughts.

Carrie forced a smile. "Well, yes, I'm a little worried, but things will work out. Tomorrow I'll go back to
Victor and see if I can find something there."

"That just ain't practical, Miss Carrie. Leastways not in this kind of weather." Effie looked down at her hands. "I been thinking," she said. "I been thinking that I could go back to work."

"Go back to work? At The Chateau?"

"Yes'm." Avoiding Carrie's eyes, she poured tea for herself and took a seat at the table. "I could give what I make to you and sometimes when I wasn't working I could still come over and see you and Sarah and—"

"No! Absolutely not!" Carrie reached out and took Effie's hand. "You're part of Sarah's and my family now, Effie. You belong with us."

"But you need money, Miss Carrie."

"I don't need it that badly. Besides, something will turn up. I'll think of something."

But what? During the next few days, Carrie racked her brain, trying to figure out how she was going to manage on the little money she had left. In spite of Effie's not wanting her to, she took the train back to Victor. But there were no jobs there, either. She didn't know whether Mrs. Primrose had visited the shops and stores there, or whether there simply weren't any jobs.

One night, alone in her room, Carrie took what money she had left and counted it. Twice. There was so little left, barely enough to buy food for another week. She sat for a moment, looking at the money, then went to the dresser and took the silver filigree brooch out of the drawer. She held it in her hand for a moment, then with a sigh put it in her pocketbook.

It was the only pretty thing her mother had ever had, a gift from her own mother. A few days before she died, she had pressed it into Carrie's hand.

"I never wore it, because your father said it was too frivolous to wear to church and that was just about the only time I ever got out of the house except when I did the shopping. I want you to have it, Carrie, and what's more, I want you to wear it.''

It meant a lot to Carrie, and it would hurt her to part with it. But she had no choice, she needed the money.

The following morning she told Effie she had to go shopping. Bundling her cloak about her, she made her way along Bennett Avenue to the pawnshop she had seen there. At the door she paused, reluctant to go in, saddened by the need to part with this tenuous link to her mother.

The window was filled with an assortment of things for sale: gold watches and watch fobs, a violin, a beautifully carved cameo, silver earrings, gold shirt studs, a trumpet. All treasures from better times.

With a smothered sigh, Carrie pushed open the door and went in.

The inside was a larger duplication of the things in the window. Here there were overcoats and boots, hunting rifles and six-shooters, pickaxes and cooking pots.

''Help ya?''

Carrie turned and saw a man peering at her out of what seemed like a wire cage. She went toward him, took the brooch out of her handbag and said, ''Yes. I'd like to...'' She wasn't sure what the word was. Pawn? Sell? ''I have this,'' she said, and put the brooch on the counter at the edge of the cage.

He picked it up and looked at it. ''Old,'' he said. ''Not worth much.''

Carrie tightened her hands around her bag. ''It's silver,'' she said.

''Gold's better.''

''It's a family heirloom.''

''That don't mean nothin' to me.''

She waited.

"I could give you a couple of dollars for it."

"I want ten dollars."

"Ten dollars!" He shoved the brooch toward her. "I can't give you nothin' like that."

"How much . . . ?" She felt as though she were begging, and hated it. She wanted to turn and run out of the shop. But she couldn't. "How much would you give me?" she asked.

"Three dollars."

"Three dollars! But it's worth—"

"Take it or leave it, lady."

Carrie bit hard down on her lip. "I'll take it," she said.

She came out of the shop just as Matt rounded the corner. He started to call out to her, then stopped when he caught a glimpse of her white face. When she turned away from him, he saw the slump of her shoulders, hunched as though in pain.

Hesitating a moment, he looked at her retreating figure, then at the pawnshop. "What the hell?" he muttered under his breath, and headed for the pawnshop.

"Maybe you could become a seamstress," Effie said, one evening after Sarah was in bed. "Those two shirtwaists you made over for me turned out real nice."

"But it took me a week to figure out how to do it." Carrie shook her head. "I'm a terrible seamstress, Effie. If I tried to make a living sewing for other folks, we'd all starve."

"You might could ask Mr. Matt if he knows anybody who's hiring. He knows just about everybody in town. Maybe he could help."

Carrie shook her head. "No," she said, "I couldn't do that."

He had not been back to the house since the evening he had brought Sarah the building blocks, the evening Carrie had watched him from the window. When Sarah asked why he hadn't come to see her, Carrie said, "I guess he's real busy, honey."

"But I miss him," Sarah said. And each night when she knelt to say her prayers she always said, "God bless Aunt Carrie and Effie and Uncle Matt."

"He 'pears to be real fond of you," Effie said now. "And of course he's just crazy about Sarah. It's real nice, how fond he is of her. Almost like she was his own little girl. Lord knows he's more of a daddy to her than her own ever was."

"I...I don't understand. I thought..." Carrie clasped her hands together. "What are you talking about, Effie?"

"I'm talking about that actor fella Miss Rosalinda got hooked up with. He was from down South somewhere. Had a fancy name. Beau...Beauregard something. She told me about him when she was sick, about how he up and left her when he found out she was in a family way."

"But I thought—" Carrie stopped. No. She didn't want Effie or anybody else to know she'd thought Matt was Sarah's father. But why hadn't Matt denied it? Why hadn't he told her that he and Rosalinda had only been friends, if indeed that's all they had been?

"Matt," she said, "Mr. Craddock...he knew Rosalinda before, didn't he?"

Effie nodded. "Miss Rosalinda met him in Wichita and I guess they got friendly there. So when she came here and couldn't get a job, he was real nice to her."

Real nice. A sigh escaped Carrie's lips, and while there was relief in knowing that Matt had not fathered Rosalinda's child, the fact still remained that undoubtedly he and Rosalinda had been lovers.

She didn't think she could ever forgive him for that.

Noah Pierce had taken to dropping by the house on Second Street, "to see how everything's going," he said. He always brought a little present for Sarah and a box of homemade fudge for Carrie and Effie. Mostly he talked to Carrie, because Effie was so tongue-tied in front of him she could barely speak. She tried to, but when she did she'd blush to the roots of her carrot-red hair and, with a stuttered "Excuse me," would beat a hasty retreat to the kitchen.

"You surely have done a lot for her," Noah said one afternoon after Effie had said there was something she had to attend to. "She's filled out real nice and she's near prettier than a picture." He leaned forward in his chair, hands on his knees. "I believe she's going to have a birthday soon."

"Next week," Carrie said. "She'll be sixteen."

"Lots of little gals get married when they're sixteen."

Carrie waited.

"I'm twenty-seven," he said. And cleared his throat. "My job over at The Chateau pays pretty good, Miss Carrie. And sometimes when there's a party, the gentlemen guests pay me extra. Course I don't plan to stay there forever. I've had offers to play the piano in some of the gambling houses, but I haven't wanted to leave Miss Charmaine because she's been real good to me. Even so, I've been thinking lately that if a man should decide to get married and start having young'uns he might should work in a place that's a little more respectable, if you get my meaning."

"I think I understand," Carrie said.

"I was wondering, since you're looking after Effie, what you'd think if I started..." He ran a finger around the collar of his white shirt. "If I was to court her," he said.

"I think you'd have to ask Effie that question, Noah," Carrie said with a smile.

"That'd scare me to death, Miss Carrie. She hightails it every time I come over. It seems like I never have a minute alone with her."

Carrie stood. "How about right now?" she asked.

"Oh, Lord, I—"

But before he could say anything else, Carrie called out, "Effie? Could you come in here, please?"

And when the girl came through the kitchen door, Carrie said, "I'm going upstairs to check on Sarah. Would you entertain Mr. Pierce for a little while?"

Effie looked at Noah Pierce. Her cheeks flushed and her hands twisted the edges of the big white apron. She shot an appealing glance Carrie's way, but with a wave of her hand, Carrie started up the stairs.

Carrie came down half an hour later to see a bemused Effie sitting on the edge of the rocking chair. "Did Mr. Pierce leave?" Carrie asked.

Effie blinked and nodded.

"Did you have a nice visit?" Carrie persisted.

"Yes. He..." Effie looked at her. "He asked if he could come calling, Miss Carrie. He asked if he could...could *court* me."

"Oh?" Carrie tried to hide a smile. "And what did you say, Effie?"

"I didn't hardly know what to say. I just sat here like a ninny, staring at him because I couldn't believe that anybody'd ever want me, after me being a...you know. I like Mr. Pierce. He's always been nice to me, but I never thought...I never thought he liked me."

"What did you tell him, Effie?"

"I don't know if I told him anything, Miss Carrie. I think I just kind of bobbed my head." She blushed again. "He asked if it'd be all right if next week, on my birthday, he took me out to the Ponderosa Restaurant for dinner." She looked at Carrie. "What do you think, Miss Carrie? Should I go?"

"Would you like to?"

"Yes, ma'am. I believe I would."

"Then go," Carrie said with a smile. "Mr. Pierce seems like a very nice man."

"He is." Effie said smiling. "He purely is."

Noah became a frequent visitor to the house on Second Street. He bought Effie a pair of earrings for her birthday, and whenever he had an afternoon or an evening free he took her buggy riding.

Effie blossomed under all the attention. She smiled and laughed and sang in a high, off-key voice as she helped Carrie with the housework. And she punctuated almost every sentence with, "Noah says" or "Noah thinks."

It was a pleasure to see her so happy, and Carrie was fervently glad that if things worked out between Effie and Noah, that never again, please God, would the girl have to work in a place like The Chateau.

But though she was happy for Effie, every day her concern for her own problems grew. She didn't have enough money for next months' rent, and barely enough for food. She was so desperate that she'd even thought of writing Josiah Wilkinson and telling him she'd marry him if he'd send her enough money to get back to Ohio.

But the thought of Josiah Wilkinson, of his ever touching her, of doing to her what husbands did to their wives when they got married, made her feel almost physically ill.

She went back to some of the places she had been to before, hoping against hope that the storekeepers had relented. The answer was always the same, they had nothing for her. She even tried to get a job doing housework. No one would have her.

Then one day when Noah came to call on Effie, he said, "I know you've been looking for work, Miss Carrie, and just today I heard of something."

"You did?" Carrie felt her pulses race. "What is it, Noah?"

"Well, ma'am, it's a job working over at the Golden Nugget as an assistant manager."

"The Golden Nugget?"

"It's a gambling establishment, Miss Carrie. A real fine place."

"But I can't...I couldn't..." Carrie shook her head. "I couldn't work in a place like that."

"There's just gambling and drinking," Noah persisted. "It's not like The Chateau. There are girls and all, to talk to the customers and dance with them, but they don't..." His face reddened. "That's all they do," he said. "And you wouldn't do that. You'd just take care of the business end and keep an eye on things. I guess you'd have to wear some fancy duds and all, but you wouldn't have to drink or dance with the customers."

Carrie shook her head. "I don't think so," she said.

Noah looked troubled. "If you change your mind, I'll go on over to the Golden Nugget with you and introduce you to Pete O'Reilly. He's the manager. Wouldn't hurt you none to talk to him. Job pays good and you might like it."

"I'm afraid not, Noah. But thank you."

When Carrie was alone, she thought, a gambling saloon! Noah Pierce had actually suggested she work in a gambling saloon! She needed a job all right, but that was something she absolutely would not do.

Absolutely not.

Three days later, when she went into the general store to buy a sack of flour, Mr. Davenport, looking red faced with embarrassment said, "I beg your pardon, Miss McClennon. I hate to say anything, but I'm afraid you're a little overdue on your rent. Miz Bisbee's daughter came in to see me yesterday and she said unless you could pay her by the end of the month you're going to have to leave."

Carrie stared at the grocer. Leave? And go where?

Once again the thought of Josiah Wilkinson flashed through her mind; once again she rejected it.

But what was she going to do? Dear God, what could she do?

The next day when Noah came to call, she told him that she had changed her mind about the job at the Golden Nugget.

Chapter Nine

The dress was wine-colored chiffon over pink satin. There were inserts of lace down the sides and around the bosom, with stitched-in tucks of pink velvet ribbon. It cinched in at the waist and came to a low vee in the front. It was the most daring dress Carrie had ever seen, let alone worn.

But daring though it was, it was not nearly as revealing as the gowns the other women wore. Their full white breasts, pushed high up by laced-up corsets, bulged over their low-cut gowns. They wore rouge on their cheeks and their lips, and makeup around their sultry eyes.

"We put boiled belladonna leaves on our eyes before we come to work," a woman named Blanche told Carrie. "It gives us bedroom eyes. Believe me, honey, that's what the men like."

Bedroom eyes. Carrie shuddered. She'd been shuddering inwardly ever since she'd walked into the Golden Nugget three days ago and asked for Pete O'Reilly.

"Over there," a man mopping the floor had told her. "The bald-headed guy with the red mustache talking to the little guy. Over there by the bar."

Carrie had taken a deep breath and, when she approached O'Reilly, she'd said, "Good afternoon. My name is Carrie McClennon, and I—"

"Be right with you," he said without looking up from the row of figures he was adding. When he was finished checking them, he handed them to the other man and said, "Show this to the boss, Stan. He'll want to check it. Tell him we did real good last night." He turned to Carrie. "Now then," he said, and stopped. Eyebrows as red as his mustache climbed. "*You're* Miss McClennon?" he asked.

"Yes." Carrie cleared her throat. "Mr. Noah Pierce told me that you were looking for an assistant manager."

O'Reilly nodded. "Yeah, but I was expecting..." He ran a hand across his bald head. "I don't suppose you've had any experience."

"No, but I—"

He sighed. "When can you start?"

"Tomorrow." Carrie clutched her handbag. "Whenever you want me to."

"Next Monday." He looked her up and down. "You'll have to have some gowns made, because sure as shooting you can't come to work looking like you do now."

Gowns made? Carrie's heart sank. She didn't have enough money for rent, and she certainly didn't have any money to buy gowns. "I'm sorry," she started to say. "I'm afraid I—"

O'Reilly reached into his pocket and handed her a hundred dollars. "This ought to cover it," he said. "You go see Miz Howard. That's Amelia Howard over on Hawthorne Street. She'll know what to do."

"But—"

"Salary's twenty-five dollars a week. Here's two weeks in advance in case you need to buy anything else."

Twenty-five dollars a week! Carrie had stared at the money, unable to believe that her financial troubles were over. That kind of salary was unheard of. Unless... She looked at O'Reilly. "I understood from Mr. Pierce that I was to be the assistant manager."

"That's right."

"He said my work would not include..." The money was hot in her hand. She had a crazy and momentary notion to take it and run. Instead she said, "I understood that the work I do here would not include socializing with the customers."

"It don't. All you got to do is help me and Stan with the books, order whiskey when it runs low, and kinda keep the girls in line. You don't have to drink with nobody or dance with nobody. Them's my orders from...I mean that's all an assistant manager does. It's kind of a prestige job, if you get my meaning."

Carrie didn't get his meaning, she only knew that when she walked out of the Golden Nugget, she had one hundred and fifty dollars in her hand.

The next day she paid her rent, then went to Hawthorne Street.

Miss Amelia Howard appeared to be a prim lady in her middle forties. After the seamstress invited Carrie in, she helped her remove her cloak, then proceeded to give Carrie a quick head-to-toe appraisal. She finally spoke.

"I know pretty much the kind of dresses you'll be needing. Now, take your suit off so that I can get your measurements."

Once that was done, she went to the many bolts of materials stacked against the wall and began selecting fabrics and colors. Beautiful colors—the lightest, most delicate blues Carrie had ever seen, bright reds, pinks and shadowy mauves, dark greens, pale greens, ivory and gold.

One by one she held them up to Carrie, nodding at the more subdued tones, putting aside the brighter colors.

"You won't be wearing a flannel petticoat under any of these," she said with a smile. "What you'll want will be some opera drawers or pantalets, and lacy camisoles over your corset. I can fix you up with everything you'll need, even the shoes. I'll have one of the dresses and some of the underthings finished by Monday. Come by in the afternoon and pick them up."

Carrie had left the seamstress in a daze, and she'd felt no different when she'd gone to collect the dress she would wear her first night at work.

Waiting until she had put on the delicate undergarments, the white bloomers and the chemise with a pink ribbon running through the top, the ribbed stockings, and the pink opera pumps, she finally looked at herself in the mirror. Never before had she worn clothes the likes of these. They looked indecent and...a smile curved Carrie's mouth. They looked pretty. They made her feel pretty.

But her hair..Carrie frowned. It was pulled straight back off her face the way she always wore it, which was quite proper of course. But somehow it didn't seem to go with the undergarments or with the dress she would be wearing. She unpinned it, brushed it out, then fluffed it into a looser fashion about her face before she pinned it back.

Finally she put the dress on, and when she did, she stared at herself in the mirror. "Mercy!" she'd said aloud.

When she went downstairs Effie too had stared at her openmouthed.

"Lord love us, Miss Carrie," she'd whispered. "If you aren't the prettiest thing I did see. You look like a princess right out of one of Mr. Grimm's fairy stories."

And Noah Pierce, who had come to escort Carrie to the Golden Nugget, grinned and said, "Effie's right, ma'am. You're really something else in that getup."

She felt like something else, Carrie thought now as she looked around her. She felt all arms and bare shoulders and exposed bosom. As for this place, it was unlike anything she'd ever seen before. She'd been here during the day when she'd come to apply for the job, but it was different now at night, all sparkling glitter and plush red velvet.

Upstairs, where she hadn't been, were the offices of the owner. "That way he can look down on what's happening," Mr. O'Reilly told her when he handed her a list of figures to check. "He isn't here every night, but when he is, he likes to keep an eye on what's going on."

Carved chairs with velvet seats were arranged at the sides of the room near the long mahogany bar. Chandeliers shone down upon the polished wood floors. A five-piece musical group played at one end of the big room near a small raised dance floor. There were gaming tables where men played poker and faro, while beautifully dressed girls circulated among them, offering drinks and encouraging smiles. Still other girls stood at the bar, chatting and drinking with the guests there. Others danced with whatever man asked them.

With the music playing, the laughter of the women, the voices of the men, and the whir of the roulette wheels, the room hummed with life.

When the music stopped, a piano was wheeled onto the small stage at the side of the dance floor and a woman, wearing the lowest cut gown Carrie had ever seen, mounted the stage.

Men gathered around and began clapping. "Whooee!" a couple of them cried. "Here comes Sally. Sing it, Sal. Let's hear it, girl!"

The woman laughed and tossed her shiny black curls back over the bare shoulder of her bright red dress, and began to sing in a loud, uninhibited voice,

"Oh, give me a man who's a cowboy,
A man who can rope and can ride,
A man who can wrangle a woman's fandangle
And once in the saddle can ride her to joy.

"Oh, give me a man who's a miner.
A man who knows how to go deep
A man who can plumb me, whose kisses can
    stun me
Whose carrot's so good I could weep."

The men roared and stamped their feet and clapped their hands. "More!" they yelled. "Come on, Sally baby, give us more."

"Gimme a drink, boys, and I'll give you anything you want," Sally LeBeau called out with a laugh.

One of the men handed her a shot glass full of whiskey. She tossed it down and reached for another, and then she began to sing a song even bawdier than the first.

Carrie stared up at the stage, unable to believe what she was hearing, that a woman, that *anybody*, would sing words like that in public.

Lord forgive me, she thought, I've fallen into a den of iniquity.

Matt watched her from the window of his upstairs office. From the moment Carrie had walked through the door tonight, she had been looking at everything and everyone with a wide-eyed expression. Pete O'Reilly, standing next to him, had said, "I sure hope you know what you're doing, boss."

Matt wasn't sure that he did, but he honestly couldn't think of another way to help her. He'd known from what Noah had told him that Carrie was running low on funds, but he hadn't known how bad her situation was until he'd seen her coming out of the pawnshop. He wanted to help her, but he knew that she wouldn't accept his help, so he'd thought of a job in the Golden Nugget. He'd had Noah tell her about the job, and he'd told O'Reilly that if and when she showed up, he was to hire her. He had also arranged for his bouncer, Worthy Magee, to take her home every night, and for the bartender, Buck Wattles, to keep an eye on her.

When she had taken her cloak off tonight, there had been a part of him that wanted to rush downstairs and put it back on her, a part of him that didn't like her exposing her creamy-white shoulders, or showing the vee in the line of her breasts. But the other side of him, that fiercely male part of him, felt a flare of excitement at seeing her like that, and yes, a sense of triumph because he'd known that, underneath her prim exterior and her schoolmarmish clothes, there was a woman just waiting to be unleashed. And like a butterfly eager to spread its wings or a flower waiting to blossom, it was time for Miss Carrie McClennon to become a woman.

A pretty woman, for with her auburn hair soft about her face and her cheeks flushed with excitement, she was one of the prettiest he'd ever seen. He knew then, as he'd known from almost the first moment he'd seen her, that he wanted her. But he'd have to be careful. Carrie wasn't like the other women he'd known in his life. She was special and that both worried and excited him.

Going to work wasn't much easier the next night or the nights that followed. But Carrie persevered. She arrived every night promptly at seven and left at one, always escorted to her front steps by Worthy Magee, a giant of a man whose job seemed to be making sure that the gentlemen acted like gentlemen.

As broad as he was tall, with a face that showed the scars of battles won and lost, Mr. Magee treated Carrie with old-fashioned courtliness. He always took her arm when they went up her front steps and waited until she was safely inside before he'd tip his hat and say, "Good evening, ma'am."

Stanley Bray, the Golden Nugget's bookkeeper, by contrast to Worthy Magee, was a quiet, bespectacled man with a humble demeanor. He showed Carrie the simple system of bookkeeping used by the Golden Nugget. He also instructed her how to count the number of bottles consumed every night, how to replenish the supply of special whiskey, the year and the make of the most expensive French champagne, and had taken her down to the cellar and showed her the kegs of beer and the barrels of what he called "homemade hooch."

For someone like Carrie, who had never had a drink in her life, this was a totally new experience.

Many of the customers at the Golden Nugget were well-dressed, prosperous-looking men, but a lot of them were rougher-looking fellows, prospectors and miners who liked their whiskey straight and their music loud. The first few nights that Carrie was there, a couple of them had sidled over to the high desk next to the bar where she checked on the price of drinks and the number of bottles taken to the tables.

Always, politely but firmly, Carrie refused their requests to share a drink or a dance, and if they persisted, Buck Wattles would suddenly appear to ask, "You having any trouble, Miss Carrie?" At which point, the men would mumble an excuse and beat a hasty retreat.

The musical group was lively, and although the music wasn't the kind that Carrie was used to, there were times she found herself tapping her toes to the beat and humming along with the songs like "Buffalo Gals (Won't You Come Out Tonight)" or "Oh! Susanna."

"You've got a mighty pretty voice," Buck Wattles said one night. "It's a lot better than Sally's, though I guess the men she's singing to pay more attention to the words than they do to the music." He shook his head. "She'd shock the likes of a mule skinner, Miss Carrie. Not only that, she drinks like one. Pours blue ruin down her throat like we were going to run out tomorrow. Look at her up there now, stewed as a turnip. Wonder she don't fall right off the stage."

Carrie turned to look at the singer, who was belting out one of her bawdy songs. Though she had been here for ten days now, she still wasn't used to Sally's singing. About the only songs she'd heard when she was growing up, and later when she sang in the church choir, were hymns and the more popular songs of the day.

Even some of the other girls who worked in the Golden Nugget were occasionally shocked by Sally LeBeau's songs. "Don't she just beat all?" a girl named Flo said to Carrie one night. "She's drinking more and more every night. Both Stan and Worthy have tried to talk to her, but she won't listen. Said she could drink any man here under the table and I guess she can."

"But she's heading for a fall," a girl named Gladys put in. "One of these days the boss is going to catch her when she's drunk, and when he does, she'll be out of here."

"Who *is* the boss?" Carrie asked. "I still haven't met him."

"Oh, he's around," Flo said as she and Gladys exchanged glances. "But I guess...I guess he doesn't come in here as much as he used to."

"When he does, I'd like to thank him for the job." Carrie smiled. "So let me know the next time he comes in."

"Sure, honey, we'll let you know."

But they never did.

Carrie had not seen Matt since she had started working there, but on Sunday, two weeks after she had started at the Golden Nugget, she met him on the way home from church.

She and Sarah were walking just behind Effie and Noah when Matt pulled his rig alongside them.

"Good morning," he said. "I see you've all been to church."

Before he could say anything else, Sarah had started trying to pull herself up to him. "Whoa," he said to his horse, stopping it, then quickly bent down and scooped Sarah up into his arms.

"Where you been?" she asked. "How come you never come to see us? Can I go for a ride in your buggy? Please, can I?"

He looked down at Carrie. "You can if it's all right with your Aunt Carrie." He hesitated. "And if she comes with us."

Sarah clapped her hands. "She'll come. Won't you, Aunt Carrie? Won't you?"

"I have to get home and start dinner," Carrie said stiffly.

"I'll fix dinner. You go along with Mr. Matt." Effie smiled up at him. "Miss Carrie's been working real hard. It'll do her good to get some nice fresh air."

Matt reached down for Carrie's hand. "Allow me to help you up, Miss Carrie."

She looked at him, at Effie, and at Sarah's expectant face. "Very well," she said primly. "But it's cold out, I have to be careful of Sarah."

"I have a lap robe. Besides, the sun's out today."

"I'll have dinner ready when you and Miss Sarah come back," Effie said.

"I thought maybe we'd ride over to Elkton and have dinner at the hotel." Matt shot a smile at Sarah. "Would you like that?"

"Yes!" She clapped her hands. "Won't that be fun, Aunt Carrie?"

Carrie clenched her jaw and glared at Matt. "I really don't think that's a good idea, Sarah. I—"

"You won't mind eating alone with Noah, will you, Effie?" Matt asked.

Effie blushed.

"You all go on. Effie and I will manage just fine," Noah assured them.

Matt nodded, and with the flick of his whip, set off down Bennett Avenue.

Carrie fumed all the way to Elkton, which didn't seem to bother Matt at all. Sarah chatted like a little magpie and asked question after question. "What makes icicles? How come they hang off the trees that way? Who makes the snowflakes? Did'ja ever taste one? When is summer going to come?"

Matt answered all of her questions, patiently, seriously. And in spite of herself, Carrie once again thought how differently he acted toward Sarah from the way her father had acted toward both her and Rosalinda. Horacio McClennon had never had the time or the patience to listen to his children.

Matt was different. Whatever else his faults, he was wonderful with Sarah.

The hotel restaurant in Elkton was pretty and cheerful, and by the time they were seated at a table near the fireplace, Carrie found herself relaxing. Matt ordered hot cider for her and Sarah, a glass of red wine for himself. After the roast chicken had been served, he said, "I understand you've found a job, Carrie. How do you like it?"

"At first I didn't like it at all," she said, after a moment's hesitation. "And there are parts of it I still don't. I certainly don't like the kind of clothes I have to wear. But..." She lifted her shoulders. "I like it better than I thought I would. I like the music, not the kind Sally LeBeau sings, but the music the band plays. And I like the work."

"But it's a gambling saloon," Matt said with a wicked smile.

"I know." Carrie toyed with her fork. "But the people there aren't what I expected. Some of the girls are very nice, and so are the men who work there."

"Any of the customers ever bother you?"

Carrie shook her head. "Once or twice in the beginning, but Mr. Wattles, he's the bartender, he told them to leave me alone and they did."

"I'm glad to hear that." Matt reached over to tie a napkin under Sarah's chin. "And you get home all right at night?"

"A man by the name of Worthy Magee always sees me home. He works at the Golden Nugget as a...I don't know what you call it, but he keeps everything in order. I mean in case there's a fight."

"Are you doing all right money-wise?"

Carrie nodded. "Yes, I am, Matt. For a while things were difficult. I even had to..." She stopped because she'd been about to tell him about taking her brooch to the pawnshop. But she was ashamed of that; she didn't want anybody to ever know about it. She'd gone back to the pawnshop as soon as she'd got that first money from Mr. O'Reilly, but the brooch was gone. "Sold it," the man in the cage had muttered.

"Everything is fine now," she went on. "It won't be too long before Sarah and I will be able to return to Ohio."

"You're still planning to go back?"

"Of course," she said, surprised. "That's my home."

He picked up his wineglass. Funny, he hadn't thought about her leaving, but now that he did, he found he didn't like the idea.

"I don't fit in here, Matt." Carrie looked across the table at him. "I don't suppose I ever will. The nice people of the town don't want anything to do with me, and the others..." Carrie shook her head.

"You mean the girls that work in places like The Chateau? The ones you have to work with at the Golden Nugget."

"Yes, I suppose that's what I mean." Carrie searched for the right words. "We're different, that's all. We don't really have anything in common. As for Sally LeBeau..." She blushed. "She's something else entirely!"

"Yes, she is that," Matt said with a laugh. He reached across the table and took Carrie's hand. "I know you don't belong in a place like that," he said. "But it won't be forever, Carrie. Things will ease up after a while. People will get to know you, and when they do, they'll forget all about Elvira Primrose's gossip. You'll find a different job, something more to your liking."

"Perhaps you're right."

He tightened his fingers around hers and stroked the back of her hand with his thumb. "I wish you'd let me get to know you better," he said.

The thumb that caressed the back of her hand sent shivers down her spine. "No," she said, as she tried to pull her hand from his grasp.

"Carrie, please..." He stopped and glanced at Sarah. She had dipped her fingers into the cranberry sauce and was busily licking them off. "I want to help you," he said in a low voice. "Let me, Carrie."

She was caught by the intensity in his deep green eyes, warmed by the touch of his hand.

"I want to take care of you," he said softly. "At least until you go back to Ohio."

"Until I go back to Ohio?" The words were like a handful of snow going down her back and she stiffened.

Matt's face flushed. "I didn't mean that the way it sounded," he said quickly. "It's just that I'm not a man who makes longtime commitments. But I do care about you. I care a great deal."

Carrie pulled her hand away. "I'm sorry," she said. "That's not good enough."

"I see." He reached for his napkin and wiped the cranberry stains off Sarah's fingers.

They finished the rest of the meal in silence.

It began to snow when they left the restaurant. Because the air was colder than it had been, Carrie put Sarah on her lap and covered her with the lap robe. In a little while Sarah's eyes began to close, and, leaning her head on Carrie's shoulder, she went to sleep.

The snow drifted down, and Carrie eased the robe up over the child's face. But she herself didn't seem to mind the weather. Her cheeks were red and snowflakes lingered on her long sooty lashes.

Looking at her, Matt felt something quite unexpected clutch at his heart.

Chapter Ten

"Sally LeBeau got drunk and fell smack dab off the stage last night," Buck Wattles told Carrie the next evening when she reported for work.

"Darnedest thing I ever saw. She was right in the middle of a song. Started wiggling her hips the way she does and wiggled herself right off the stage. Broke her leg in two places. Doc Taylor says she'll be laid up for five or six months."

"That's terrible!"

"Sure is. Mr. O'Reilly's mighty upset. Been looking all over town today for a new singer, but he hasn't had any luck. He's going over to Independence and Victor tomorrow. Figures he can maybe find a gal in one of the better gambling halls in one of those places."

"But do you really need a singer?" Carrie asked. "The band is awfully good. Isn't that enough?"

Wattles shook his head. "There's lots of the gents who come here just to gamble, and there's others who come to drink and dance with a pretty girl. But there're some who want to listen to a gal sing." He stopped cleaning the bar and looked at Carrie. "You sing real good," he said with a grin. "Maybe you could take old Sally's place."

"Me?" Carrie shook her head. "I don't know any of the songs that Sally sang, Mr. Wattles. Even if I did I'd never sing them."

"I didn't think you would, Miss Carrie, and I was only funning when I said that." He took a clean rag and started polishing some glasses, but stopped after a moment. "But what if you were to sing some nice songs? You know, the kind of songs that are sung in those fancy music halls?"

"No," Carrie said firmly.

"Anyways, I don't guess the gents would go for that sorta music, being as how they're used to what Sal dished out. Does seem a shame though. You got a real fine voice, Miss Carrie."

"But not that kind of a voice," she said firmly.

A week passed. O'Reilly went to most of the towns around Cripple Creek looking for a woman to replace Sally LeBeau. He even spent two days in Denver, sure that in a city that large he'd be able to find a saloon singer. But he didn't find what he was looking for, and by the second week he was desperate.

"I gotta get me somebody," he told Buck Wattles. "If I don't come up with a singer soon, we're gonna be losing business."

Wattles looked at Carrie and winked. "I know a gal who can sing," he said.

"Why didn't you say so?"

"Well, truth to tell, Pete, she's not too keen on singing here. Even if she was, she wouldn't sing the kind of songs the fellas are used to."

"Can she carry a tune?"

"Yep, I heard her. She sings like an angel."

"It's not an angel I'm looking for."

"Then I don't guess you'd be interested in the girl I'm talking about."

Carrie frowned and her gray eyes flashed a warning.

O'Reilly slapped a beefy fist on the bar. "Who is it?" he demanded. "Where is she?"

"She's standing right behind you."

"What? Who're you talking about?" O'Reilly turned and looked beyond Carrie toward the already-crowded gambling room. "Which one of the girls?" he asked.

"Miss Carrie," Wattles said.

"Carrie!" O'Reilly's eyes bulged. "You gotta be kidding!"

"Nope." Buck Wattles laughed. "And she's mad as sin at me right this minute for telling you."

"You sing?" O'Reilly asked her.

"No," Carrie snapped.

"Then why'd Buck say you did?" He scratched his bald head. "I got a lot of men coming here tonight. If they don't hear what they want to hear they'll go someplace else."

"Then let them go."

"I wouldn't like that. I wouldn't like it at all." O'Reilly's eyes were level with hers. "You make a mighty nice salary here, ma'am. I'd hate to tell the boss that you refused to do something I asked you to do."

Carrie chewed her bottom lip. "Really, Mr. O'Reilly, I don't have the kind of voice you're looking for. The only singing I've done was in my father's church choir back in Ohio."

"I don't want no hymn singing. What other kind of songs do you know?"

"Just songs," Carrie said.

"What songs?"

"'I'll Take You Home Again Kathleen,' 'London-derry Air,' things like that. The men who come here wouldn't want to hear them."

O'Reilly scratched his chin. "Probably not," he said gloomily. "But I gotta have somebody. You could fill in tonight and—"

"Tonight?" Carrie looked at him wide-eyed, her mouth suddenly gone dry. "No, I couldn't."

"If I say you can, you can."

She looked from him to Buck Wattles, who frowned and said, "Lord, Miss Carrie. I'm sorry. I was just funning a little. Leave her alone, Pete, she doesn't want to do it so, just let her be."

O'Reilly hesitated. From somewhere in the middle of the room a man called out, "What about some enter-tainment?"

Another man joined in, saying, "Yeah, when's Sally coming back?"

Other voices were muttering the same protests, then somebody said, "Let's go on over to the Silver Fox. They got a gal over there that's almost as good as old Sal."

"Hold on, boys," O'Reilly called out in a loud voice. "We just found us a singer that'll knock your boots off." He took Carrie's arm and propelled her forward. "It's our own little Carrie McClennon, who was sing-ing her heart out back in Ohio before she came here."

Carrie tried to hang back, but O'Reilly held firm as he led her toward the stage.

"Listen," she whispered. "I can't! Mr. O'Reilly, please!"

"You just think about that twenty-five dollars a week we're paying you," he whispered close to her ear.

"But—"

He lifted her up onto the stage and motioned to the musical group. "Play anything the little lady wants," he told them.

The men gathered around. The piano player looked at her. She looked at O'Reilly.

"Sing us one of Sally's songs," one of the men yelled.

"Yeah. How 'bout, 'Oh Gimme A Man Who's A Miner'?" a short, bandy-legged man called out.

"I . . . I'm afraid I don't do that one," Carrie said.

"Well sing *something*, darlin'!" another man said.

Carrie wet her lips and turned to the piano player. "Do you know 'Bird in a Gilded Cage'?"

"I know it," the piano player said. "But—"

"Then play it," O'Reilly ordered.

"You don't know what you're asking, boss. I play a song like that these buzzards'll kill me."

"Play it!"

The piano player shrugged, and with a sigh, muttered, "You asked for it."

And Carrie began to sing, "'I'm only a bird in a gilded cage, a pitiful sight to—'"

"You're pitiful all right!" a man called out.

Her voice wobbled.

"Sing, dammit!" O'Reilly said.

Hands clenched at her sides, Carrie sang in spite of the catcalls, the boos and the whistles. A boot thudded up to the stage near the piano player. The musician dodged but kept on playing. A tin of tobacco bounced off the keys.

"Cut that out!" One of the miners slugged the man who'd thrown the tin. "Give the little lady a chance."

"A chance? What she needs is singing lessons!" somebody else called out.

Carrie faltered. She looked down at O'Reilly.

"Fer God's sake, keep singing!" he roared. "Maybe it'll quiet these bastards down."

Carrie struggled on, singing in her sweet, clear voice, and at last the men, except for a few disgruntled mutters, grew quiet.

Matt stood at the back of the room. He'd heard the commotion from below and looked down to see Carrie on the stage, hands clasped to her sides, looking scared half to death. When one of the miners hurled the boot, Matt had started down the stairs. He didn't know who in the hell's idea it was to get her to sing, but whoever it was was going to hear from him.

He had hurried into the gambling room and pushed his way through the throng of gamblers toward the stage, but before he could get there, the men had quieted down.

"Sing us another'n, honey," one of them said.

Carrie looked toward the piano player. He gave her an encouraging smile. "How about 'Red River Valley'?" he asked. "Do you know it?"

"Yes, but I..." Carrie took a deep breath. "Yes, I know it," she said, and began to sing, "'From this valley they say you are going...'"

As Matt watched, the hard-rock miners quieted down. Their expressions changed. They looked thoughtful, almost wistful. In the other part of the room, some of the gamblers stopped to listen, and little by little the whole saloon grew quiet.

When Carrie finished the song the men clapped their hands and stamped their feet. She bobbed her head, thankful that it was over, but as she turned to leave the stage, a man called out, "Do you know 'I'll Take You Home Again Kathleen,' ma'am?"

Carrie looked down at the man. His clothes were rough. He had a worn and grizzled face and a beard that came halfway down to his chest. His eyes were a watery blue, and there was something in them, a longing, a memory perhaps, that touched her.

"Yes," she said. "I'll be happy to sing it for you, sir."

Matt folded his arms across his chest and stepped back out of the way so that Carrie wouldn't see him. As he listened to her singing, he looked around the room at the faces of the miners and the gamblers, the drinkers and the con men, all of them touched by the sweetness of Carrie's voice, the innocence of her expression.

As he was touched.

She reminded him of home, of the mother he had lost when he was sixteen, of the first girl he'd ever kissed. She reminded him of green fields, of the sun shining down on stalks of golden corn, of summer picnics and harvest moons. Of youth and love. Of things that had been and were no more. And he knew that the other men, listening as he listened, were as affected as he was. This time when Carrie finished the song, there was only silence.

"You're all right, little gal," a man called out. "You sure hidey are all right."

The crowd cheered her and asked for more. As Matt edged his way back toward the stairs that led up to his office, Carrie began to sing "Green Grow The Lilacs." He listened for a moment, a bemused expression on his face. Then smiling to himself, he murmured, "Looks like a star is born."

Matt told Pete O'Reilly that Carrie was to have new gowns made, and he described to Amelia Howard the style of gowns he wanted. They were to be made of the finest material, fashionable but not too revealing. Carrie was to have a new cloak, dark blue velvet trimmed with black sable, with an attached hood that framed her face, and a sable muff to match. If she protested about the new clothes or the velvet cloak, she was to be told they'd been ordered by her employer because, as the new star of the Golden Nugget it was part of her job to look fashionable.

He also told O'Reilly to increase her salary to fifty dollars a week.

"Fifty dollars! That's plumb crazy, boss. No dame's worth that much."

"This dame is," Matt answered with a smile.

Carrie was worth it though, and more. Word had gotten around Cripple Creek that there was a new singer at the Golden Nugget, and that she was something special. Men flocked to the gambling parlor, not just from Cripple Creek but from as far away as Victor, Cameron, Gillette and Goldfield. They drank and gambled and danced with the other girls, but the main reason they came was to listen to Carrie sing.

She stuck to the songs she knew, songs like "Londonderry Air," "Aura Lee," and "Beautiful Dreamer." If somebody talked while she was singing, they had one of the hard-rock miners to deal with. A thump on the head usually insured silence.

Matt was proud of her. He had given her the job at the Golden Nugget because he knew how desperately she needed money, even though he'd known she didn't belong in a place like his. And she hadn't belonged, not at first. She'd been as out of place as a two-legged mule at a horse race and just as uncomfortable. The night she'd started singing, with the men hooting and holler-

ing up at her, looking scared and alone, he'd known
he'd been wrong to trick her into working at the Golden
Nugget. She should have been singing in a church choir
instead of a gambling saloon, and he'd started downstairs to take her away from the stage to a place where
she'd be spared the humiliation and the embarrassment she was suffering.

But when the miners had stopped to listen, so had he,
and he'd been just as mesmerized as they had been.
Carrie was an angel, pure, untouchable.

But Lord help him, how he wanted to touch her.

Night after night, as Matt watched other men look at
her with longing in their eyes, he was overwhelmed with
the need to take her away to some quiet place where they
could be alone. He wanted to lay her down on a big
feather bed and hold her. He wanted to slowly slip the
silken gown off her shoulders and rest his face against
the creamy whiteness of her breasts. He wanted to touch
and stroke her, to hear the whisper of her voice and
watch her eyes go smoky with desire.

It was hell seeing her every night with her not knowing he was there, not being able to talk to her because
he knew that if she ever discovered he owned the Golden
Nugget and that he was the one who'd had her hired,
she'd leave. But Matt needed to see her and talk with
her. So, with the help of his friend, Noah Pierce, Matt
got himself invited to dinner by Effie on a Sunday night
when Carrie wasn't working.

Partly because she felt it was Effie's house, too, and
partly because she had missed Matt, Carrie acqui-
esced.

Matt arrived at the house on Second Street with a new
doll for Sarah and a chocolate cake from the bakeshop. He shook hands with Noah Pierce and told Effie

she was getting prettier every day. To Carrie, he said, "I hear you're Cripple Creek's newest star. Congratulations."

"Thank you," Carrie replied with a blush.

"Do you like singing there?"

Carrie nodded. "I still don't feel comfortable, wearing the kind of dresses I do, but yes, in a strange kind of way I do like it." She challenged him with her eyes. "You've never come to hear me, have you?"

"No," Matt said. "I've never come to the Golden Nugget as a guest."

"I suppose you're busy with other things."

"Maybe not that busy. I'll drop by tomorrow night."

Watching Matt gently wipe the chocolate from Sarah's fingers, Carrie was reminded again of the way he had with children. Sarah loved him, and he returned that love with tenderness and caring. Carrie was grateful that he did, but just for a moment she felt a pang of sorrow because neither she nor Rosalinda had experienced that kind of tenderness when they were young. She made a silent vow that Sarah would never suffer as she and Rosalinda had suffered. She would raise her sister's child with love and with gentleness.

Reaching out, she smoothed the red curls back off Sarah's forehead.

It was later in the evening that Effie mentioned the girls from The Chateau.

"I miss them," she said wistfully. "'Specially Miss Charmaine and Babette."

"I guess it'd be all right if you stopped by to visit them sometime," Noah said with a smile.

Carrie looked up from her plate. "I'd really prefer that Effie not go back there, Noah."

Effie looked from Noah to Carrie and blinked back sudden tears. "I won't if you don't want me to, Miss Carrie," she murmured.

Carrie bit her lip, and knew she had hurt the girl's feelings. Relenting, she said, "I'm sorry. I suppose it would be all right if you went in the morning. You can go tomorrow if you'd like to."

"Well, now isn't that nice." Noah patted Effie's hand.

Matt looked at Carrie from over the top of his wine-glass and smiled.

She's changing, he thought. Little by little, and probably without realizing it, she's changing from the straitlaced woman who had annoyed the hell out of him into a woman he wanted to know better. A whole lot better.

The following night, having warned the men who worked for him to treat him as though he were a paying guest, Matt appeared at the Golden Nugget. He played a few hands of poker, won a little over two thousand dollars, and had a brandy at the bar.

"That Miss Carrie is something else," Buck Wattles told him. "Whoever would'a thought she'd be packing the men in with the kinda songs she sings."

"Any of the customers give her any trouble?" Matt asked.

"No, sir! Any of 'em tried, old Worthy'd give 'em what for, and so would half a dozen of the other fellas." He leaned across the bar. "She's different than the other girls, boss. There's something special about her."

Something special.

Matt watched her walk up onto the stage. Tonight Carrie was wearing a pale blue silk taffeta gown that draped down low over her shoulders and showed the rise of her bosom. It nipped in tight around her waist and flared full and long so that he could just see the tip of her blue satin slippers. Her auburn hair was curled in little ringlets about her face and fastened in the back with a blue satin bow. The spots of color on her face were from excitement, not from rouge.

She began with "My Sweetheart's the Man in the Moon."

As she sang, Matt moved closer to the stage and when she finished, someone called out "'Beautiful Dreamer.'"

He had heard the song sung before, but surely never the way Carrie sang it. As Matt watched her the words took on a new meaning. "Beautiful dreamer, wake unto me."

Wake unto me, Carrie, he thought. Let me be the one to show you how it feels to hold and be held. Let me be the one to take you down the many paths of love.

Matt observed the faces of the men around him and felt a flare of anger. He didn't want anybody else looking at her like that. He wanted Carrie for himself, wanted to hide her away from all eyes but his. He wanted to be the one to touch those bare shoulders, those creamy breasts. He wanted to be the one to love her to wakefulness.

"Wake unto me," she sang.

Carrie's eyes found his among the crowd of men, and it was as though she were singing for him. Only for him.

Suddenly Matt's eyes narrowed and his nostrils flared. He wanted Carrie McClennon, and by all that was holy, he was going to have her.

Chapter Eleven

" 'In my sweet little Alice blue gown,' " Carrie sang, and although this was the usual raucous Saturday-night crowd, men gathered near the stage to stop and listen and watch.

Tonight she wore the lilac satin gown. The plunging neckline that revealed the rise of rounded breasts was discreetly shadowed by chiffon of an even more delicate shade of lilac. Her auburn hair was worn piled high on her head, with only one long curl lying free over her bare shoulder. She wore white satin slippers and elbow-length gloves, and held a lace fan woven with ribbons in one hand.

Carrie finished "Alice Blue Gown," then began singing "After the Ball," and as she sang she gently swayed as though she were dancing. The gambling saloon, the hubbub of voices, the whir of the roulette wheel and the faces of the men gathered around her faded as she pictured herself in a beautiful ballroom, dancing among elegantly dressed men and women. Chandeliers shone down upon the handsome couples, a real orchestra played, and she was dancing with the handsomest man of them all. His arms were strong. His

hair was black as velvet, the eyes that looked into hers
were as green as Ohio spring grass.

The song ended, but for a moment Carrie was lost in
the dream, lost until the men who were gathered around
the stage began to applaud and stamp their feet. She
looked down at them, unaware for a moment that, after all, she wasn't in a beautifully elegant ballroom, but
was here on the stage of the Golden Nugget gambling
saloon.

Suddenly she was overwhelmed by the desire to be
held, as Matt Craddock had once held her. And to belong to someone who really cared. With a smothered
sigh, she summoned a tremulous smile and, blowing
kisses with the tips of her gloved fingers, left the stage
and went to a place near the far end of the bar that had
been designated as her special table.

"I can keep an eye on you here," Buck Wattles had
told her. "Anybody tries to bother you, either me or
Worthy can ward 'em off and send 'em packin'."

But this was a Saturday night and the Golden Nugget was jammed with customers. Men were lined up
three deep at the bar and it was all Buck and his two
helpers could do to keep up with the shouted orders.
The same was true with Worthy Magee. After a hard
week's work in the mines, the miners, the gamblers and
the traveling salesmen were out to have a little fun. They
wanted to dance with the saloon girls, gamble away
some of their hard-earned money, get drunk as skunks,
and just generally raise hell. Every now and then, when
somebody took a swing at somebody else, Worthy Magee would break up the fight and toss the offenders out
into the snow.

It was after midnight; one more show and Carrie
would be through for the night. After that she would

have to wait until Worthy was free to take her home. Once or twice, when he had been busy, she had left the Golden Nugget alone, only to have him come running after her, saying, "Now you know you're not supposed to leave without me." Other times, when he hadn't been able to get away, either Stanley Bray or one of the bar helpers walked her to her door.

Carrie was tired tonight and she decided that if she didn't see Magee after she finished singing the next time, she wouldn't wait. She'd get her cloak from the room that led off the side of the bar and slip out before he noticed that she was gone.

"So this is where you're hiding!"

Nathan LaRue rested both hands on her table. He smelled of whiskey and cheap cigars. "Now don't this beat all," he said. "Whoever would'a thought you'd be singing in a classy saloon."

Carrie looked quickly over toward the bar. Buck was way down at the other end, almost obscured from her view by the men crowded around demanding drinks. She frowned up at LaRue. "I haven't anything to say to you," she said.

"Well, ain't you Miss High-and-Mighty," he sneered. "Too good to work for me, but not too good to work for Matt Craddock."

"I don't work for Mr. Craddock and I'd appreciate it if you'd leave me alone."

He lurched against the table. "How about a dance?" he said, reaching for her hand. "Come on and dance."

"I don't want to dance with you, Mr. LaRue, so please leave me alone."

"You gotta dance with me. That's what Craddock's paying you for. You gotta dance with the customers, and I'm a customer."

"I don't know what you're talking about. Leave me alone or I'll call the bartender."

"Bartender's busy." He reached for her. "What else is Craddock paying you to do?"

"Get away from me!"

"Whazza matter? I'm not good enough for you?" He waggled his head back and forth. "Just like your sister. Thought she was too good for me, too, but she wasn't too good for him. Damn little whore—"

Rising from her chair, Carrie hit him as hard as she could, a stunning blow across his face that sent him reeling back. She turned and started toward the bar, but before she could reach it, LaRue grabbed her.

"She was doing it for him same as you are," he muttered as he shoved her hard up against the end of the bar. "He owns everything in town and now he owns you."

Carrie struggled to get out of his grip, but he held her there. She could feel his whiskey breath on her cheek and she looked around for Buck. "Buck!" she cried. "Help me! Help me!"

But he didn't hear her. No one heard her.

Matt had gotten into a game of faro earlier at the High Stakes. He'd lost a little, he'd won a little, and had finally come away with over five thousand dollars in his pocket. On his way to the Golden Nugget he'd checked the action, as well as the receipts at the Silver Dollar and the Dirty Shame. It was a typical Saturday night; both places were filled and the money was rolling in.

It was after twelve by the time he got to the Golden Nugget. The place was jam-packed. The gaming tables were filled, men surrounded the roulette wheels, all of the dance-hall girls had partners, and men were lined up at the bar.

Carrie was up on the stage singing, and he paused for a moment to listen to her. She looked very beautiful tonight with her hair piled high on her head and that one silky curl hanging down her bare shoulder. She was singing "After the Ball," swaying with the music, a dreamlike expression on her face, a look of longing that he had never seen before.

He thought suddenly how it would be if he took her away from here, to places like Chicago or New York, even to Paris. He wanted to show her fine restaurants and theaters. He wanted to dance with her, to hold her close and know that when the dancing stopped he would take her to some quiet place where he'd make love to her.

The dance ended, and still Carrie stood there, that same wistful look on her face, a look that made him want to go to her. But he didn't. He turned away before she could see him and went to the stairs that led up to his private office.

A few minutes later Stanley Bray came with the receipts and two bags of money. Without counting it, Matt put the money into the safe and began looking over the receipts.

"Looks good tonight, Stan," he said. "Business is booming."

"It's been better than ever since Miss McClennon started singing here," Bray said. "Hope she isn't taking business away from your other places."

Matt smiled and shook his head. "I made my rounds before I came here and it's business as usual." He went to the window and looked down on the crowd below. "But it's certainly booming in here tonight. Think we'll

stay open till two. The way things are going..." He
stopped, frowning.

"What's the matter, boss?"

"Just saw somebody come in who's not welcome
here."

Bray looked down at the man weaving his way toward the bar. "Nathan LaRue," he said with a nod.
"Nasty fellow."

"I don't want him here, Stan. When you go back
down, tell Buck or Worthy to get rid of him." He turned
away and picked up the receipts. He spread them out on
his desk and began going through them. Several minutes passed. He put the receipts aside, tapping his fingers on the desk, then got up and went back to the glass
to look down below.

His gaze searched the men crowded around the bar.
He didn't see LaRue. He was about to turn away when
suddenly he froze. "What the hell," he muttered under his breath, then turned and ran out of the office.

Bray looked down on the scene below, eyes darting,
trying to see what Matt had seen. Then he saw it. Nathan LaRue had Carrie McClennon up against the far
end of the bar. She was struggling to get away from him.
With a muttered oath he took out after Matt.

LaRue pressed his face close to hers. "Think you're
too good for me," he said. "Think you're Miss Highfalutin up there singing, showing everybody what you
got." He rammed his body against hers.

"Let me go!" Carrie tried to brace herself against the
bar, tried to push Nathan LaRue away. He grabbed the
back of her head, forcing her toward him, so close she
could see his bloodshot eyes, smell his drunken breath.

"Help me!" she cried. "Somebody—"

Suddenly LaRue spun away from her and she saw Matt, his face angry white, his lips drawn back in a snarl. He hit the other man with his fist. LaRue staggered back, cursing, screaming out a venom of hate.

Carrie caught a glimpse of startled faces, of Buck Wattles springing over the bar.

"Stay away!" Matt called out. "He's mine!"

Nathan LaRue got to his feet. Matt hit him again and LaRue slammed hard against the bar. Head down, he rushed Matt. Matt smashed an uppercut to the chin and LaRue went down. Blood running from his mouth, he staggered up.

"Bastard!" he roared. "I'll get you for this." He swiped at the blood running down his chin. "One of these days I'll get even with you and with her and with every other whore in the tenderloin."

"Get up!" Matt roared, and started toward him.

"I'll kill you," LaRue screamed, and quick as a striking rattler, he reached into the breast pocket of his coat.

Carrie saw the snub-nosed gun. Saw the flash of fire. Saw Matt stagger back against the bar, and the blood, bright red against his white forehead.

As though from a distance, she could hear the screams of the other girls, the shouts of the men.

"Get a doctor!" Buck Wattles cried.

"Don't let that bastard get away!" a man yelled.

Another shot rang out.

"He's heading toward the door!" someone hollered.

"Get him! Where's Magee? Where in the hell is Magee?"

"I saw Doc Taylor come in a few minutes ago. Somebody find him," Gladys called out over the din.

Carrie fell on her hands and knees beside Matt. She cradled his head in her arms and, yanking off her white gloves, tried to stanch the blood running from his forehead. He was unconscious, his breathing shallow.

"Matt!" she cried. "Matt!"

"Let me see him, Miss Carrie."

Doc Taylor knelt beside her. "That's it, hold him there. I want to look at his head."

The doctor probed with long lean fingers. "Bullet just grazed him," he murmured. "Probably a concussion. He might be out for an hour or two, maybe longer. I'll need to examine him better when we get him home. Right now we'd best get him outta here and over to where he lives."

"Take him to my house," Carrie said.

The doctor looked up. Flo's chin dropped, and Gladys said, "To *your* house?"

Doc Taylor said, "You sure? He's going to need a lot of taking care of in the next few days."

"I'm sure."

"All right then. Somebody give me a couple of towels so's I can stop the bleeding. I'll bandage him when we get to Miss Carrie's."

Buck Wattles handed him two clean towels. "Soon as the doc is ready, I want you men there to pick Mr. Matt up real careful. Flo, you go and get Miss Carrie's cloak."

"Let me help you up, ma'am," Stanley Bray said, taking Carrie's arm to help her to her feet.

Carrie stood, arms crossed over her chest as though for protection, watching Dr. Taylor wrap a makeshift bandage around Matt's head, wincing when Matt mumbled and tried to turn away. She reached down and took his hand. And held it all the way to her house on Second Street.

Matt's head hurt. He tried to open his eyes, but when he did, the pain hit him so hard he moaned aloud.

"Shh," a voice said beside him. "It's all right, Matt. Go back to sleep."

He felt a cool hand on his brow, soothing him, quieting him, and thought that he was dreaming.

He slept again, and when he awoke, a voice that sounded like Carrie's voice, said, "Try to drink some broth, Matt."

He dreamed that she sang to him, so softly he could barely hear. She stroked the hair back off his forehead and the pain went away. And once he dreamed he felt her lips brush his cheek. He tried to awaken because he wanted to bring her down beside him and enfold her in his arms. "Carrie," he tried to say. But the words would not come.

She was always there. She spooned medicine into his mouth. She fed him hot broth, and she bathed him. She did everything for him.

Once he opened his eyes to see Doc Taylor bending over him.

"How you doing?" Dr. Taylor asked. "Head still hurting?"

"Hell, yes!" he said with as much strength as he could muster.

The next time he awoke he saw the lace curtains at the window and knew that this was a place he had never seen before. He turned his head and saw Carrie beside him.

"Carrie?" He tried to sit up, but pain stabbed at him, and with a groan he closed his eyes. "Where . . . where am I?"

"You're with me, Matt. At my house."

"Don't understand." He searched his brain, trying to remember. "What happened?"

"You were shot," she said.

"Shot?" So that's why his head hurt. He reached up and touched the bandage. "Who shot me? I don't remember . . ." His expression changed, hardened. "Nathan LaRue," he said. Pictures formed in his mind. LaRue had Carrie jammed up against the bar. LaRue had his hands on her and he'd wanted to kill LaRue because he had touched her, had hurt her.

There'd been a fight, he remembered that now. He remembered hitting LaRue. But that was all. That and the pain in his head.

"Did they catch him?"

"Not yet, but they will. The sheriff has men out looking for him. Try to rest now."

"Why?" he asked, looking at her.

"Why what, Matt?"

"Why did you bring me here, Carrie?"

She looked at him, her face still, thoughtful. There was something in her eyes he had never seen before.

"I wanted to take care of you," she said.

"Why, Carrie?"

She shook her head. "I don't know," she whispered.

"You know."

Pink color rose in her cheeks. "You live alone. You needed somebody. I was afraid that Flo or Gladys or one of the other girls . . ." She shook her head. "I wanted to be the one to take care of you," she said.

"You still haven't told me why." He looked up at her. "Tell me, Carrie."

"Because you needed me. And because I needed to."

He reached for her hand. She tried to pull it away, but he held on to it. "No," he said, and closed his eyes. Still holding her hand, he fell asleep.

Carrie sat there beside Matt for a long time. His face was more relaxed, his breathing was even, and a slight smile curved the corners of his mouth.

He had asked her why she had had him brought here. She had told him that she needed to, but even now wasn't sure why she had felt such a need, why it seemed right that Matt be brought here. There had been no conscious decision on her part.

She barely remembered running through the snow beside the men who carried him, Dr. Taylor cautioning them to be careful. Or of Stanley Bray saying over and over again, "He's going to be all right, Miss Carrie. He's going to be all right."

When they reached the house, Effie had let them in, her face shocked. Then, at Carrie's bidding, she had raced up the stairs to fold back the blankets of Carrie's bed.

In a blur Carrie had watched Dr. Taylor stitch the wound at the side of Matt's forehead and held Matt's hand when the needle pierced his skin and he moaned aloud.

She had stayed at his bedside all that long first night. And prayed as she had never prayed before.

Again and again she recalled that terrible moment when LaRue had pointed his gun and fired. She remembered Matt's blood staining her gloves, and her fear, her terrible fear that he was dead.

She recalled later, Dr. Taylor telling her that Matt was going to be all right. She had wept then, there beside the bed, clasping Matt's hand and whispering his name.

But she still had not let herself think why she had brought Matt here. She had told him that she needed to. But even she did not quite understand that need.

Matt slept with the vision of Carrie's face behind his eyelids, and awoke with the sound of her name on his lips. Her voice and the touch of her hand were more dear to him than anything he had ever known.

Finally one morning he awoke with a clear head. Sunlight streamed in through the window and Carrie was standing beside him.

"You're better," she said, smiling down at him.

"Yes." Matt pulled himself to a sitting position. "How long have I been here?"

"Five days."

"Five days!" He ran a hand across his cheek and felt the stubble of beard. "How'd I get here?"

"Some of the men from the Golden Nugget carried you."

He remembered then that one of the times he had awakened he had asked her why they had brought him here. "You needed someone," she said.

"Thank you," Matt said now. "Thank you for bringing me here, Carrie. For taking care of me."

"There's no need—"

"Thank you," he said again.

Her gaze met his. "This is where I wanted you to be."

"Why, Carrie?" He took her hand and pulled her down onto the bed beside him. "Tell me why."

"I don't know why, Matt. I only know that I—"

"Uncle Matt?" Sarah stood in the doorway. "Are you better, Uncle Matt?"

Matt smiled and Carrie got to her feet. "I'm better, Sarah," he said, holding his hand out to her.

The girl came slowly across the room. "Are you really all right?" she whispered.

"Of course I'm all right, and hungry as a bear." He growled and reached down to give her a hug. "Do you suppose you could talk your Aunt Carrie into bringing me some real food?"

"What would you like?" Carrie asked with a smile.

"Bacon and eggs, biscuits and coffee. A lot of everything."

"I'll fix it," Effie offered from the doorway.

But Carrie shook her head. She needed time to be away from Matt, time to think. "No," she said. "I'll do it," and hurried out of the room before Effie could stop her.

Doc Taylor was pleased with how rapidly Matt was improving. "I know you must be champing at the bit to be out of bed," he told the patient. "Another day or two and you'll be fit as a fiddle and out on the town."

But Matt wasn't eager to be out on the town. He wanted to stay right where he was. He liked waking in the morning and having Carrie bring his breakfast in to him. He liked looking at her, talking to her.

She hadn't gone back to the Golden Nugget. "I don't want to go back until you're better," she said. Then she hesitated. "Nathan LaRue told me that you own it. Do you?"

"Yes, Carrie." Matt waited for her anger. Instead she only looked thoughtful.

"You set it up with Noah Pierce," she said at last. "And with Pete O'Reilly." The suggestion of a smile curved her lips. "Poor Pete," she mused. "I remember the first time he saw me. He looked me up and down, and I knew he couldn't imagine why in the world I was there."

She met Matt's gaze. "But I know," she said. "I know you were trying to help me, Matt. I understand now about the outrageous salary, the gowns, all of it."

"You're not angry?"

Carrie shook her head. "Maybe I should be," she said. "But I'm not, because I know you were trying to help me. And you did, Matt. You saved my life and I'm grateful." She looked down at him. "But I can't keep taking your money."

"I'm afraid you'll have to." He grinned at her. "You're a star, Miss Carrie. If I tell my customers you're not coming back, those hard-rock miners will tar and feather me." He reached for her hand. "But you don't have to go back unless you want to, Carrie. If you hate it—"

"I don't hate it. Besides, I'm saving money. Soon I'll have enough to take Sarah back to Ohio, even enough to buy a little house in Norwalk." She smiled. "And I *won't* have to marry Josiah Wilkinson."

"Who in the hell is Josiah Wilkinson?" Matt asked with a scowl.

"He's the preacher who took my father's place. He warned me about coming West. He said sin was rampant and temptation waited." She looked down at her hands. "He wanted to marry me," she said. "I thought about it when things were bad, when I'd almost run out of money. I thought about writing him. He would have sent me the money to go home. But I..." She shook her head. "I couldn't," she said. "I just couldn't do that."

She went to the window and looked out at the snow. "Now I won't have to. Thanks to you I've got enough money to take care of Sarah and myself until I find a job teaching."

"You could stay here." Matt cleared his throat. "I don't want you to go," he said. "I want you to stay here, with me."

Carrie turned away from the window. "I don't think I can do that," she said carefully.

Matt reached out his hand toward her. "Carrie, I—"

"Uncle Matt! Guess what, Uncle Matt?" Sarah said from the doorway.

And with one last fleeting look, Carrie hurried from the room.

Chapter Twelve

The following morning when Carrie went into the kitchen to fix Matt's breakfast tray, Effie said, "I saw Miss Charmaine when I was out shopping yesterday and she asked me if I could..." She stopped, hesitant, and lowering her eyes, began to dry her hands on the kitchen towel.

"She asked you if you could what?" Carrie prompted.

"She said Babette was ailing and she asked me to ask you if sometime I could bring Sarah over for a visit."

"To The Chateau?" Carrie frowned. "I don't think that's a good idea, Effie."

"No, ma'am, I don't suppose it is."

"What's the matter with Babette?"

"Along about Christmastime she got word that her little boy, the one who's back in Arkansas where she came from, she got word he was bad off. She's been real worried and she's been sending money and all. For a while she didn't hear anything and then last week she got a letter from her mother saying little Timmie had died. Miss Charmaine says Babette's been grieving something terrible and she thought maybe, seeing as how Babette was so crazy about Sarah, and Sarah being the same age as her Timmie, that maybe seeing Sarah would cheer her up."

Effie dabbed at her eyes. "I can understand about your not wanting Sarah to go, but if it's all right with you I'd like to go over and spend the afternoon with Babette."

"Yes, of course it's all right." Carrie hesitated. She really didn't want Effie to go back to The Chateau, and certainly she didn't want Sarah there. The townspeople already thought that she was a fallen woman and if someone like Mrs. Primrose saw Effie taking Sarah down to the tenderloin district, word would be all over Cripple Creek that she'd allowed her niece to visit there. She was sorry about Babette's little boy, but she really couldn't allow Sarah to go back to The Chateau.

From the living room by the fire where Sarah was playing with her dolls, she heard Sarah say, "Drink your milk, Mary Agnes. If you do I'll give both of us a cookie." Then Sarah laughed, a happy chortle of sound that seemed to fill the whole house with warmth.

A child's laughter. Was there anything more beautiful? Carrie thought of a little boy's laughter that had been forever silenced, and of the mother who grieved for him. In such a short space of time, Sarah had become so incredibly dear to her. How frightened she had been when Sarah had the croup. How would she feel if she ever lost the precious little girl?

Babette was grieving for the little boy she had lost, a little boy she hadn't been able to keep with her because of how she made her living.

And suddenly Carrie thought, to hell with the Mrs. Primroses of the town. I don't care what they think.

"I've changed my mind," she told Effie. "Go ahead and take Sarah with you. Perhaps you're right. Perhaps it will help Babette to spend some time with her."

"You sure you don't mind?"

Carrie put her arm around the girl's shoulders. "I don't mind," she said. "And tell Babette that as soon as I can, I'll come by to see her, too."

So it was that Carrie found herself alone with Matt that afternoon. When she took his luncheon tray up to him, he was standing by the window, waving down to Sarah and Effie. Stanley Bray had brought him some clothes a few days ago, and he was wearing a black quilted robe. He turned and smiled at Carrie as she entered.

"Sarah looks all excited," he said. "Where is she going?"

"To The Chateau."

He raised one black eyebrow in question.

"Babette's little boy died, Matt. Effie saw Charmaine the other day and she told her how sad Babette was, and that she thought it might cheer her up if she could see Sarah." Carrie put the tray down on the dresser. "I didn't want her to go back there, but I..." She shook her head. "I don't know. Maybe her being there will help Babette."

For a moment Matt didn't say anything. Then he smiled and said, "You're a nice woman, Carrie."

A slight smile curved Carrie's lips. "You said once that I was a narrow-minded biddy."

"That was before." He crossed the room and put his hands on her shoulders. "That was before so many things," he said.

Carrie was suddenly aware how quiet the house was, and that she was alone with him. "You really should be back in bed," she murmured.

Matt put a finger under her chin, forcing her to look at him. "I'm all right, thanks to you, Carrie. I'm all right because you sat by my bed at night, because the sound of your voice and your touch made the pain go away. I haven't told you before what that meant to me, just knowing you were with me." He rested his palm on the side of her face. "It meant everything to me, Carrie. Everything."

Carrie didn't know why, but suddenly she felt the sting of tears behind her eyelids. She couldn't help herself as she leaned her face into his shoulder. "I was so afraid," she whispered. "When LaRue shot you, when I saw you fall . . ." She rubbed her face back and forth against the smoothness of his robe. "I thought he'd killed you. I thought—"

"Shh, Carrie. Don't, sweetheart."

She raised her tearstained face to his, and in a way Matt could not explain, it seemed to him as though he were seeing her for the very first time. He looked deeply into her gray-blue eyes, eyes that he could drown in. Her lips were sweetly parted, as though waiting for him to claim them.

"Carrie," he said again. And he kissed her.

For a moment she stiffened. Then with a muffled cry, her mouth warmed and her lips melted against his. A flame that she had tried so hard to deny curled deep within her. She wanted Matt to kiss her, to kiss her and hold her and never let her go.

His lips were firm yet soft against hers. His mouth was warm, and, when he touched the tip of his tongue to hers, the flame became a fire and she moaned deep in her throat. But did not pull away.

He cupped her head between his hands. He kissed her closed eyes, the corners of her mouth. He ran his tongue across her lower lip and took it between his strong white teeth to tease and to suckle. He kissed her until her knees went weak, until her body trembled and she had to cling to him lest she fall.

She felt the warmth of his hand against her breast and she whispered, "No, you shouldn't do that. It isn't nice."

But, oh, it was nice. It made her feel all kinds of wonderful feelings she had never felt before. She leaned closer, her body warming in a way she didn't really understand. And when he fumbled with the buttons of her white shirtwaist, she did not try to stop him.

His hand crept under her chemise, so cool against her skin that she flinched. He held her there, warming his hand with the heat of her flesh, cupping the firm roundness and lightly, so lightly, caressing her.

She cried out, and when she did, he kissed her deep and hard. He cupped her breasts and drew his fingers up around the peaked and almost painful nipples to stroke and soothe her there.

Desire shivered through her like hot fingers of need. A liquid fire burned in her veins, sizzling its tortuous way down to her belly, down to that most secret part of her.

She clung to him, moaning into his mouth, loving his touch, not wanting him to stop.

He put his hand against the small of her back and pressed her close. She felt the whole hard length of his body and, afraid, tried to move away. He wouldn't let her.

"This is what happens to me when I touch you, Carrie," he whispered against her lips. "This is the way it is for me. This is part of me. Don't pull away from me, Carrie."

He pressed her even closer and suddenly that most intimate part was on fire. She tried to tell herself how bad this was, how wicked, even as she felt herself moving against him. It was as if she had no control over her body, as if getting closer to him would somehow ease the unbearable tension growing within her.

He moved his legs apart and brought her closer to that throbbing part of him. She whimpered in need. He rubbed her breasts and squeezed one tender nipple. The breath came ragged from her throat. Her mouth sought his and she groaned against his lips.

"Carrie," he murmured, and with a cry, he picked her up and carried her to the bed.

"No," she whispered. "Oh, please, I . . ."

Matt pulled at the buttons of her shirtwaist and shrugged it off her shoulders. He untied the blue ribbon of her chemise and slipped it down.

"Look at you," he said hoarsely. "Oh, Lord, just look at you."

He cuddled her breasts, and frightened, she attempted to push herself away, to protect herself from the hot, moist mouth pressed against her flesh. But Matt held her there, pinned her with his body.

"You're beautiful," he said. "Oh, Carrie, you're so beautiful."

He flicked his tongue across her nipples, eliciting a cry so shrill it was as though she had been touched by lightning.

"Oh, yes," he whispered. And he began to suckle her there, to take one rigid tip between his teeth to gently tug and tease.

Carrie throbbed with desire, and turning her head from side to side in an agony of need, she whispered, "Don't. Oh, don't." But even as she said the words, her hands stroked the thickness of his hair and she held him there.

At last he let her go and looked at her, his eyes hooded and dark with desire. He kissed her mouth. He whispered her name against her lips in a voice made hoarse by all that he was feeling. And when he let her go, he unfastened her heavy dark skirt and pulled it down over her ankles.

"No!" she cried. "What are you doing? No!" And tried to cover herself.

He came up beside her and took her in his arms again. "We're going to make love," he told her. "And it's going to be good, Carrie. I promise you, it's going to be good."

He kissed her again, very gently, and though she hid her face in the pillow and though she said, "You musn't," she did not struggle when he tugged the white silk opera bloomers down over her ankles.

She pulled the blanket up to cover her shame. But he said, "No, Carrie," and with a slight smile took the blanket out of her hands and laid it back.

With hungry eyes he looked at her, and, as though to himself, he murmured, "I knew. I knew this is the way you would look." He ran his hands over her breasts, and continued to caress her, gently stroking her, watching her when she gasped. Then, slowly he went down her body, down over the smallness of her waist, the flatness of her belly, down, down to the apex of her legs.

"You mustn't do that," she said softly.

Matt held her with his gaze. "I need to touch you like this," he said. "I've wanted to for such a long time, Carrie."

He curled his fingers through the crisp spring of curls. She grabbed his wrist to stop him, but he said, "Shh, Carrie. It's all right, sweetheart." He took her hand away and held it, while his other hand continued to caress her. "So warm," he whispered. "So moist and ready."

Her body moved under his, and moved as though with a will of its own, even as she tried to struggle away from him. She had never felt like this before, and while there was a part of her that wanted Matt to stop, there was a part of her that didn't want him ever to stop. His fingers were so warm, so capable. The mouth that moved to capture her mouth was warm, too, and his tongue was silky soft.

"Carrie," he said in a strangled voice, and moved away from her. She opened her eyes then, and saw him taking off his robe, tearing at his pajamas.

"What are you doing?" she cried. "What..."

He lay beside her and took her back into his arms. "Have you ever made love before?" he asked in a gentle voice.

With her head buried in the hollow of his shoulder, she shook her head.

"Do you want to now?"

"If you want to," she whispered, and felt his smile when he kissed her.

"I want to," he said.

The kiss deepened, and in spite of her fear, the fire began again, for while he kissed her, he fondled her breasts. If this was what lovemaking was, if this is what people did when they married, then she liked it. She enjoyed the kissing, the touching. Like a lazy cat Carrie stretched beneath him, sighing her pleasure, embracing his shoulders, moving her mouth against his as he had moved his mouth against hers; caressing, suckling, coaxing.

Then, he came over her. She felt the whole length of him. And felt his hardness as she cradled him between her thighs. That startled her, frightened her. What was he going to do? What . . . ?

He held her hips. He said, "I'll try not to hurt you, Carrie. But we have to do this, sweetheart. We have to." Gripping her hips, he plunged that hardness into her.

Pain ripped through her. She cried out and tried to move away from him.

"I'm sorry, sorry," he gasped against her lips. "But it will be all right now, Carrie. I promise you, sweetheart. I promise you."

He began to move against her, carefully, gently. He kissed her mouth. "It will be all right now, Carrie dear," he said softly against her lips. "I won't hurt you again."

The pain eased and in its place there came a warming. A sweetly sensuous feeling flooded through Carrie. She felt him grow and throb with life, pulsate inside her. Her body quivered with reaction and she moved ever so tentatively against him.

"That's my sweet girl," he murmured. "Put your arms around me, Carrie. Lift your body to mine, sweet. That's it, Carrie. That's it, love."

She hadn't known, had not even imagined that anything could be this incredibly good, that anything could make her feel like this.

He kissed the side of her face. He told her how good this was, how much it meant to him to be with her like this.

And she loved it. Lord forgive her, she loved it. She wanted it to go on and on. She didn't ever want to stop, because she knew that nothing could ever be this good again. She felt his breath against her breasts, heard his whispers of pleasure and felt a thrill unlike anything she had ever known because she knew she was pleasing him.

He thrust more deeply into her and his movements quickened.

"Matt," she said. "Oh, Matt." And suddenly, with the sound of his name a strange and frightening thing began to happen to her.

"Oh stop!" she protested weakly. "Something's happening to me. Matt...? Oh please!"

He kissed her mouth, and his breath came hot and quick against her lips. "Yes, Carrie," he encouraged. "Yes, love. Let it happen, Carrie. Let go, sweetheart. Let it happen."

"No...no, I..." Then there were no words. She spun out of control, clinging to him as he began to gather more momentum. Higher and higher, scarcely able to breathe, on the verge of fainting with sheer pleasure. He surged against her and she heard him cry her name in a paroxysm of pleasure.

His arms tightened around her and she clung to him, her body shaking in an agony of release while he soothed her and told her how fine she was and what this had meant to him.

For a long time they lay like that, bodies entwined, breathing hard, not speaking. But when at last their breathing evened Matt slid to her side and gathered her in his arms.

"I'm sorry I hurt you," he said. "It's only for the first time, Carrie. It won't be like that again." He raised her face and gently kissed her. "I knew the first time I kissed you it would be like this between us, Carrie." He began to stroke her back. "Are you all right?"

"I'm not sure. I feel strange, like my body is..." She looked at him. "I don't know how to explain it, Matt. I feel more alive than I've ever felt before. Like I'm...like I'm singing inside." She blushed and hid her face against his shoulder. "I didn't know anything could be like what we did," she whispered. "I didn't know it could be so nice."

Matt kissed the top of her head, then gently raised her face so that she would look at him again. "Tell me," he said. "Tell me what you're thinking now."

She caught her lower lip between her teeth, suddenly shy and embarrassed.

"Tell me," he said again.

"I...I didn't know that was what people did."

His eyes widened with surprise. "You didn't know?"

Carrie shook her head. "I thought babies came from kissing, from touching, but I didn't know..." She shook her head. "I know what we did was wicked, Matt, but there's a part of me that wonders why anything that feels so good is bad. I mean if two people really care about each other. If they..."

Hot color rose in Carrie's cheeks, but before she could say anything else, Matt said, "Two people care, Carrie. That's what makes lovemaking special."

"But the girls at The Chateau..." The blush deepened. "Is this what they do?"

Matt nodded. "Yes, dear, but it's different." He kissed her bare shoulder. "When two people feel the way we feel..." He shook his head, trying to find the words to explain how different it was when a man made love to a woman he cared about.

Matt had made love to many women, women he had paid for, and women who had come casually into his life. But with none of them had he experienced what he had experienced with Carrie. She had been awkward and unsure of herself, and though at first she had been afraid, she had responded with a sweetness of passion such as he had never known. Somewhere deep down inside himself he knew that no other woman would ever thrill him the way Carrie had. He knew, too, that Carrie wasn't a part-time girl, and that this was not a casual lovemaking.

That gave Matt pause. How serious were his intentions? he asked himself. He was thirty-six years old, free and unattached, and he wanted to keep it that way. Yet the thought of ever leaving Carrie, of not being able to be with her, to make love with her again, sent a cold shiver of fear down his spine.

They were such different people: he was a gambler, she was a straitlaced... Matt grinned. Well, not as straitlaced as he had once thought.

But there were problems. For one thing, she thought that he and Rosalinda had been lovers.

He eased himself up onto the pillows. "There's something I want to tell you," he said. "It's about Rosalinda."

Carrie didn't want to hear it, not now, not after what she had just shared with Matt. For a little while she had forgotten that once he had Rosalinda... She turned away, at the thought that once he and Rosalinda had been together in the way she and Matt had.

But when she said, "I don't want to hear it," and started to get up, Matt put his arm around her waist and brought her down beside him. "It's something you need to hear," he said.

Arms crossed over her chest, her jaw set and firm, Carrie stared straight ahead.

"I met Rosalinda almost four years ago in Wichita," he said. "I had gone with friends to see a theatrical group perform a musical comedy. Rosalinda was the star." He tightened his arms around Carrie. "You would have been proud of her, Carrie. Her acting was good and so was her singing, though she didn't have the voice you have. But she was dear and funny and appealing and she carried the show.

"I went backstage with my friends afterward and somebody introduced us. She knew some of my friends, and when we invited her to dinner, she accepted. We talked a lot that night and we became friends."

"I see," Carrie said in a cold, precise voice.

"There was something about Rosalinda that touched me, Carrie. She was so young and she seemed so alone, and I had the feeling she wasn't doing too well moneywise. I took her out to dinner whenever I was in town. I tried to give her money, but she wouldn't accept it, so once in a while I bought her a gift—earrings, a hat I saw her looking at, a fur muff."

"How nice."

Matt took hold of her chin and said in a firm, nononsense voice, "I was not her lover, Carrie. I liked Rosalinda, and I worried about her, the way I would if she had been my younger sister. But I wasn't in love with her. Nor was she in love with me."

Carrie's eyes widened. "But when I accused you of being her lover, you didn't deny it."

"I didn't see any reason why I should. Maybe it's stiff-necked pride, but I've never felt that I had to defend myself or explain myself to anybody." His eyes burned into hers. "But I'm doing it now," he said. "You need to know how it was."

He moved slightly away from her. "The actor who played opposite Rosalinda left the show and they hired a new fellow to play the part. His name was Beauregard Jones."

"Beauregard...?" Carrie turned to look at him. "Effie told me about him. She said that he was Sarah's father."

Matt nodded. "Yes, it's true. That sorry son of a bitch was Sarah's father."

Carrie shivered, and he reached down and pulled the blanket up around them. "I tried to warn Rosalinda about him, but she wouldn't listen. Maybe people never do when they're in love." Matt shook his head. "Anyway, about that time I decided to move to Cripple Creek, so I didn't see your sister for a while. I didn't know she was pregnant, that she'd had a child, or that Beauregard had left her."

"But why did she come here? Was it because of you? Because you had been her friend?

Matt hesitated. Yes, he wanted to say, that's why. But he couldn't. Carrie needed to hear the truth. He wanted her to know exactly what had happened, because she had the right to know.

"She came to Cripple Creek with Nathan LaRue," he said.

"With . . . ?" Carrie's face went as white as the sheet that covered them.

"He talked her into coming here with him by promising her a job singing in a saloon. But once they got here . . ." Matt reached for Carrie's hand. "Once they got here, he tried to put her into a crib."

"A crib?" She stared at Matt, horrified. She remembered the first time she had seen the tenderloin, remembered the broken-down pine shacks there in the place called Poverty Gulch, and the girls leaning in the doorways, shawls over their shoulders. Their eyes looked old, their pinched faces were splotched with rouge and despair.

"But Rosalinda didn't . . ." Tears were running down Carrie's face now. "She couldn't have . . ." She tried to pull her hand from Matt's, but he held on to her. "What about Sarah?" she cried.

"Rosalinda kept Sarah with her."

"In one of those places?" Carrie covered her face with her hand. "Oh, my God." She wept. "My God."

Matt tightened his hand around hers. "Rosalinda tried to get away from LaRue. She wouldn't do what he asked. She wouldn't prostitute herself. And because she wouldn't, he beat her."

He was painfully aware of Carrie weeping beside him. He wanted to stop, but he knew that he had to go on. She had to know everything.

"She managed to sneak away to one of the other cribs. The woman there hid her out and managed to get word to me."

Matt closed his eyes and saw again the crib where Rosalinda had been hiding. He had found her there, huddled in a corner of the room, the frightened child on her lap. One of her eyes had been blackened and there had been a bruise the size of a peach on the side of her face. Her arms were black and blue.

That was the first time he had seen Sarah. She had been wearing a ragged little dress and she was barefoot. Her eyes had been wide with fear.

"This is Sarah," Rosalinda had said.

When he'd held his hand out to help Rosalinda up, the child cried out and clung to her mother. "No," she had whimpered. "Don't hit my mommy."

He knelt beside them. "I've come to take you and your mother away from here," he told Sarah. "I have a big house and a very nice lady who helps me. Her name is Tillie. I have a dog, too. His name is Big Boy and he doesn't have anybody to play with."

"You have a doggie?" Some of the fear went out of Sarah's eyes.

"Yes, I do. He's brown except for a white circle around his tail. Would you like to see him?"

"Uh-huh."

He had held out his arms and she had come to him. "It's going to be all right now, baby," he had told her. "Nothing is ever going to hurt you again."

"I found them," he told Carrie. "I took them home with me. Rosalinda was ill and my housekeeper took care of her. When she was better, I found a respectable rooming house where she could live with Sarah."

He let go of Carrie's hand and brought her close to him. "When word got out that I was looking for LaRue—he skipped town. After a while Rosalinda insisted on getting a job, and when she asked me to, I gave her a job singing at the High Stakes. I shouldn't have, Carrie. I shouldn't have listened to her, because she really wasn't well. But God, she had spunk. She'd been knocked down by two men, but she wasn't out. Whatever happened, she came up fighting.

"One night LaRue came into the High Stakes. He saw Rosalinda there. Before I could get to him, he'd grabbed her and started dragging her out of the saloon." Matt looked down at her. "The way he tried to grab you. I knocked the hell out of him, Carrie. I beat him worse than I'd ever beat a man in my life."

He tightened his arms around her. "When I saw him moving in on you at the train station in Denver, the way he'd moved in on Rosalinda, I knew I had to step in and stop him any way I could. That's why I wouldn't let him get on the train with you."

"Oh, Matt." Carrie leaned her face against his shoulder and they remained like that, without speaking, until she said, "But why did Rosalinda go to live in The Chateau?"

"She hadn't been well, and after the incident with LaRue she seemed to get worse. And I think she was afraid that he would return. She wasn't able to work, so I said I'd keep on paying her rent at the rooming house or that she could move back to my place. But she wouldn't do that, she said she wasn't going to let me go on taking care of her.

"Charmaine and I had been friends for a long time, and when she heard about Rosalinda and Sarah, she insisted I bring them over to The Chateau. They had a bedroom off the kitchen, Carrie. Nobody bothered them there. Rosalinda never—"

"I know," Carrie said. "I know."

"She told Charmaine she had a sister, and Charmaine told her to write to you. I'm sorry she didn't write sooner, Carrie."

"Yes, so am I." She leaned back against him. All of the things he had told her had been difficult to hear, yet she had had to hear them. She wanted to weep for the sister she had lost. She wanted to kill Nathan LaRue for what he had made her suffer.

"I'm glad you told me," she said at last.

"Rosalinda was a brave and a wonderful young woman, Carrie. She had a special kind of charm, a grace—"

"And joy," Carrie said. "That's what I remember about her, Matt. Her pleasure at little things—a field of buttercups, the lilt of a song, a butterfly, a child's laughter. I'm glad she had Sarah to love. And I'm..." Her eyes filled with tears. "I'm glad she gave me Sarah to love."

Matt kissed the top of her head. "I wish I could have helped her more than I did. I wish I could have saved her so that the two of you could have been together again." He held Carrie away from him and looked down into her eyes. "I cared about Rosalinda, Carrie, but I never..." He shook his head. "I never felt for her what I feel for you. I never shared with her what I have just shared with you. Do you understand?"

Carrie touched the side of his face. "Yes," she said. "I understand."

He brought her back into his arms and held her there, comforted and petted her until the tension went out of her body and she relaxed against him.

He thought about Rosalinda and of how it had been for her. And he thought about Carrie. He remembered how, that night on the train, he had sat next to her and covered both of them with his coat. When she slept, her head against his shoulder, he had thought with a certain smugness that it was the first time he had ever slept with a woman without making love to her. And that maybe he'd do something about that.

But he had felt no smugness in having made love to Carrie. Though she had been afraid, she had yielded to him. And yes, perhaps in that first moment when he had known she would, a sense of triumph had surged through him because he had won, because he had conquered her.

But that feeling of triumph had changed when he joined his body to hers. As her warmth closed about him, he had felt a oneness with another he had never known before. And when she lifted her body to his, he had known a sense not of triumph but of gratitude and of wonder.

In that final moment when she had whispered his name he'd thought his heart would burst with joy unlike anything he had ever known.

Carrie. He kissed the top of her head and held her close while she slept.

Chapter Thirteen

Carrie awakened in Matt's arms, his hand on her bare thigh, the warmth of his breath on her cheek. She lay there, scarcely daring to move or to breathe. She didn't want to rouse him; she needed this time to sort out what had happened.

Her body felt lighter, freer. She didn't understand that, nor did she understand why she wasn't overwhelmed with guilt. She should have been, for surely what she had done wasn't something nice women did. She waited for the guilt to come. It didn't. Instead she smiled, because it seemed to her as though she had just discovered a delicious secret that nobody else in the world knew about.

What she had experienced this afternoon with Matt had been the most pleasurable, the most exciting thing that had ever happened to her. It had been like falling off the end of the earth. No, that wasn't right, it had been like soaring above the earth.

She had been shocked and frightened when Matt had joined his body to hers. All she had felt in that first moment was pain and embarrassment. Is this what making love is? she had wondered. It hurt, and besides that, it was awkward and unpleasant. She'd liked it when they kissed and touched, but she didn't like this. Then something very strange began to happen to her. The heat she had felt before started again, but with an even greater intensity. It came in a great flooding of warmth, a yearning to be closer to Matt, to meld her body to his. It was so good she didn't want it to stop, because surely nothing could ever be this good again.

She had heard muffled cries of pleasure, had been barely conscious they were her own, but was unable to stifle them. She had loved what Matt was doing to her so much that all thoughts of what was proper and what was not had fled from her brain. In that final moment when her body shattered with an immensity of feeling, she had clung to Matt, trembling in his arms as sensation after sensation shook her, helpless and yielding in his embrace, totally his in that final moment of what she knew now was pure ecstasy.

Carrie wasn't sure how all this had happened, or why it had happened. Matt Craddock wasn't like any other man she had ever known, certainly he was as different from Josiah Wilkinson as night was from day. He was a gambling man, a man her father would have said was a sinner headed straight for hell.

A sinner? He had befriended Rosalinda, had taken in a woman and her child when they had no one else. And he had extended a helping hand to her from the very first moment they had met. Before they had met, actually, when he had thrown Nathan LaRue off the train bound for Cripple Creek.

He had defended her, as he had once defended Rosalinda, from LaRue. He had been shot trying to help her. The thought of LaRue chilled her. She prayed that he was far away and that he would stay far away.

She studied Matt's face. His velvet black hair, still with a light bandage where he had been shot, was tousled, and one thick strand lay over his wide forehead. She had a sudden urge to smooth it back, but was afraid if she did she would awaken him. There were shadows beneath his eyes, his lashes were long and thick. He had a straight, strong nose, wickedly full lips, and a cleft in his chin that intrigued her and made her want to kiss him there.

Matt, she thought. Oh, Matt. And she began to edge away from him. Embarrassed by her nakedness, and shivering with cold, she slid out of bed. Gathering up her clothes, she went into the bedroom she had shared with Sarah ever since Matt had come into their home.

Pulling a robe around her, she went to stand in front of the mirror above the dresser to study her face, to see how she had changed. Because she *had* changed. She touched her lips still swollen from his kisses. She looked into eyes that though they seemed the same, were not. They had looked into a man's eyes and found something special there. They held a wonderful secret now, and they would never again look at the world in quite the same way.

She was not sorry that she had made love with Matthew Craddock, but it was something she needed to think about.

She dressed and went downstairs to the kitchen. Adding more wood to the fire, she pulled up a rocking chair and sat there, alone with her thoughts, until she heard the front door open and Sarah call out, "Aunt Carrie? Where are you, Aunt Carrie?"

"In the kitchen," Carrie answered. She got up, opened the kitchen door and called out, "Come in here where it's warm."

They came in, Effie and Sarah, their cheeks apple red from the cold. Carrie kissed Sarah, and, taking her hand, led her closer to the fire and began to unbutton her coat. "Did you have a nice afternoon?" she asked Effie.

"Yes, ma'am. We really did. Poor Babette was awfully glad to see Sarah."

"Me and Babette had a tea party, and Aunt Charmaine made me little cakes and Dorrie sang and Lorelei and Conchita danced," Sarah told her. "You should'a been there, Aunt Carrie."

"Yes, I guess I should have." Carrie looked at Effie. "How's Babette doing?" she asked.

"She looks real done in, Miss Carrie. But seeing Sarah cheered her up a whole lot."

"Then I'm glad you went."

"It's Dorrie's birthday tomorrow. They're going to have a little party. Just the girls I mean. It'll be early, before any of the gentlemen come. Dorrie asked me to ask you if maybe you'd let Sarah come back. She—"

"Please, Aunt Carrie? Can I go? Please can I go?"

"I think it would be nice if you did," Matt said from the doorway of the kitchen.

"Uncle Matt!" Sarah launched herself at him. "Are you all well?"

Matt picked her up and kissed both of her cheeks. "Yes, I'm all well, thanks to you and Effie and your Aunt Carrie." His gaze sought Carrie's from across the room. "You took care of me," he said. "You nursed me back to health."

Caught by the intensity of his gaze and the warmth of his green eyes, Carrie couldn't speak. She only stood there, looking at him. He wore the black quilted robe, and his hair was still damp from washing up. The same lock had fallen down over his forehead, and again Carrie had the overwhelming desire to smooth it back.

"You'd better sit down," she said, motioning him to a chair. "You musn't overdo."

"I'm all right. As a matter of fact I don't know when I've slept so well or felt so good. Maybe spring is in the air. Or maybe..." He smiled a deceptively innocent smile at Carrie. "Or maybe it's you...your good home cooking I mean."

When Carrie blushed, he went to the rocking chair and sat down with Sarah on his lap. "Did you have a nice time today?" he asked the child.

"Babette and me—"

"Babette and I," he corrected.

"That's what I said. Babette and me had a tea party and tomorrow Effie and me are going back for Dorrie's birthday."

"Well, isn't that nice?" He looked at Carrie over the top of Sarah's head. "You'll let her go?"

She looked at Sarah, then at him. "Yes," she said. "I'll let her go."

Later, after Carrie and Effie had fixed supper, the four of them sat around the table in the kitchen. Still later, while the women washed the dishes, Matt sat beside the fire and rocked Sarah until she fell asleep, her head on his shoulder, her small hand curled inside his.

"I should take her up," Carrie said.

Matt shook his head. "Let me do it."

"You go on, too, Miss Carrie," Effie said. "I'll finish cleaning up here in the kitchen."

"All right, Effie." Carrie patted the girl's shoulder, and when Matt rose, she followed him up the stairs to Sarah's room.

He put the sleeping child down on the bed, waiting while Carrie undressed her. And when Carrie slipped the red flannel nightshirt over Sarah's head, he pulled back the blankets, and together they eased Sarah into bed.

"She's had a busy day," Carrie said. "She'll sleep till morning."

"You've had a busy day, too." Matt rested his hands on Carrie's shoulders and brought her around to face him. "Are you all right?" he asked in a gentle voice. "I didn't hurt you?"

She shook her head and, not meeting his eyes, tried to move away. But he held her there. "Don't be sorry about what we did," he said.

"I'm not."

"It was the nicest thing that ever happened to me." His eyes were serious, intent, warming as he gazed down at her. His hands tightened on her shoulders; he moved closer.

"Matt," she whispered.

"We'll be alone again tomorrow," he murmured. "Think about that tonight before you go to sleep, Carrie."

Then he kissed her and let her go.

Sarah and Effie left the house the next morning at eleven. The sun was out and there was the hint of spring in the air.

Matt had come down for breakfast, and later he had bundled Sarah into her coat and her boots, and given her five silver dollars to buy a birthday present for Dorrie.

"You really should go upstairs and rest," Carrie said when Sarah and Effie had gone. "Dr. Taylor said you needed a couple more days to recuperate."

"I've recuperated." He grinned. "In fact I feel better than I have in a long time."

"Matt..." She backed away from him.

"Carrie..." The grin widened wickedly.

"You really have to rest."

"I intend to." He reached for her.

"I have to clean up the kitchen."

"Later."

"No, I—"

He stopped her words with a kiss. "I thought about this all night," he said against her lips. "I thought what it would be like to hold you again, to kiss you again." He drew her closer, his hand against the back of her head, holding her as he studied her face. "Do you know what you do to me, Carrie? Do you have any idea how I feel when I look at you, when I touch you?"

It started again, the same warmth, the same delicious weakening of her knees. The same feeling of doubt that she shouldn't be like this with him.

He took her face between his hands and kissed her, his mouth warm against hers, searching, probing. She felt herself giving way, felt her body warm and soften. He put one hand against the small of her back to bring her closer, and she became startlingly aware of the hard tautness of his body.

She tried to move away, but he said, "No, Carrie. No, sweetheart," and pressed her closer. "Ah, Carrie," he whispered against her lips. "My sweet girl. My lovely Carrie."

He unbuttoned her shirtwaist and Carrie felt the heat of his hand against her breast. "Come upstairs with me, Carrie," he said. "Come with me now."

"No." She tried to struggle out of his embrace. "What we did yesterday..." She shook her head. "It was wonderful, Matt. But we shouldn't have. People shouldn't do what we did, especially if they aren't married. We shouldn't..."

He cupped her bottom and brought her closer, so close that she could feel the hardness of that most intimate part of him burning against that most intimate part of her.

He began to move against her while he held her there. He took her mouth and touched his tongue to hers. He kissed her deep and hard. A shock wave surged through her body, and her fingers dug hard into the taut flesh of his arms.

"What are you doing to me?" she managed to gasp.

He kissed the words away and held her there, moving against her, urging her ever closer. Shocks of pure fire burned where he touched and she moaned into his mouth. He lifted her, drawing her to him, pressing insistently against the small of her back, all the while his hungry mouth was devouring hers.

"Carrie," he whispered against her lips. He suddenly let her go and, picking her up in his arms, headed for the stairs.

Carrie buried her head against his shoulder, dizzy with an emotion she still didn't understand. He made her feel wanton, made her forget all the rules she'd been raised with, things she'd been brought up to believe.

"Wait," she said when they reached the bedroom and he put her down. "You have to listen to me." She gulped for breath. "We shouldn't do this again, Matt."

"Why not, sweetheart?" He resumed opening the remainder of the buttons of her shirtwaist, then slipped it off her shoulders.

"Because we..." She tried to speak reasonably, calmly, but he'd started nibbling on one earlobe, and it was hard to concentrate with a shiver of thrills running up and down her spine. "But we... we did it yesterday. People don't—"

He ran his tongue around the curve of her ear. "They don't what, Carrie?"

"They only do it... I think you're only supposed to do something like we did just once in a while."

"Once in a while?" One dark eyebrow cocked.

She remembered her father ordering her mother into the bedroom, and the sermon that followed the next morning.

"It's a sin of the flesh," she whispered. "My father said that. He..." She shook her head, unable to go on.

Matt stared down at her, then taking her hand, he led her to the rocking chair by the window. He sat down and brought her into his lap, and he held her as he had held Sarah last night. Yesterday, carried away by a passion she didn't understand, Carrie had yielded to him. But she'd had time to think about what she had done, and the old fears, the old beliefs and prejudices had surfaced. Though his body throbbed with wanting her, he knew he would not force her to do anything she didn't want to do.

For a little while he just held her there, soothing her, quieting her before he said, "Carrie, what happened between us yesterday was just about the nicest thing that can happen between a man and a woman. It's the closest two people can come to each other. It's giving and receiving, it's as elemental as life itself."

He kissed her forehead, and, holding her close, he tried to understand how it had been for her and for Rosalinda. Rosalinda had told him about their father, about his coldness and his cruelty, about the whippings. "We grew up with sin," she'd said. "It was our heritage, our daily lesson, our bible."

"Carrie was the good one," Rosalinda said. "I don't know if she believed everything our father preached, but she was obedient. She always did what she was told except when she tried to protect me." Her eyes had been sad, her mouth pinched with remembered pain. "It never did much good because Papa always had his way. But she tried, Matt. She tried and she took a lot of lickings because of me."

Rosalinda had run away, but Carrie had stayed and been the dutiful daughter. What had it cost her? he wondered now. What fears of right and wrong lay beneath her calm demeanor? What childhood terrors still lingered?

He kissed her again, but not as he had before. This time he kissed her gently, tenderly, and only when her lips parted under his did he let the kiss deepen and grow.

Carrie sighed against him and he shifted in the chair, holding her closer, cradling her body against his. He kissed her eyelids, her cheeks, her nose. When she whispered his name, he took her mouth again. He cupped her breast, and though she murmured a protest, she didn't draw away.

Little by little a sweet lethargy crept over Carrie, and she was barely aware when Matt slipped the camisole lower so that he could stroke her breasts. She turned toward him then, and with her arms around his neck, began to answer his kisses.

His hands were gentle, but his skin was rough against her softness, and she loved the roughness. That slight scratch of skin against skin excited and aroused her. He palmed her breast, and when his thumb grazed her nipple, she whispered her pleasure.

Matt tried to content himself with this, because he wanted to allay her fears, to make it so good for her that her feelings of guilt would disappear. He wanted to go slowly, but she was coming alive under his ministrations. Her small moans and gasps of excitement were driving him over the edge, arousing him to a point of no return.

She pushed aside the opening of his robe to unbutton his pajamas. Slipping her hand inside, she began to caress him as he caressed her, curling her fingers through the dark thatch of chest hair, loving the feel of it and of his skin.

"Carrie?" It was a plea of hunger, a plea of need against her lips. She buried her face against the hollow of his shoulder, and when he picked her up and carried her to the bed, she did not protest. Nor did she protest when he stripped her clothes away. But she was still afraid to look at him, and turned away and covered herself when he took off his robe.

He lay down beside her and gathered her in his arms. "Carrie," he said against her lips. Again, as he had before, he made himself wait while he stroked her to readiness, and only when her body began to tremble against his, only when she yearned toward him, murmuring his name in a litany of desire, did he join his body to hers.

Carrie tensed, remembering yesterday's pain, but when he said, "It's all right, Carrie," she relaxed against him and lifted her body to his the way he had told her to.

And it was as it had been. He filled her, he became a part of her. Shivers ran through her body. Her nerve ends tingled and her body heated as small shocks of pure desire quivered through her veins. He kissed her throat, he nibbled her ears until she thought she would go wild. He rained kisses over her face and took her mouth, thrusting his tongue as his body moved over hers.

He left her mouth to suckle her breast, rolling the peaked and painful nipple with his tongue, sucking hard, driving her to ecstasy.

She cried his name. Her body writhed under his and she tried to get closer, tried to merge herself with him, to become part of him.

"Sweetheart," he gasped. "Ah, Carrie, Carrie." He cupped her buttocks to bring her closer. "Tell me," he whispered. "Tell me if it's too much."

But she was beyond words, beyond thought. She gripped his shoulders and sought his mouth and lifted her body to his, weeping out in anguished joy as the waves of sensation flooded through her.

"Yes!" Matt cried. "Oh, yes!" And his big body thundered against hers, driving her on and on until, close to fainting, she cried out his name and heard his answering cry.

He held her close, so close she could barely get her breath. He stroked her and told her how fine she was and how she made him feel. He kissed the side of her face, he brushed the tangled hair back from her cheek, and when she started to move from him, he said, "No, honey, stay for a moment. I love the feel of your body under mine, I love the softness of you holding me this way."

Her body was wet with perspiration, her heart rocketing in her chest, but as he stroked her, she began to relax. She liked the feel of his body over hers this way, the texture of his skin. She ran her hands along his back, down to his rounded buttocks. And when he asked, "Am I too heavy for you?" she shook her head.

"No, stay like this," she whispered, and felt him relax against her.

He breathed in her scents, rubbing his face against the fall of her hair and her throat. He wanted to make her a part of him, to hold her like this and never let her go.

And that scared the hell out of Matt. As did the fact that he'd never felt for a woman what he was feeling right now with Carrie. She was an innocent, inexperienced. Yet she had responded to him with a warmth and a giving that had set his blood on fire. Repressed though she had been, she was all woman. When her body had quivered under his, when she cried his name and lifted herself to him in that final moment, he had felt a thrill of exaltation unlike anything he had ever felt before.

And with the thought of how it had been, it began to happen again. She felt him grow. Her eyes popped open and she said, "What are you doing?"

"I'm making love with you again."

"Oh." She looked up at him. "I didn't think...I mean I...I thought you were only supposed to do it once."

"Or twice." He smiled. "Or more."

"More?" Her eyes widened. Then she answered his smile with a smile that set the blood zinging through his veins. "Do you like this?" he asked her.

She turned her head into his shoulder, still shy, and in a voice so low he could barely hear her, whispered, "Yes, Matt. Yes, I like it."

"Say my name again."

She looked up at him. "Matt," she said. "Matt."

He kissed her and began to move against her. He wanted it to last for a very long time and so he moved slowly, letting it build, loving her whimperings of pleasure, her murmured, "Oh, Matt," as she lifted her body to his. "Oh, yes. Oh, yes. That's good. That's so good."

She entwined her arms around his neck and sought his mouth. They kissed softly, deeply. All the while, his body moved against hers, and when she began to tremble and her breath came in short, frenzied gasps, he said, "Yes, Carrie? Yes?"

Again, as it had been before, she could do no more than whisper his name. As her body moved like a frantic thing under his, she bit hard down on her lip so that she would not cry out.

He thrust hard against her, once, twice, and it was too much for him and for her. They cried each other's names, and held each other, heart to beating heart, as wave after wave of white blinding passion gripped and shattered them.

When at last their heartbeats slowed, Matt shifted and rolled so that Carrie lay over him. He held her there, stroking her to calmness. "Carrie," he whispered. "My Carrie."

Matt left the next day after breakfast, telling himself and Carrie that he had fully recovered from the gunshot wound and it was time he went back to work.

But that wasn't the real reason Matt was leaving. He was running scared, scared of the power of Carrie's kisses, of the arms that held him, of the sweet womanly body that eagerly met his. Scared? Hell, he was running for his life.

Chapter Fourteen

Matt stayed away from Carrie for four miserable days.
He didn't sleep well, he barely touched his food. He
missed her voice and the sound of her step on the stair,
her softness and her scents. His arms felt empty without her.

Before, he had always been able to walk away from a
woman without any lasting emotional problem. He had
always been generous, both before and at the end of the
relationship, and maybe that's what helped him walk
away with a clear conscience.

This time it was different. He wasn't sure how it had
happened, why Carrie McClennon affected him the way
she did or why he had absolutely no desire to walk away
from her. It was something he had to think about.

He spent his afternoons playing poker. He had always enjoyed the game and he was a lucky gambler, able
to bluff the men playing with him with a grin and a
slight lift of an eyebrow. But his luck had changed, he
was losing more than he was winning. The night he
folded holding a jacks-high full house he knew he was
in trouble. He left the game and headed for the house
on Second Street.

It was after midnight when Matt pulled his rig up in front of Carrie's place. There was a light in her room and he thought of her up there alone, getting ready for bed. He closed his eyes and it seemed to him he could see her there, untying the ribbon of her lacy camisole, pulling the satin bloomers down over her hips.... He ran a hand over his face and tried to quell the sudden tightening of his body. He was acting like a lovesick schoolboy, mooning under the window of his girl. Feeling like a fool, he muttered a string of curses under his breath and took hold of the reins. But before he could flick them across the horse's back, he saw her coming down the street toward him.

He wanted to tell the horse to "Giddap!" and leave before she saw him. But it was too late.

"That you, boss?" Worthy Magee asked, surprise in his voice.

"Yes." Matt looked down at Carrie. "It's late," he said, angry and embarrassed that she had seen him here. "Where have you been?"

"At the Golden Nugget," she said, obviously puzzled.

God, he was losing his mind! How could he have forgotten she worked this late?

"I don't like it," he said.

"You don't like what?"

"I don't like your working there."

"But it's your place," she said reasonably. "You arranged for me to work there."

He glowered down at her, and to Magee he said, "You can leave now, Worthy. I'll see Miss McClennon to her door."

The other man nodded and tipped his hat. "See you later, boss," he said as he departed.

"Get in," Matt said.

Carrie looked up at him, flustered, not understanding.

He reached a hand down to her. "Get in," he said again.

Not sure that she should, Carrie held out her hand and climbed up beside him. "Where are we going?" she asked.

"I don't know. Somewhere…" Matt shook his head. "I don't know where."

"Matt…" She touched his arm. "Matt, what is it?"

"I'm damned if I know," he said under his breath, and, flicking the whip over the horse's back, headed toward the edge of town.

He looked straight ahead, his face in the night shadows stern and unhappy. She wanted to say something, to ask him what had happened to upset him. But she said nothing.

She'd had a lot to think about since Matt had left, and she had gone through a whole confusion of emotions: uncertainty over having become intimate with him, guilt because she had, and a nagging fear that she was headed straight to hell.

Coupled with her guilt had been the fear that because Matt had had his way with her she would never see him again. After four days of not seeing or hearing from him, she was sure that was the case. But now he was here, looking thundercloud grim. Was he about to tell her that they had made a terrible mistake? That they shouldn't have made love?

She clasped her hands together inside the fur muff and looked straight ahead. The trees on either side of the narrow rutted road were bare, and though it hadn't snowed for over a week the air was frosty cold.

Matt didn't speak. When the town was behind them, he pulled off the road and stopped near a stand of ponderosa pines. Without saying anything, he jumped down, then held up his arms to Carrie.

She moistened her lips. "I don't understand," she said. "Why did you bring me here?"

"Come down," he said, and she put her hands on his shoulders and let him lift her out of the rig. He spanned her waist, but instead of setting her on the ground, he slid her slowly down the length of his body and kept her there, pressed tightly against him.

"Carrie." The word was a strangled sigh whispered against her lips. He kissed her hard, with all the pent-up anger and frustration he'd been harboring for days.

His face was cold against hers, but his mouth was warm. Her lips parted and the kiss grew deeper, stronger. She felt the strength of arms that held her, and she clung to him, whispering his name against her lips.

When at last he put her down, she shivered with reaction.

"You're cold." He opened his coat and enfolded her with it. The fur was warm, his body warmer. She snuggled against him and he groaned aloud. "I've missed you," he said against her hair. "Lord, Carrie, how I've missed you."

"You didn't come back," she said. "There was no word from you. I thought you didn't want to see me because we did what we...what we did." She shook her head. "I thought you didn't want to see me again."

"No! Oh, God, no! It wasn't that, honey. Never that. It was..." He looked down at her and shook his head.

"What, Matt? What was it?"

He took a deep breath. "I had to sort out my feelings." He held her away from him. "I've never felt toward a woman what I feel for you, Carrie. I'm not sure I understand it, I'm not even sure I like it. I only know that when I'm not with you I'm so damned miserable I can't think straight." He brought her back into his arms. "I want you with me, Carrie. I want you beside me when I go to bed at night, and when I wake in the morning." He tightened his arms around her. "I want you, Carrie."

Relief flooded through her. Matt cared about her. He loved her and missed her, wanted her. Surely now he was talking about marriage.

"Carrie?"

She looked up at him and said, "Yes, Matt? Yes, darling?"

"I want to live with you, Carrie."

She took a trembling breath.

"Move in with me," he said. "You and Sarah, and Effie, if you want her to." He tightened his arms around her. "I can't stand being away from you, Carrie. I need you."

"Are you...are you asking me to marry you, Matt?"

"Marry...?" He frowned. "No," he said uncertainly. "I'm asking you to live with me."

She stepped away from him. "I see."

"That doesn't mean I don't care about you. That I don't want—"

"That you don't want me." She felt cold, frozen all the way to her bones.

He took hold of her arms, but when he tried to pull her back into his embrace, he felt her resistance. "I'll treat you real fine," he said. "Maybe in time—"

"No." She turned away. "It's late. I'd like to go back to town."

"Carrie..." He tried to find the words to tell her how he felt, to explain that though he felt deeply about her, he wasn't ready for marriage, that he might never be ready.

She stood beside the rig, her back straight as a stick, her jaw set and firm. He took her arm to help her into the rig. She didn't look at him.

"I didn't mean to offend you," he said when he came up beside her. "I care about you and I love being with you, but..." Matt shook his head.

"But you're not the marrying kind," she said.

His mouth tightened. "No, I'm not."

Carrie looked him square in the eye. "Well, I am," she said.

They rode all the way back to town without speaking.

"I'm a mite worried, boss." Charlie Riggs, the manager of the Dirty Shame Saloon, paused in wiping off the bar. "A fella that was in the other night told me he'd seen Nathan LaRue over in Victor. LaRue was drunk as a pie-eyed skunk and bragging about how he near killed you and that one of these days he was coming back to finish the job."

"Drunken talk," Matt said. "Besides, the word is out, Charlie. He sets foot back in Cripple Creek he'll be in trouble with the law. Don't worry."

But Matt was worried, not so much for himself but for Carrie. LaRue was a good-for-nothing slicker, a panderer who beat up women and made his money selling their bodies. Matt had taken Rosalinda away from LaRue and protected her from him, the same way he'd protected Carrie from LaRue at the Denver railroad station. But LaRue still had his eye on Carrie and that worried him. For though both Buck Wattles and Worthy Magee kept tabs on her at work, she was vulnerable whenever she was alone. He had no idea what LaRue might try, but he didn't want to take any chances with Carrie's welfare.

He knew how she felt about him, but he had to see her, to warn her that LaRue had been seen in Victor and that he might cause trouble again.

As soon as she arrived at the Golden Nugget the next night, he sent for her. She came up to his office, escorted by Stanley Bray.

"You wanted to see me?" she said when they were alone.

Matt pointed to a chair. "Sit down. I want to talk to you."

"We have nothing to say."

His jaw clenched and firmed. "It's about LaRue," he said.

"LaRue?" Her eyes widened. "Is he here in Cripple Creek?"

Matt shook his head. "No, but he's been seen in Victor."

"I see. If he's that close then he might come here." She gripped the arms of the chair and a knot of fear welled up in her throat, not for herself, but for Matt. LaRue had threatened to get even with him. He'd almost killed Matt before. If he came back . . .

"Don't look like that." Matt got up from behind his desk and came around to where she sat. "I've been thinking," he said. "Maybe you'd better take some time off, just until things cool down. Until he leaves the area or we know he's safely put away. I can have one of the men from the saloon watch your house."

"I don't want to take time off."

"If you're worried about money, we'll continue to pay you."

"It isn't the money," she said impatiently. "I like singing here and I'm not going to run away like some frightened rabbit."

"But—"

"No buts, Matt." Carrie stood and faced him. "If you'll excuse me now it's time I went back to work."

"I'll take you home tonight."

She shook her head. "Mr. Magee usually sees me home."

"He's busy. I want him here."

"Then I'll go by myself."

Matt's face hardened. "I'll have my rig brought round at twelve-thirty," he told her.

Hands on her hips, Carrie glared at him.

He glared back at her. "Twelve-thirty," he said.

She stamped her way downstairs, and when it was time to sing, she added three extra songs to her show. Let Matt wait, she thought angrily, mad enough to spit if she'd been a spitting woman.

She'd been mad enough to spit ever since the other night when he'd told her he wasn't the marrying kind. He was what her friend, Margaret Louise Fairbanks, would have called a cad, a love-'em-and-leave-'em man. He had taken her innocence. He had changed her, and she would never be the same again.

It cut down deep into her soul that what they shared hadn't meant as much to him as it had to her. That while he had wanted to sleep with her he had absolutely no thought of marrying her, that he'd actually blanched when she mentioned the word *marriage*.

Still fuming, Carrie put on the dark blue velvet cloak, and, pulling the hood up to cover her hair, went to meet

Matt. There would be no rides out of town tonight, she decided. He could take her home, but that's all he could do.

Worthy Magee accompanied her out to the rig and helped her up. "Good night, Miss Carrie," he said. "Night, boss."

"Good night, Worthy. Keep an eye on things, will you?"

"Sure thing, Mr. Craddock. See you tomorrow night."

Matt said, "Giddap," and that was the last word spoken until they arrived at Carrie's house. "I'll see you to your door," he said then, and offered his hand to help her down.

She took his hand but stood well away from him when her feet touched the ground. "That won't be necessary." She gathered the cloak around her. "I'm quite capable of going up the steps by myself. Good—"

"Wait!" Matt held up a cautioning hand. "I thought I heard something."

"I didn't." Carrie started up the front walk, but Matt stopped her, his hand on her arm. Still holding her there, he reached into the pocket of his overcoat and she saw him pull out a small, snub-nosed revolver.

"What are you doing?" she whispered. "What—"

"Shh." As quietly as he could, Matt opened the front gate. "Get in the house," he started to say but stopped when he heard another sound. Quickly, he yanked Carrie inside the gate and shoved her down behind it. "Stay where you are," he ordered in a whisper. "Don't move."

Carrie looked up at him, frightened enough now to do what he said.

Bending low to the ground, Matt started around toward the back of the house. From somewhere down the street a dog barked. Matt waited, then began to edge forward. A branch snapped and before he could turn, a figure rushed at him through the darkness. He saw the upraised arm, the glint of a blade as the knife slashed down. As he brought his arm up, the blade cut through the heavy fabric of his coat and he dropped the derringer.

Carrie screamed. The attacker struck again and Matt staggered back, regained a foothold and lunged at the man with the knife. The two of them grappled. Carrie saw the flash of steel, saw Matt dodge out of the way. The moon came out behind the heavy clouds, and she screamed again when she saw Matt's assailant.

Nathan LaRue, his face distorted with rage, knife clutched in his fist, struck again. But Matt was ready for him. His fist doubled, he hit LaRue a stunning blow on the jaw. LaRue went back, but he didn't fall. Before Matt could reach him, he'd scrambled up, spun around and headed down the street.

Matt started after him.

"No!" Carrie screamed.

Matt went down on one knee, hands flat on the ground, holding himself so that he wouldn't fall.

The front door opened. Effie called out, "What's happening? Miss Carrie? Miss Carrie? Are you all right?"

"It's Matt!" She ran to him. "He's been hurt. Help me."

"I'm all right." He managed to get to his feet. "Don't make such a damn fuss."

She put an arm around his waist. "Shut up!" she cried, almost hysterical with reaction. "Just shut up!"

They got him into the kitchen and sat him down. The left arm of his overcoat was ripped from shoulder to elbow, and bloody. Carrie eased his coat off, then the tweed jacket of his suit. It too was torn and bloody.

"I can do it," Matt said.

"No, you can't," Carrie scolded. "Get a pillowcase and tear it into bandages, and antiseptic," she said to Effie. Stripping off his shirt, she winced when he winced. The wound was almost three inches long. She stanched the blood with a clean kitchen towel and held it there, her other hand on his shoulder, supporting him.

"It isn't bad," Matt said. "Don't look like that, Carrie."

"LaRue could have killed you," she whispered.

"But he didn't." He would have if he'd had a gun, Matt thought. Why hadn't he? His eyebrows drew together in a frown. Dammit, of course! It hadn't been him LaRue was waiting for, it had been Carrie.

The thought chilled him. She'd been angry tonight. What if in a fit of pique she had left without him and found LaRue waiting for her? What would LaRue have done? Would he have forced her into the house? Or had he planned to take her away with him?

Matt felt a cold trickle of sweat run down the middle of his back. The thought of the other man putting his hands on Carrie was like a physical pain that hurt more than the knife wound. It was Carrie who was in danger. LaRue had decided to get back at him through her. Well, by God, LaRue wouldn't get away with it.

It would be easier to protect her if she would agree to move in with him. He had a housekeeper, a cook and a handyman. He could pull in one of the miners from the Lucky Lady to watch his house at night. But when he'd asked her to move in with him, she'd bristled like a hen turkey with her tail feathers ruffled.

Still he knew she cared for him. He'd known that when he'd made love to her. He knew it now by the way she touched him, and the way her eyes filled when she dabbed the antiseptic to the wound. He felt it in the gentleness of her hands.

He closed his eyes. Carrie, he thought, what am I going to do about you?

Later, because he would not leave her, they sat in front of the fireplace in the parlor, Matt stretched out on the love seat, Carrie in the rocking chair. She had wanted to go for Dr. Taylor, but he wouldn't let her.

"The wound is superficial," he said. "If you'll feel better about it, I'll stop in tomorrow and see the doc. But I'm staying here tonight."

And though she had objected, he refused to leave. Tomorrow he would speak to the sheriff, and he'd have the sheriff notify the neighboring towns to be on the lookout for LaRue. He'd hire two men, one to watch the house during the day and another at night. If Carrie refused to move in with him, he was going to make damn sure she was protected.

He shifted on the love seat and she said, "What is it? Are you all right? Does your arm hurt?"

"It hurts," he said. "But it'll be all right. Don't worry." He held out his hand to her. "Come sit beside me, Carrie. I want to talk to you."

For a moment Carrie hesitated, then she crossed the room and sat next to him.

"I know you were frightened by what happened tonight," he said. "I used to think LaRue was just a cheap hustler. That's what he is all right, but now I know how dangerous he is." Matt took her hand. "I wish you'd change your mind about moving in with me, Carrie."

Her chin firmed, but before she could speak, Matt went on. "You don't have to share my bedroom, but I'd like you to be where I know you'll be safe if LaRue decides to try again."

Carrie stared at him. "LaRue isn't after me. It's you he wants."

Because he didn't want her to know what he suspected, Matt didn't argue the point. "I know, Carrie. But I still think it would be a good idea if you and Effie and Sarah moved in with me."

"That's out of the question. This is my home and this is where I intend to stay until I go back to Ohio."

"I don't want you to go back to Ohio," he said before he thought. But once the words were out, he knew that it was true. He didn't want her to leave.

He took her hand, and, when she tried to tug it away, he held on to it and said, "We have to talk, Carrie. I know I hurt you the other night when I told you that I wasn't ready for marriage and I'm sorry. But I've been on my own for a long time, I'm used to living the way I live. I don't want to be accountable to anyone."

A furrow creased his brow, clearly showing his concern. "If I'm in an all-night poker game I don't want to have to worry about hurrying home to a waiting wife. If I want to drink and raise a little hell over at Charmaine's, I want to be free to do it. Maybe I'd take a sudden notion to get on a train and go back to Chicago or to New York, maybe on down to Mexico. The thing is, Carrie, I've been a free man since the day I left school and went out on my own. I don't think I'm ready to give up that freedom."

"I'm not asking you to," she said between clenched teeth.

He knew she was angry, and that he should stop, but something made him go on. It was important to him that she understand.

"There's something else," he said. "I'm not sure that marriage really works. I saw what happened to my mother and father, I saw how she held him back. All his life my dad worked on the Erie Canal, and he hated every minute of it. For years he begged my mother to go out to California with him. He had maps, Carrie, maps and books and newspaper articles, everything he could find on California. It was his dream, his obsession. It was all he talked about, all he ever thought about. But he never got there because my mother held him back. And I decided..." He looked at her, his face set and serious. "I decided that I'd never let a woman do to me what my mother did to my father."

"All women aren't like your mother," Carrie said.

"Maybe not." He turned his gaze toward the fire, and, taking another tack, he asked, "How many happy marriages have you known, Carrie?"

She thought of her parents' marriage. "I haven't known many," she answered truthfully. "But that doesn't mean that marriage can't work if two people..." She stopped. My God, it sounded as though she were pleading with him to marry her. "You're right," she snapped, angry again. "Marriage is a terrible institution."

For a few moments they didn't speak, then Matt said, "I've never felt for a woman what I feel for you, Carrie. It's a new emotion for me, it takes a little getting used to." He stroked the back of her hand. "At first you were a challenge and I—"

"A challenge!" she said, looking outraged.

Matt smiled. "You were so straitlaced and prim that I couldn't help wanting to know what kind of a woman you were underneath all that starch."

Carrie shot him a withering look, but he went on. "Little by little you began to get under my skin. It wasn't just that I was curious, or that you were pretty. I began to see the kind of a woman you were. I saw the way you were with Sarah, and that touched me because she means a lot to me."

Matt hesitated, wondering how much he should tell her. He decided to continue. "Rosalinda told me all about your father. She made me promise that if anything happened to her, I'd never let him have Sarah." He tightened his hand around Carrie's. "I would have kept that promise, and because I didn't know you, I decided that if you were anything like him I was going to do everything I could to keep Sarah away from you."

Carrie stared at him, her eyes wide with shock.

"But you're nothing like your father, Carrie. You've loved Sarah from the very first day. You treat her gently and I know you'll be as good a mother to her as Rosalinda would have been."

"I will be, Matt," Carrie said softly. "I promise you I will."

"I've seen your struggle and your pride," he went on. "I know how hard you tried to keep going so that you could take care of Sarah and Effie." With his good hand, Matt reached into his vest pocket and brought out a tissue-wrapped package. "I saw you sell this," he said, and placed it in her hand.

Carrie opened the paper and stared at the filigree brooch that had been her mother's. Her eyes filled with tears. "I tried to buy it back," she said. "But the man in the pawnshop told me someone had bought it."

"I saw you leave the shop." Matt closed her fingers around the brooch. "I've been waiting for the right moment to give it to you, Carrie."

"Matt . . . ?"

He kissed the tears from her cheeks. "You're so fine," he said. "You're everything I've ever dreamed a woman could be." He held her a little away from him so that he could look deep into her eyes. "Give me some time, Carrie," he said. "Give me a chance to see if I can be the kind of a man you want me to be."

"Matt, I—"

He stopped her words with a kiss that was neither fierce nor demanding, but rather a sharing of warmth. "Don't shut me out," he said. "Don't keep me away."

Carrie felt herself soften inside, and when he drew her closer, she did not pull away, but let her head rest against his chest.

They stayed like that far into the night, he with his good arm around her, her head on his shoulder as they gazed into the fire, each with their own thoughts, their own doubts and fears.

At times he stroked the hair back from her face or kissed her brow. He held her without passion, for what he felt went deeper than passion, it went into his very heart. He did not understand it, he only knew he was filled with an overwhelming tenderness and with a need to take care of her.

Carrie, he thought. And held her there, close to him, until they both went to sleep.

Chapter Fifteen

A month passed without any trace of Nathan LaRue. But though some of his tension eased, Matt still insisted on keeping the men he hired to watch the house on Second Street. And that after Carrie had finished for the night at the Golden Nugget, either he or Worthy Magee escorted her home.

Every day Carrie's popularity grew. News of her singing spread across the state. The owner of the Crystal Palace in Denver came to try and hire her away from Matt.

"I'll double what he's paying you," Thomas T. Trainor said. "What're you making here?"

"Fifty dollars a week."

"Fifty dollars! I doubt Miss Jenny Lind herself made that kind of money. But by damn, I'll pay it. A hundred dollars a week and you start next Saturday night."

"But you don't understand, Mr. Trainor," Carrie said with a smile. "I don't want to leave Cripple Creek."

Or Matt.

Carrie and Matt had been tentative with each other these past four weeks. They were polite and friendly, but as though by mutual consent, they avoided any closer contact.

Carrie had thought a great deal about their conversation the night of Nathan LaRue's attack, and she had tried to sort out her feelings about Matt and his attitude toward marriage.

He had said he wasn't ready to give up his freedom. She tried to understand that perhaps men needed the feeling they were free more than women did, but it was difficult for her. Being with Matt, making love with Matt, had made her long for a home and family of her own. She wanted to do things for Matt, to be there for him. She didn't need any more freedom than the freedom to be in his arms.

He had said, too, he didn't want to be accountable to anybody, that if he wanted to gamble all night that's what he would do. Or if he wanted to go to Chicago or New York or Mexico he had to be free to leave.

What was so wonderful about staying up all night gambling? she wondered. And when he got on a train to go somewhere, why couldn't she go with him?

He had spoken of the unhappiness of his mother and father's marriage, and because of the bitterness of her own parents' marriage she understood. If marriage was for better or for worse then certainly for her mother it had been for worse. In the case of Matt's parents, it had been his father who suffered. Held back by a wife afraid to venture out in the world, he had lost his dream.

She did not think she would ever be the kind of wife Matt's mother had been. But how could she be sure? When a couple married, they took a vow to love and cherish each other forever. But how long did forever last? How long before the wants and needs of one conflicted with the wants and needs of the other? Why did love have to end? Why did the small selfish ways and the small cruelties begin? The hurt feelings and the pain.

She understood Matt's fears because they were her fears, too. But surely if a man and a woman loved each other...

Love. This was the first time Carrie had allowed the word to enter her conscious mind. She was afraid of it; she savored it. She said it aloud in the silence of her room and knew that it was true. She loved Matthew Craddock.

He came to dinner most Sunday afternoons. So did Noah Pierce, and usually after dinner Noah and Effie went buggy riding. Matt stayed until it was time for Sarah to go to bed, and when it was, he kissed the little girl good-night, and, like a family friend, kissed Carrie with the same tender affection. Though at times Carrie could see the hunger in his eyes, he never went beyond that one affectionate kiss.

"Noah's crazy about Effie," he said one night after the other couple had left. "One of these days he's going to ask her to marry him."

"Effie's only sixteen," Carrie answered. "That's too young to marry, but I would certainly rather have her marry Noah than go back to The Chateau."

"Charmaine was saying the other day how much Effie had changed since she's been with you. She's pleased about Noah's courting Effie and—"

"You've seen Charmaine?" Carrie's eyebrows rose. "You've been to The Chateau?"

Matt nodded. "With a man from Durango I'm doing some business with."

Carrie frowned and her lips drew into a disapproving line.

"For drinks."

"Really?" She looked at him, then away. "Well, it certainly isn't any concern of mine."

"Isn't it?"

"No."

"A lot of men go to The Chateau for a drink and a little conversation, Carrie. Not all of them go upstairs." He got up from the love seat and went to stand in front of her. "I didn't go upstairs, Carrie, if that's what's bothering you."

"It isn't," she said, and averted her eyes.

Matt reached down and pulled her out of the rocker. "There hasn't been anyone—"

"Uncle Matt?" Sarah looked up from where she'd been playing with her dolls in front of the fireplace. Dressed in the long pink flannel nightshirt and fuzzy slippers that Carrie had put on her earlier, her little face was wrinkled with concern. "Are you mad at Aunt Carrie, Uncle Matt?"

Matt glared down at Carrie for a moment, then he let her go. "Of course not, sweetheart," he said to Sarah. "Sometimes grown-ups have serious things to say to each other, that's all."

"Is Aunt Carrie mad at you?"

Matt looked at Carrie, then back to Sarah. He went over and picked her up and kissed both her cheeks. "No, baby. But your Aunt Carrie and I need to have a serious talk. How about if I take you up to bed and tuck you in?"

"Will you tell me a story?"

"You bet I will." And to Carrie, he said, "You don't mind if I take her up?"

"Of course not." But she didn't look at Matt when she kissed Sarah and said, "Night-night, lovey. I'll be up in a few minutes."

She watched him carry the little girl up the stairs, then went to stand in front of the fire. It isn't any of my business what Matt does, she told herself. I haven't any right to object. But the thought of him holding another woman the way he had held her, of doing all the things with someone else that he had done with her, sent a stab of pain through her so fierce that she covered her mouth with her hand lest she cry out.

She was still standing there ten minutes later, her back to the room, when Matt came downstairs. Without a word he went to her, and before she knew what he meant to do, he took hold of her arms and turned her around to face him.

"I went to The Chateau," he said. "I had a drink, I talked to the girls, and I did some business with the man I went there with. That's all I did, Carrie." When she didn't answer, he gave her a little shake. "There hasn't been anybody since the last time you and I were together. I don't want anybody else, I only want you."

Carrie tried to pull away from him, but he held her there, gripping her shoulders. "I want you," he said. "*You*, Carrie. Not Charmaine or Lorelei or Conchita or anybody else. You've spoiled me for any other woman." His hands tightened. "And frankly, my dear, that makes me mad as hell."

He held her away from him, and suddenly all of his anger and frustration boiled to the surface. His eyes flashed sparks of hot green fire, his mouth firmed into a cruel hard line. "Damn you," he said. "Damn you, Carrie McClennon."

He kissed her, his mouth fierce, hungry, passionate. He held her there, one hand behind her head so that she couldn't move away from him, the other hand cupping her bottom, pressing her so close she could feel the tension of his body, the rigid part of him burning against the fabric of her gown.

Heat rushed into her loins. Her hands came up to push him away, but instead flattened against his chest. Her lips parted under his and she moaned aloud into his mouth.

Beyond all reason, burning with a flame that threatened to consume him if he did not have her, Matt plunged his tongue into her sweet hot mouth and kissed her hard and deep.

When she murmured a protest, he reached for her breasts, cupping them in his big hands, running his thumbs over the peaks of her nipples, squeezing, tugging, feeling them grow under his fingers.

He heard the rasp of her breath against his lips and felt the softening of her body against his hardness. He wanted her. He would take her. He could, here on the floor in front of the fire. Strip her clothes off. Join his body to hers. Feel that soft, moist, heated part of her close around him. He could . . .

With a growl he let her go. Gripping her shoulders so hard that she flinched, he looked down at her with angry eyes.

"Damn you," he said again. Before she could answer, he scooped his coat up off the chair and ran out the front door as though the devil himself were after him.

Carrie stood there, dazed, unable to move. She touched her bruised and swollen lips, and with a broken sob, sank down onto the love seat and covered her eyes with her hand. "Matt," she wept. "Oh, Matt."

Carrie did not see him or hear from him for a week.

The weather changed. The air warmed and softened. And Sarah got the measles.

Rosalinda had had them when she was a child, so Carrie knew what it was as soon as she saw the eruptions on Sarah's body and felt her feverish forehead.

"Go get Dr. Taylor," she told Effie. "Then go to the Golden Nugget and tell them I won't be in for a few days."

That night when Matt stopped in at the gambling saloon and saw that Carrie wasn't there, he said, "Where's Miss McClennon? Why isn't she here?"

"Her little niece is sick," Stanley Bray told him. "A girl came by this afternoon to say that Miss Carrie wouldn't be in."

"Sarah's ill? What's the matter with her?"

"Measles, the girl said. She'd already gone for Doc Taylor." Bray shook his head. "There's going to be a hullabaloo when the customers find out Miss Carrie isn't going to be here tonight. They've already started asking where she is."

"It won't be for long," Matt said. And it wouldn't be, if everything went all right with Sarah. If there were no complications.

The next morning he knocked on Carrie's door.

"Miss Carrie's upstairs with Sarah," Effie said when she answered it. "Poor little tyke is sicker'n a dog. All over, a rash and a fever, and feeling plumb poorly."

"Is it all right if I go up?"

Effie bobbed her head. "She'll be real glad to see you, Mr. Matt."

He took the stairs two at a time and stopped at the open doorway. "Hello, princess," he said. "I heard you weren't feeling so good."

Sarah looked up at him. "I'm sick," she said, sniffling.

"I know, baby." He went to her bedside and took her hand. "What did Doc Taylor say?" he asked Carrie.

"It's the measles. She'll be in bed for a week."

"You look pretty done in, Carrie. Why don't you go downstairs and let Effie fix you a cup of tea. I'll stay with Sarah."

Carrie hesitated, then she patted Sarah's hand and said, "I'll just be downstairs, honey. You can visit with Uncle Matt while I'm gone."

As she left the room, she heard Sarah say, "Come sit 'side me, Uncle Matt."

Matt came every day to see Sarah. He held her when she didn't feel well, told her stories when she fussed, and rocked her to sleep when she was tired. He brought her presents, and when Carrie protested that he was spoiling Sarah, he said, "All little girls should be spoiled and petted, Carrie." He smiled. "And so should not-so-little girls."

When she looked away without answering, he said, "I've missed you."

For a moment her gray eyes softened and he saw the slight tremble of her lips.

"Carrie," he said.

"No," she whispered. And before he could stop her, she turned and left the room.

By the end of the week Sarah was well enough to come downstairs. Matt built up the fire, and when the parlor was warm, he wrapped Sarah in a blanket and carried her down.

Carrie had prepared her favorite dinner of fried chicken, and Effie had made chocolate cupcakes. After they had eaten, Sarah beamed a smile at each of them and said, "This is just like a party."

"All we need now is some music," Effie said.

"I agree." Matt looked at Carrie. "Will you sing for us?"

Sarah clapped her hands. "Yes, sing, Aunt Carrie."

Carrie hesitated, uncomfortable with Matt looking at her the way he was, then hesitantly began to sing "Sweet Betsy from Pike," substituting the name Sarah for Betsy, which made Sarah clap her hands and chortle with pleasure. After that Carrie sang "Skip to My Lou," and when Matt said, "One more, please," she nodded and began to sing "Greensleeves."

Firelight turned her auburn hair to flame and cast soft shadows on her face. The lace of the collar of her white shirtwaist edged the line of her throat. There was a touching sweetness of expression when she looked at Sarah and sang the old and lovely words,

> "'Alas, my love, you do me wrong,
> To cast me off discourteously,
> When I have loved you so long,
> Delighting in your company.'"

Matt's eyes grew thoughtful as he watched her. Had he done wrong to Carrie? Had he cast her off discourteously after she had so willingly given of herself, given of her love? Had he been selfish, thinking only of his desire without giving thought to the consequences for her?

"That was beautiful, Miss Carrie," Effie said when the song ended. "I swear, you sing like an angel."

Matt said, "Yes, it was beautiful, Carrie."

Carrie looked at him and there was something in his eyes she hadn't seen before—a questioning, a shadow of doubt. And a hunger.

"I'll take Sarah up," Matt offered, turning away and gathering the child in his arms. As Sarah's head nodded on his shoulder, he made his way up the stairs.

"Mr. Matt is just about the nicest man I ever met," Effie said.

Carrie, still lost in the dream of his eyes, only nodded. Then, because she didn't want to talk about Matt, she forced a smile and asked, "What about Noah?"

"Well, he's nice, too." Effie blushed and bobbed her head. "He's *real* nice, Miss Carrie. He treats me like I was somebody special and he never says a word about my having been at The Chateau. It's just like I never was as far as he's concerned. He's so good and he treats me like I was good, too."

Carrie took the girl's hand. "You are good, Effie. You're one of the nicest girls I've ever known."

"But you know what I was, Miss Carrie."

"I know who you are, Effie. That's all that matters. Who you are now."

"Yes, ma'am." Effie toyed with the edge of her skirt. "Noah's asked me to marry him, Miss Carrie."

Carrie had been expecting it, but still she was surprised. "What did you say?" she asked.

"I told him I had to ask you. I...I don't have any kin except my pa and I wouldn't ask him for the time of day." She looked beseechingly at Carrie. "What do you think I should do? Should I marry Noah?" She twisted her hands together. "I just don't know what to do."

"Do you love him?"

Effie's eyes filled. "Yes'm, I love him something terrible."

"Then I think you should marry him, Effie." Carrie moved closer to the girl and put her arm around her. "Noah's a fine man," she said. "You'll be happy with him."

"But I don't want to leave you and Sarah."

"We'll see each other often. Besides, Sarah and I will be going back to Ohio one of these days." She squeezed the girl's thin shoulders. "It makes me happy to know that you'll be taken care of when I'm gone."

At Carrie's words, Matt stopped at the bottom of the stairs, his hand on the newel post. He sucked breath into his lungs, steadying himself before he asked, "What's going on?"

"Noah has asked Effie to marry him," Carrie said.

"Well, now." Matt strode into the room. "That's mighty good news, Effie. When's the wedding going to be?"

"I don't know, Mr. Matt. I don't want to leave Miss Carrie until Sarah's all better. And Noah's got to find us a house. He's wanting to do it next month and I guess . . . I guess if it's all right with Miss Carrie, that's when it'll be."

"Of course it's all right with me," Carrie said with a smile. "Would you like to have the wedding here?"

"I'd love to, Miss Carrie. This is the nicest house I've ever lived in, and I've been happy here with you and Sarah. It would mean a lot to me to get married here. But I . . . I don't think I should." Effie lowered her eyes. "You see, I'd like to ask Miss Charmaine and the girls and I know you wouldn't cotton to that so maybe it'd be better if me and Noah went to the justice of the peace and—"

"You'll do no such thing," Carrie said indignantly. "You'll be married here and if you want to invite . . ."

She swallowed hard and tried to ignore the glint of humor in Matt's eyes. "If you want to invite Charmaine and the other girls, you can."

Effie looked at her, wide-eyed. "Really? Really, Miss Carrie?"

"Really," Carrie said, and hoped she wouldn't live to regret it.

The wedding was set for the second Sunday in April. Carrie would stand up for Effie, Matt would act as Noah's best man, and Sarah would be the flower girl.

Carrie and Effie began preparing the house for the wedding. Floors were scrubbed, rugs were hung on the clothesline and beaten with flat sticks to get the dust out. The curtains were washed and the furniture polished.

Carrie was polishing the silver on the afternoon Matt came to call. She was wearing an Old Mother Hubbard dress and had her hair tucked up under a scarf.

He took one look at her, raised an eyebrow and said, "I've come to take you away from all this."

"I'm busy," she said.

"It's a beautiful day and you need a break." He took the cleaning cloth out of her hand. "I'll wait while you change."

Carrie tried to look severe. "I can't, Matt," she said. "I have to finish cleaning the silver."

"The silver can wait."

"Course it can," Effie said from the kitchen doorway. "You go along with Mr. Matt."

Carrie looked from Effie to Matt.

"The columbine is in bloom," he said.

Carrie took a deep breath. "You win. It'll take me a few minutes to get ready, if you don't mind waiting."

"I'm a patient man, Miss Carrie," he said with a deceptively innocent smile. "I found out a long time ago that anything good is worth waiting for."

Carrie's stomach fluttered with anticipation. "I'll only be a minute," she murmured, and headed for the stairs.

Twenty minutes later she came down wearing a black wool skirt, a handkerchief-linen blouse with a pleated front, and a short blue velvet jacket with a fur collar and a matching muff. Her hat, of the same blue velvet, was trimmed with a fluff of veil.

A smile tugged at the corners of Matt's mouth, and he thought how Carrie had changed in the months he had known her, how far she had come from the gray church mouse he had seen that blustery day at the Denver station to this well-dressed stylish woman.

"I don't want to be gone too long," she said.

"You won't be." He smiled at Effie and, swooping Sarah up in his arms, gave her a hug before he took Carrie's arm and led her out to his rig.

Matt was right, the mountain meadows were covered with columbine. Purple thistles softened the winter-dry fields, and the mountains were bright with yellow clover. As she looked around her, Carrie felt herself beginning to relax. She was glad she had come out—it was a beautiful day, spring was in the air, and she was with Matt.

"I thought we'd ride out to the Lucky Lady," he said. "I've got a man who runs the mine for me, but every once in a while I like to take a look at it."

"What made you decide to buy a gold mine?"

"I didn't buy it, I won it playing poker." He chuckled. "There were only two of us left in the game and we were playing five-card stud. I had a pair of queens showing and the man across from me, the one who owned the Lucky Lady, showed three sixes. I raised as high as I could go. He thought I was bluffing so he kept raising the stakes. When we were both just about out of money I wagered the Dirty Shame and he wagered the Lucky Lady. I wasn't bluffing. My down card was a queen." Matt grinned. "My Lucky Lady," he said.

Carrie shook her head. She knew nothing about cards and she couldn't understand a man who would wager so much on a game of chance. Again, as she had before, she realized just how different she and Matt were.

When they arrived at the mine, Matt introduced her to his foreman, a ruddy-faced man by the name of Sam Carruthers. He showed her the mining office and the tracks that led into the mine, and the cage that took the miners underground.

"The men are working at seven hundred feet," Carruthers told Matt. "It's rich as damn sin down there and seems like every day is better'n the day before." He grinned and scratched his bald head. "Keeps going like it is, you're going to be the richest man in Colorado."

"Let's hope so," Matt said with a laugh, and taking Carrie's arm, he led her back to the rig.

The richest man in Colorado. Matt had it all: looks, money and charm. He could have any woman he wanted, and what bothered Carrie was that just maybe he wanted as many of them as he could get before he settled down.

When Matt saw the pucker of worry linger between Carrie's eyebrows, he asked, "What's the matter?"

Carrie shook her head. "It's nothing, Matt. Nothing important."

"Maybe you're hungry."

"Maybe." She forced a smile. After all, it was a beautiful afternoon, she was with Matt, and she was going to enjoy it. The sun was warm on her face, the aspen were in bud, and spring was almost here. And, yes, she really was hungry.

"What would you say to fried chicken and biscuits, fresh country cheese, apple pie, and a bottle of red wine?"

"It sounds wonderful. We're not too far from Victor. Is that where we're going? To a restaurant there?"

"Nope." Matt pointed up toward the mountains. "See that overhang of rocks?" he said. "That's where we're going."

"But there isn't anyplace to eat up there."

"Sure there is. There's a meadow and pine trees and sunshine. There's even an orchestra."

"An orchestra?" Carrie looked at him and shook her head. "What in the world are you talking about, Matt?"

"Birds," he said. "Best music in the world except maybe for your singing." He grinned. "Look behind you, Carrie. Fried chicken and all the trimmings."

Carrie lifted the lap robe and saw the picnic basket. "Lunch," she said, pleased. She looked up at the high meadow and thought what it would be like up there, alone with Matt.

The lofty ponderosa pines with their cathedrallike spires surrounded fields of columbine and yellow clover. Except for the spontaneous chirping of the birds, it was quiet here, as quiet as a church on a Sunday morning before anyone came.

"It's so beautiful," she whispered, not wanting to break the silence. "It's as though we were the only ones left in the world, isn't it?" She looked up at him.

"Thank you for bringing me here, Matt. It truly is a special place."

"My place," he said. "I've never brought anyone else here, Carrie."

They walked to the edge of the pines and spread the lap robe on the ground. When they were seated, Matt opened the basket and took out the fried chicken, the china plates, the silver and two crystal wine glasses. He served the wine, pouring his glass half-full, carefully measuring only a little for her. Then handing Carrie hers, he said, "Let's drink to spring."

"To spring." She touched her glass to his.

The fried chicken was crisp. They ate cheese with the biscuits, sipped the red wine and finished almost half of the apple pie.

When Carrie was done eating, she took her jacket and her hat off and lay back on the lap robe. The sun warmed her face and clover scented the air. She hadn't been this relaxed in weeks. Tonight she would go to work at the Golden Nugget. Tomorrow she would cook and clean and take care of Sarah, but for now, for this glorious afternoon, she hadn't a care in the world. She could just lie here looking up at the trees and listening to the birds.

She was aware of Matt beside her, his back against the trunk of a tree, his long legs stretched out in front of him, his face shadowed by pine branches. She watched him take a cheroot out of the pocket of his brown corduroy jacket, bite the end off and light it.

"You don't mind?" he asked.

"No, I like it." It was a good smell; when she had kissed him the scent of it was on his breath, a part of him, of his masculinity.

She closed her eyes. Only for a moment, she told herself, but suddenly she was drifting, dreaming. The sun was warm and the meadow hummed with a life all its own.

Matt snubbed the cheroot out and moved away from the tree. "Let me hold you," he said softly, and lifting Carrie's shoulders, he rested her head on his lap.

"It's time we left," she murmured, half-asleep.

"Shh," he soothed. "Close your eyes, Carrie. Rest."

"For a minute."

"Yes, dear. For a minute."

Her breathing evened. Matt watched the gentle rise and fall of her breasts and smiled. He stroked loose tendrils of her rich auburn hair back from her face. He ran his fingertips over her forehead, her cheeks and her lips. He traced the lobes of her ears, the line of her throat.

Between sleeping and waking, Carrie murmured her pleasure, shifting so that she was turned toward him as he continued to stroke her. She felt his fingers at the top button of her handkerchief-linen shirtwaist, and still she did not open her eyes or move away.

He opened the shirtwaist and tugged at the pink ribbon that threaded through the white camisole. The sun warmed her breasts and she opened her eyes.

"Don't move away," he said. "Not yet."

"I won't," she whispered.

He touched her with gentle hands, caressing the roundness of her breasts, watching the sudden peak of rose-tipped nipples.

"My sweet Carrie," he murmured. Shifting so that he lay beside her, he leaned to kiss her breasts.

Carrie felt the warm earth beneath her back, the sun, and the warmth of his mouth. She threaded her fingers through the black thickness of his hair. She felt his breath against her skin. "Matt," she said, and gave herself up to his hungry mouth.

His mouth was gentle, his tongue like a sweet fire burning against her nipples. It was agony, it was ecstasy, and when it became too much, she said, "Wait," and sat up.

There was a question in his eyes, but he didn't try to stop her.

She touched the side of his face, then, with her gaze meeting his, she shrugged the shirtwaist off her shoulders, then the camisole. Next she took off her low-cut opera pumps and unfastened the buttons of her black wool skirt.

"Carrie?" Matt questioned in a voice grown thick with desire. But still he did not touch her or move toward her.

She took off the cotton-and-lace petticoat, and all that was left were the white ruffled pantalets.

"Now you," she said.

Never shifting his gaze from hers, Matt took off his clothes. This time she did not look away. Instead she looked at him, her eyes smoky with desire. His shoulders were broad. His waist and his hips were narrow, his legs long and finely muscled. His skin was bronzed by the sun.

He laid her down on the robe and put his corduroy jacket beneath her head. His hands shaking with eagerness, he took off her white ruffled pantalets.

She was glorious. Her skin, touched by the sun, was like pale pink ivory, but unlike ivory, it was warm and alive to the touch. His touch.

He ran his hands slowly down the silky-smooth length of her. Though his body thrummed with desire, he made himself wait. As he made her wait.

He kissed her mouth gently, slowly. Her lips parted under his, and her mouth was sweet. The whisper of her breath mingled with his. He trailed a line of kisses over her face. He kissed her ears and her throat while she moaned softly against him, and her arms came up to caress his shoulders and his back. He took both breasts, cupping them while he tasted the tender nipples.

"Oh, please," Carrie whispered, her body on fire. "Please, Matt."

Kissing her with all of the pent-up longing he had held in check too long, he grasped her hips and entered her with a moan.

He moved against her hard and fast. For though he had told himself he would go slowly, he could not. It was heaven to be with her like this, to feel her warmth close about him. To look down into her face and see there the same desire that burned within him.

Carrie rolled her head from side to side, lost in the heat of sensation, loving the movement of his body over hers, offering her lips when he took them, whispering his name in a frenzy of desire. When he groaned with pleasure, her body swelled with pride, because she knew that she was pleasing him. And she wanted to. Oh, yes, she wanted to please Matt. She wanted to give of herself, to be everything he wanted her to be because she loved him. God help her, she loved him.

"Carrie," he whispered softly against her lips. "My Carrie."

She began to climb toward that final moment when the world would explode, and she clung to him, her fingertips digging into his shoulders, crying his name with wild abandon.

"Yes!" he whispered. "Oh, yes!" And together they crested the unbelievable high that lovers have known since time began.

When at last their breathing evened, Carrie looked up at the sun filtering through the pines and knew a happiness unlike anything she had known before. For this glorious afternoon, she and Matt were one. He might leave her, she might leave him, but in this perfect moment they were one, their bodies and their hearts joined here in this quiet meadow. Here beneath the April sun.

Chapter Sixteen

The Reverend Hubert Barnside, a tall spare man in his late sixties, lowered his glasses on his thick, red-veined nose and frowned at Effie. "It'd be a lot more fittin' if you got married in the church," he said.

"But Miss Carrie said I could be married at her house and that's what I..." She looked at Carrie, then back at the forbidding man seated across the desk from her. "That's what I want to do," she finished.

"Weddings should be in a church," he insisted. "I don't rightly like performing 'em in somebody's house."

"But that's what Effie and Mr. Pierce have decided they want," Carrie said.

He frowned at Carrie. "Far as I'm concerned that's not the way it should be."

"Very well." Carrie stood. "Thank you for your time, Reverend Barnside." With a nod to Effie, she said, "Let's go."

The minister's face got red. "I didn't say I *wouldn't* do it. I just said it oughta be here in the church. No need for you to get on your high horse, woman. I was just discussing, that's all."

Carrie sat back down.

"You religious a'tall?"

"My father was a minister."

"Then I reckon you are, or leastways you were." He lowered his glasses even farther down on the bridge of his nose. "Maybe you've had more'n your share of churchgoing."

"Maybe." Then relenting, Carrie smiled and said, "I come to church, Reverend Barnside. And so does Miss Davis."

"Then maybe we can work something out," he muttered.

And it was arranged.

Invitations were issued to Charmaine, Miss Binty and the girls. Buck Wattles, Stanley Bray and Worthy Magee would attend, so would the men in the musical group who were all friends of Noah's.

The only two people Carrie knew on the "right" side of town were Mr. Davenport and that sour-acting Elvira Primrose. Sorely tempted to send an invitation to that lady, she smiled at the idea of Mrs. Primrose, dressed in her Sunday best, sitting between Conchita and Lorelei in *their* Sunday best.

Over Effie's protestations that a pretty shirtwaist and a new skirt would do her just fine for the wedding, Carrie insisted on taking her to Miss Amelia Howard's, where she ordered a wedding dress made. She also ordered a new dress for herself and one for Sarah.

A week before the wedding, heavenly smells of cakes and cookies, cranberry-nut bread, and apple fruitcake filled the house. "Weddings are even better'n Christmas," Sarah commented. "Can we bake more cookies. when you get married, Aunt Carrie?"

Carrie wiped a smudge of flour off Sarah's cheek. "We'll see," she said.

She had tried not to think about that subject, but had instead resigned herself to the way things were. Again and again she told herself that somehow it would work out between her and Matt, that surely he could not be the way he was with her if he didn't care. She had seen the expression in his eyes when he looked at her. She knew his need to touch her, the hand that rested on her hand, the arm around her shoulder, the gentle squeeze around her waist when no one was looking.

There had been no opportunity to be really alone since the day they had gone buggy riding. Sometimes in bed at night she thought about that afternoon, how they had made love there in that open field beneath the sheltering pines, and waited for the guilt feelings to come. But they didn't come. All that she felt was a gladness in her heart that at last she knew what it meant to love someone, to hold and be held, and to share a passion that was as beautiful as it was exciting.

It will be all right, she told herself. He will come to love me as I love him and then he won't be afraid. All I have to do is be patient, to wait for that moment when he realizes how right we are for each other, that our marriage will be different than either of our parents' marriages.

She had only to wait. And to keep on loving him.

The second Sunday in April dawned bright and clear and perfect. At the first light of dawn, Effie knocked timidly at Carrie's door, and when Carrie mumbled a sleepy "Yes?" Effie said, "I'm so nervous I could bust. Could we maybe talk for a little while?"

Though it had been after one when Carrie had gotten to bed that morning, she put a robe on and went downstairs with Effie. They drank coffee while she assured the younger woman that everything was going to be just fine, that as long as she loved Noah there was nothing to worry about.

"And we'll see each other every day," Carrie said, for it had already been arranged that because Noah worked almost the same hours as Carrie did, Effie would come over every night and stay with Sarah, and that after Worthy Magee had seen Carrie safely to her door, he would then walk Effie the two blocks to the house she and Noah had rented.

"You're a part of Sarah's and my lives," Carrie said now. "We'll never really lose each other."

Little by little she managed to calm Effie down. When Sarah awakened, the three of them had breakfast, then Carrie made Effie go up and try to rest.

The wedding was at four. At two-thirty, Carrie said that it was time for them to start dressing.

"You're going to look just beautiful," she told Effie when she laid the gown on the bed.

"It's almost too pretty to wear, isn't it?" Effie said, touching the creamy smooth satin. "It's the most beautiful dress I've ever seen, Miss Carrie." She shook her head, a look of wonder in her eyes. "I sure hidey never even dreamed I'd have a wedding or a dress like this. I thought when we were picking it out that maybe I shouldn't be wearing white, me being what I was and all. But now...now I think it's all right." She raised her eyes and looked at Carrie. "It's a new beginning for me," she said softly. "I'm starting over. But I wouldn't be if it hadn't been for you. You took me away from The Chateau and brought me here into your own house, knowing what I was."

"I knew what you were, Effie," Carrie said with a warm smile. "I knew you were a dear and loving girl and that's all that mattered."

"I don't reckon there's any way I can ever thank you, Miss Carrie. But I do. I thank you with all my heart for taking me in, for letting me have the wedding here, and for the dress. It's kinda a shame to be wearing it only once, isn't it?"

"You can save it for your daughter to wear at her wedding." Then, feeling a sudden and unaccountable twinge of sadness, Carrie said, "Come now, let's get you dressed."

First came the silk undergarments, the tightly laced corset, the lace camisole, the pantalets and the petticoats, and finally the white satin wedding gown. The sleeves were capped with a lace flounce. The bodice was trimmed with lace, the hem with a flounce of ruffled satin.

Carrie fastened all of the buttons up the back, then stepped back and looked at Effie. "You look..." She swallowed hard. "You look just beautiful," she said. "Come and see." And taking Effie's hand, she led her to the full-length mirror next to the window.

For a moment Effie couldn't speak. She gazed at herself in the mirror with startled eyes, then a slow, sweet smile curved the corners of her mouth. "I can't hardly believe that's me." She took a big, shaking breath, and in a shy voice, asked, "Do you think Noah's going to like me like this?"

"I think he's going to love you." Carrie gave the girl a quick hug, then led her to a straight-backed chair and said, "Sit here and try not to get wrinkled. I'm going to dress Sarah."

Which was no easy task, because the little girl was so excited she could hardly stand still. She jiggled and hopped from one foot to the other until Carrie tied the pink sash of the ruffly pink dress. Just as she finished brushing Sarah's hair, Miss Binty, who had offered to come early to help usher in the guests, arrived. Carrie went down to meet her, with Sarah following behind.

"You go on up and do whatever you have to do," Miss Binty told Carrie. "I'll take care of things down here." She smiled at Sarah. "Lord sakes, just look at you. If you aren't the prettiest little girl I've seen in all my born days. And look at that pretty dress. I swear you look like a little pink angel."

She took off her coat, and when she started into the front parlor, she stopped and said, "Oh, my goodness, doesn't that look nice!"

There were bouquets of wildflowers near the windows, and pots of buttercups and daisies on either side of the fireplace where the Reverend Mr. Barnside would stand. The two rows of chairs that Matt had sent over from the Golden Nugget were lined up facing the fireplace.

"This is a real nice place for a wedding, Miss Carrie," Miss Binty said. "It was real kind of you to have it here."

"Effie is a special friend of mine," Carrie answered. "I wanted things to be nice for her."

"They're going to be, ma'am. With you for her friend and Noah Pierce for her husband, Effie's going to be just fine. Now why don't you go on up and get dressed. Sarah and I will take care of whoever's coming. When it's time I'll send her upstairs. Soon's you hear the music you and Effie come on down."

So Carrie went upstairs to bathe and dress in her own new gown of pink-and-gold brocaded satin. She unpinned the hair she'd so hastily rolled into a bun this morning, brushed it until it was smooth, and fixed it in a loose pompadour with small tendrils about her face and the back of her neck. That done, she went in to Effie.

The girl was pacing up and down her room.

"I'm in a nervous twit," the girl said when she saw Carrie. "I just can't sit still. My stomach has got the nervous flutters and my throat's so dry I'm spittin' cotton."

"But you look beautiful," Carrie said with a smile. She sat Effie down, smoothed the girl's hair, then placed the crystal-beaded coronet on her head and fastened the veil into place.

Without a word, she took Effie's hand and led her once again to the full-length mirror. "Be happy, dear," she whispered. "Be happy."

The piano player struck a chord; the wedding march commenced.

The three of them came slowly down the beribboned stairway, Sarah leading the way, looking solemn and a little frightened, scattering rosebuds as she walked. At the entrance of the parlor, she hesitated, unsure what to do next until Matt motioned her forward.

Like Noah, Matt wore a black frock coat and pinstriped pants, with a sprig of columbine in his lapel. And like Noah he turned to watch the two women come down the stairs, Carrie first, looking as beautiful as he had ever seen her, and Effie, pretty as a picture in her wedding dress, a bouquet of lilacs in her arms.

He looked at Noah looking at Effie. The groom's Adam's apple bobbed up and down. He gulped, and there was in his eyes an expression of such love, of such wonder, that for the smallest fraction of a moment Matt felt his own throat constrict with unaccustomed pain.

The Reverend Mr. Barnside cleared his throat. Effie and Carrie took their places. He and Noah stepped forward. Noah reached for Effie's hand.

And it began.

How many times, at how many weddings in her father's church had Carrie heard these very same words? But now they took on a new significance and touched something deep within her. She was so very aware of Matt standing only a few feet away from her, but she tried not to look at him when the Reverend Mr. Barnside said the old familiar words.

"To love. To honor and to cherish."

She could not help herself, she had to look at Matt. He was watching her, his dark eyebrows drawn together, his eyes strangely troubled. Anguish and love and need welled up inside her, and she cast her eyes down so that he would not see all that she was feeling.

"Do you, Effie?"

And her shy, sweet answer.

"Do you, Noah?"

And his hearty, "Yes! I mean I do. Yes."

"Till death do us part," they repeated in unison.

Till death do us part. A lifetime commitment, one man and one woman bound together in love.

This was the way it should be, for marriage, after all, was the culmination of love. It was the natural process of the order of things. When a man and woman fell in love, they married. That was the way it was meant to be.

She looked at the girls from The Chateau, with their brightly colored ruffled dresses, their frizzed hair and rouged cheeks, and saw in their eyes the same bitter-sweet longing she felt.

"By the power vested in me, in the sight of God..."

In the sight of God. Carrie closed her eyes.

"I do pronounce you husband and wife. May the sun shine on this day and all the days of your lives together."

Matt saw the tears well up in Carrie's eyes. The breath caught in his throat and, without thinking, he took a step toward her, then stopped, remembering where they were.

"You may kiss your bride, Mr. Pierce," the Reverend Mr. Barnside said, and, blushing scarlet, Noah took Effie in his arms and soundly kissed her.

"*Bravo!*" Conchita cried.

The piano player began to play (There'll Be) "A Hot Time in the Old Town Tonight," and everybody laughed. The girls from The Chateau rushed to kiss Effie, while Buck and Worthy and Stanley Bray shook hands with Noah.

Only Carrie and Matt stayed where they were, still caught in each other's gaze, unable to turn away. He took a step toward her, but at that moment Dorrie grabbed his arm. "Come on and kiss the bride, Matt," she said.

He looked at Carrie, then with a whispered, "Sorry," let Dorrie lead him away.

Carrie shook hands with Noah. She kissed Effie's cheek, then, embarrassed by her tears, hurried out to the kitchen to help Miss Binty.

"Let me help, too," Charmaine said, and before Carrie could answer, Charmaine began picking up the plates of cakes and cookies to carry into the dining room.

"That was just about the nicest wedding I've ever seen," she said as she put an apple cake on the table. "It was nice of you to invite us."

"You're Effie's friends," Carrie said a bit stiffly. "Of course I'd invite you."

Charmaine raised one arched eyebrow. "Of course," she said.

Dressed in a bright blue taffeta suit and a matching hat with plumed ostrich feathers, the older woman looked as bright as springtime. Hands on her narrow hips, she looked at Carrie. "It isn't often the girls and I are invited over to this side of town where the so-called nice folks live."

"Nice folks like Elvira Primrose?" Carrie shook her head. "I guess just about everything in this life looks different depending on where you're standing, Charmaine. Nice folks? I wonder what that really means."

Charmaine's lips twitched. "I do declare, Miss Carrie. I think maybe you've come down a peg or two. It wouldn't have anything to do with Matt, would it?"

A flush rose to Carrie's cheeks. "I . . . I don't know what you're talking about."

"Don't you?" Charmaine grinned. "Well, something or somebody's sure loosened your laces," she said. Her expression sobered as she glanced toward the wedding guests. "Matt Craddock is as fine a man as I ever met, Carrie. I don't know what's going on between the two of you, but I sure do hope, for both your sakes, that whatever it is works out."

"So do I," Carrie murmured so low that Charmaine could barely hear her.

"Then you do care?"

"Oh, yes. I care." Taking a deep breath, Carrie said, "We'd better get the rest of the food on the table."

Matt had brought several cases of French champagne, and Buck Wattles insisted on acting as bartender. The Reverend Mr. Barnside, after having declared that he was not a drinking man, accepted a glass to toast the bride and groom.

"A toast," Matt said, raising his glass, "to Effie and Noah. Through all your years of wedded bliss may you be as happy as you are today."

"Hear, hear," the Reverend Mr. Barnside said, and downed his glass.

More toasts were drunk and congratulations were offered. The musicians began to play, and Dorrie said, "It's sorta the custom for the bride and groom to dance together, Miss Carrie. Would it be all right if we rolled back the rug?"

"Could we?" Lorelei asked. "Please, Miss Carrie, could we?"

"Of course," Carrie said, mostly because she didn't really have any choice. While the men proceeded to move the furniture, Carrie went into the kitchen where Miss Binty had prepared platters of cheeses, meatballs and small brown sausages.

When she went back into the parlor, the band began to play one of Mr. Johann Strauss's waltzes. Noah bowed low from his waist and said, "May I have this dance, Mrs. Pierce?"

Effie, her face suffused with pink, took his hand, and while their friends watched, they danced to Mr. Strauss's "The Blue Danube" waltz.

And again, though she had not meant to, Carrie found herself looking at Matt. He was watching the newly married couple, and there was in his eyes an expression of tender affection, and something else, something she could not define.

He turned and saw her watching him, but just as he started toward her, Sarah tugged at his sleeve and said, "I wanna dance, too, Uncle Matt."

With a smile he bowed, took her hand and led her into the circle of dancers.

"Just look at her," Babette said, coming to stand beside Carrie. "Did you ever see anything as sweet as that little girl? You're real lucky to have her, Miss Carrie. There's just nothing like a little child to make you feel like you're something special yourself. That's the way I felt with my little boy. I . . ."

Babette shook her head, unable to go on. Knowing that the girl was close to tears, Carrie put an arm around her. "Why don't you come out and help me in the kitchen for a little while?" she said, tightening her arm around the girl's shoulders and leading her away from the dancing couples.

In the kitchen she told Miss Binty to go and enjoy herself. And when she and Babette were alone, she said, "I'm so sorry about your little boy."

Babette swiped at her tears with the back of her hand. "I just can't help thinking it was my fault." She bowed her head. "If I'd been a better mother . . . if I coulda kept little Timmie with me . . ."

"I'm sure your folks did the best they could."

"I know, Miss Carrie. They're real good people. I know they did what they could for him."

Carrie poured the tea and handed a cup to Babette. "Have you ever thought about going home?" she asked.

"Yes'm, I've thought about it. I thought about it a lot. But I don't guess I could. Not now. It's too late for

me." She looked at Carrie over the rim of the teacup. "I
hated the farm," she said. "I hated slopping hogs and
milking cows and hauling manure and picking potatoes until my back felt like it was broke. Ever since I can
remember, all I ever thought about was getting away
from it. First chance I got I left."

"Did your parents try to stop you?"

"I didn't tell them I was going, Miss Carrie." Babette put another spoonful of sugar into her tea and
slowly stirred. "A traveling salesman fella come by to
sell my pa some new kind of chicken feed. Pa put him
up for a couple of nights and when he left I left with
him. I was fifteen."

Only a year younger than Rosalinda had been when
she left, Carrie thought.

"He took me to Wichita and I was so excited I didn't
hardly know what to do. We stayed in a hotel and he
bought me some clothes and we went out to restaurants
and to the musical theater, and I guess for about two
weeks I was the happiest I've ever been."

Babette's face clouded. "Then one day he told me he
was out of money and he guessed I'd have to help him.
I told him I didn't have a dime to my name and he said,
'I know that, Baby, but I sure know how you can get
some.' I told him I didn't have no talent for singing or
dancing or anything like that. And he said . . . he said
what I had to do didn't hardly take any talent at all."

Babette looked down into her cup. "So I did what he
wanted me to do, Miss Carrie. But after a while he
started being real mean. He beat me up pretty bad one
night when I didn't make as much money as he thought
I should've, and the next morning when he was sleeping, I took some of the money back I'd earned and left.

"I'd heard about Cripple Creek from some of the men I'd...I'd met, and how it was a boomtown and all. I thought maybe I could get me a job waiting tables. But I couldn't, and finally when I didn't have any money left, I went to Miss Charmaine's and she took me in."

She raised her gaze and looked at Carrie. "It's long too late for me," she said matter-of-factly. "I couldn't never go home again."

It's never too late, Carrie wanted to say. But she knew it wouldn't help. Perhaps Babette was right, perhaps it was too late for her, just as it had been too late for Rosalinda.

Miss Binty came back to the kitchen to say that they needed more champagne. "That preacher fella is sure drinking his share," she said. "Tossing it down faster'n Buck can fill 'em up." She looked at Babette. "You all right, hon?" she asked.

Babette nodded and got up. "I shouldn't been bending your ear the way I was," she told Carrie.

"You can bend my ear anytime," Carrie said.

Couples were dancing when they went back to the parlor, even the Reverend Mr. Barnside, who waltzed Charmaine around the floor and declared that she was just about the best looking woman this side of the Continental Divide.

The hour grew late. Carrie didn't dance. Instead she busied herself running back and forth to the kitchen. When she saw Sarah dozing in a chair beside the fireplace, she picked up her little niece and carried her to her room.

There'd be no story tonight, Carrie thought with a smile as she undressed Sarah. The little girl was so sleepy she could barely keep her eyes open.

From downstairs she could hear the music and the laughter. It had been a busy and exciting day and she was beginning to tire. But it was a good sort of tired. The wedding had gone well. Effie was happy, and everybody seemed to be having a grand time.

Carrie smoothed her hair and left the room, closing the door behind her before she started down the stairs.

Matt was waiting for her.

"We haven't danced," he said.

"I don't know how."

"I'll teach you." He held out both of his hands and, as though mesmerized, Carrie came down into his arms.

"I really don't know how," she said.

"Just follow me." He looked into her eyes. Holding her close, they began to dance there in the hallway, away from the others.

She rested her head against his shoulder, and he clasped her hand and brought it up to rest against his chest.

Little by little Carrie began to relax, to follow his lead and the movement of his body.

"That's it," he whispered against her hair. "That's it, Carrie-love."

Carrie-love. She closed her eyes and drifted with the flow of the music. He feathered a kiss against her temple. She closed her eyes and moved closer in his arms.

"Carrie," he said, and, holding her away from him, he looked down at her.

His eyes were soft with an emotion she had never seen before.

"Carrie-love," he said, and kissed her with passion and with tenderness.

"Matt," she whispered. She cupped his face between her hands, and her lips parted under his as she answered his kiss.

I love you, she wanted to say. I love you with all my heart, Matthew Craddock.

But she did not say the words she so longed to say. She only held him and he held her, and answered his kiss with a passion and tenderness to match his own.

And danced with him, there in the hallway, to the sweetly sad music of "After The Ball."

Chapter Seventeen

In the days that followed Effie's wedding, Carrie was torn between feelings of love that warmed and nourished her, and a troubling uncertainty that, after all, what she and Matt had done was wrong.

Insidious feelings of guilt disturbed her sleep and invaded her dreams. Night after night she awakened trembling and fearful, the vision of her father shaking a skeletal finger at her, crying, "Wanton! Jezebel! Harlot! You will burn in eternal hell!"

One night she dreamed of herself in Effie's wedding dress, standing alone in front of the Reverend Hubert Barnside while he shook his head and said, "He's not going to come. I reckon he just doesn't love you enough to marry you."

But in spite of the dreams that troubled her and the doubts that shadowed her days, Carrie knew deep in her heart that while Matt could not give voice to his feelings, he really did care about her. She saw it in his eyes, she heard it in his voice when he spoke her name. Over and over again she told herself that he could not be as he was with her if he did not love her, and that perhaps it was only a matter of time before he declared his love.

Be patient, she told herself. Be loving and he will love you in return.

Several times he came to the house to take her and Sarah out riding in his rig. She saw him at night, too, and often when it came time for her to sing, she would look out through the faces of the men and see Matt standing to one side of the big room. When she did, she would turn to the piano player and whisper, "Greensleeves." And when she came to the words, "And I have loved you so long," her gaze would linger on his for the briefest fraction of a moment.

I have loved you. The words echoed in her mind. I have loved you, Matt.

Effie and Noah returned from their wedding trip to Denver and once in a while, when Carrie knew she would be working late at the Golden Nugget, she took Sarah to Effie's to spend the night.

The first time she did, on a night when Matt escorted her home, instead of Worthy Magee, he kissed her and said, "Let me stay with you tonight."

Carrie shook her head. "No, we can't do that, Matt. It wouldn't be right."

He put his arms around her, and, tilting her face to his, he said, "I want to go to sleep with you, Carrie. I want to lie beside you. I want to reach out my hand and know that you are there. I want to make love to you."

She looked up at him, looked deeply into his eyes and saw the desire there. Love and need, and an overwhelming sense of right and wrong quivered through her. "We shouldn't," she said. "It isn't the right thing to do, Matt."

"It's incredibly right," he said. Then he kissed her, his mouth hot and hungry against hers, and before she could get her breath, he swept her off her feet and carried her up the stairs to her bedroom.

"No," she said. And meant it. At least she told herself she meant it. But when he took off his coat and loosened his tie and came toward her, she did not move away, but stood there by the light of the lamp, waiting.

"We shouldn't do this," she protested. "We—"

But he took her words, smothering them with his lips, and when he let her go, he began to slowly undress her.

He took off her cloak and her gown. He unfastened the ribbon of her camisole and slowly unbuttoned it. He unlaced her corset, shaking his head when he did, saying, "I'm damned if I know why you women wear these fool things."

Once she tried to stop him. "Matt," she said. "Matt, you can't stay."

But he appeared not to have heard. He sat her down on the bed and took off her shoes and the ribbed stockings. And when he had slipped the satin and lace pantalets down over her ankles, he knelt in front of her. He kissed one bare ankle. Holding it, he trailed a line of kisses up her leg. He held her there while she shivered from the touch of his lips against her skin.

He kissed the insides of her thighs and she closed her eyes, shivering more violently.

"Please," she whispered, not even sure what it was she pleaded for.

"Where is your robe?" he asked, and when he had put it on her, he said, in a voice thick with all that he was feeling, "Take your hair down," and watched while with trembling hands she took the pins out of her hair.

She shook it out and it fell, thick and luxurious about her shoulders. He took her hairbrush. Standing over the bed, he began to brush her hair from scalp to tangled

ends, stroke after stroke, brushing until it shone bur-
nished red in the lamplight.

He took handfuls of it and rubbed them against his
face, breathing in the scent of her. He spread his fingers through the silky strands and she felt his hands
against her scalp, massaging, warming, lulling her to
surrender.

"Matt," she whispered.

"Soon, Carrie-love. Soon."

Carrie-love.

His hands were so warm, so strong yet gentle, she
gave herself up to them, becoming his in complete surrender.

He slipped the robe off her shoulders, and when he
had turned back the blankets, he laid her naked on the
bed. Without taking his gaze from hers, he undressed
and climbed in beside her, drawing her into his arms.

"Carrie," he breathed against the spill of her hair.

He kissed every inch of her that night, kissed and caressed her until she trembled with need and cried out.

They made love, fiercely, tenderly, and at that final
splendid moment, with her lips muffled against his
shoulder so that he could not hear, she said the words
she had so longed to say. "I love you, Matt. I love you."

They slept, and woke to love again, each softly
speaking the other's name there in the stillness of the
night.

Carrie woke before Matt in the morning and lay there
beside him, lost in the wonder of it all. Except when she
and Rosalinda were very small, she had never slept with
anyone before. It was strange and comforting to feel the
warmth of another's body against hers, to feel his
breath against her throat, to watch the rise and fall of
his chest.

Carefully she folded the blanket back and looked at the hand that rested against the whiteness of her breast. She remembered all of the ways his hands had touched her in the night. She remembered, too, her muted cries, her pleas for a release of a passion she could no longer bear. She remembered how he had soothed and held her. She remembered everything.

"Carrie?" He opened eyes that were as green as the fresh new buds of spring in the early-morning light. He smiled a knowing smile and the fingers on her breast began to make slow, smooth circles.

"It's morning," she murmured. "We have to get up. I have to get Sarah. I have to—"

"All you have to do is love me," he said against her lips. And it started again, that slow, sweet heat that crept through her body, warming her, thrilling her.

And as he had before, Matt felt a sense of wonder that Carrie could be like this with him, that he need only to touch her and her body would meld into his. He had never before known a woman who gave as she gave.

She was everything he had ever wanted in a woman, yet even as he joined his body to hers, there was a part of him that held back, that could not give as freely as she gave. He did not want to lose a part of himself. He did not want to surrender to a love that would change him. If he gave in to everything that he was feeling, he would lose the freedom he so dearly cherished.

He wasn't ready for that, he might never be ready.

She lifted her body to his. She whispered, "Oh, Matt. Oh, darling," and her slender arms tightened around his neck.

His heart swelled with an emotion he had tried for so long to deny. But even as his body thundered over hers and he convulsed with a surge of passion that took his breath and shook him to the very depths of his soul, he would not say the words he knew she wanted to hear.

"I heard you had a real nice wedding," Mr. Davenport said to Effie with a smile. "And I heard you were the flower girl, Miss Sarah," he added to the little girl. "Bet you were pretty as a picture, too."

Sarah nodded. "I had a new pink dress and I carried a basket of flowers and I dropped them all over the floor so's Effie and Aunt Carrie could walk on them."

"Now doesn't that just beat all." He opened the glass that held the candy. "Do you think your Aunt Carrie would mind if I gave you a licorice stick?"

Sarah looked up at Carrie. "You don't mind, do you?" she asked hopefully.

"No, I don't mind," Carrie said with a laugh. "Just be sure you say thank-you to Mr. Davenport."

"Thank you, Mr. Davenport," Sarah immediately replied.

"What can I do for you today, Miss McClennon?" the storekeeper questioned as he handed the candy to Sarah.

"I need a pound of coffee, a five-pound bag of flour, and—"

The bell over the door jangled as it opened and Mrs. Primrose walked in. She looked at Carrie, then at Effie, and her mouth pursed in disapproval. Chin elevated, averting her gaze, she marched to the counter. "I want three pounds of sugar, a box of chamomile tea, a—"

"I'm sorry, Mrs. Primrose," Mr. Davenport said, clearing his throat. "I'm afraid these ladies are ahead of you."

"Ladies?" Mrs. Primrose looked at Carrie first, then at Effie. "Really, Mr. Davenport, if you persist in catering to people of this type, I shall have to take my business down the street to Mr. Armitage."

"You do that, Mrs. Primrose. You just go on and do that."

Hot color spotted the woman's cheeks. She turned away from the counter and bumped into Sarah, the sleeve of her coat brushing against the well-licked licorice stick. "Get out of my way, you brat," she snapped.

Sarah looked up at her, wide-eyed. Her chin started to wobble.

Carrie put a reassuring hand on her shoulder. "The lady didn't mean that," she said.

"Indeed I did!" Mrs. Primrose drew her coat closer about her. "Women like you haven't any business here in Cripple Creek. You don't belong here and if you had any decency at all you'd take your sister's bastard child and get out of town."

Carrie tightened her hand on Sarah's shoulder. She had never wanted to hit a woman, but she did now, and she would have if Sarah hadn't been looking up at her with stricken eyes. Before she could say anything, Mr. Davenport came around the counter. He went straight for the door, opened it and said, "Good day, Mrs. Primrose."

The matron hesitated for a moment, then turning on the heel of her boot, swept out of the store.

"I'm mighty sorry about that, ma'am," he said to Carrie.

"It's not your fault, Mr. Davenport."

Effie, who up to now had been speechless, said, "That's the meanest woman I ever set eyes on. I don't know how in the world she could be so mean, 'specially to Sarah.''

Sarah looked from Effie to Carrie. "What's a basserd?" she asked.

Carrie knelt down and put her hands on Sarah's shoulders. "*Bastard* isn't a nice word," she said. "And I'm afraid Mrs. Primrose isn't a very nice lady."

"But what is it?"

"It's an ugly word." Carrie hesitated. "I know a nice word that will make you forget all about it," she said. "It's angel and that's what you are, Sarah. You're a very special angel." She hugged the little girl. "Now why don't you and Effie and I go home and have some of that chocolate cake that Effie brought over yesterday. Would you like that?"

Sarah nodded, but she looked troubled and on the verge of tears. "That was a mean lady," she sniffed.

"Amen to that," Mr. Davenport said.

The three of them returned to the house and had chocolate cake. And though Carrie tried to act as though nothing had happened, Mrs. Primrose's words, "You don't belong here," echoed in her mind.

That night, Matt sent Stanley Bray to ask Carrie if she'd come up to his office. When she came, he took both her hands, kissed her and said, "Sit down for a few minutes. There's something I want to tell you."

"You're firing me," she said with a grin.

He laughed and shook his head. "If I did, you're likely to take that offer to go to Denver and I wouldn't like that." He took a cheroot out of the small mahogany box on his desk. "I just wanted to tell you that I'm going to be busy this weekend and I won't be able to see you."

"Oh?" She sat down on the chair facing the desk. "Are you going out of town?"

"No, I'll be here but I'll be tied up." He snipped the end of the cheroot and struck a match. Keeping his gaze on the flame, he said, "I've got some businessmen coming in from the East on Friday and I've reserved The Chateau for the weekend."

"The Chateau?" Carrie stared at him.

"It's business. These same men were here a year ago and we met there then. I had a telegram from John Calhoun a few days ago. He's the head of a conglomerate that wants to buy into the Lucky Lady and he's requested that we hold our meeting at The Chateau. Charmaine is closing the place to everybody else and she's hired extra help to work in the kitchen." He looked at her, smiling a reassuring smile. "We'll do some drinking and gambling, but mostly we'll talk business. If the price is right—"

"I don't want you to," Carrie said.

"What did you say?"

"I said I don't want you to spend the weekend at The Chateau."

He studied the glowing end of the cigar. "I don't think you understand," he said carefully. "This is business, Carrie. Calhoun and his men are interested in buying the mine and I'm interested in selling it. If The Chateau is where they want to hold the meeting, then that's where it will be."

Anger turned her cold. "I see," she said.

"No, you don't see." He came to her and put his hands on her shoulders. "Business meetings have been held there before. Some of the men will spend the night with the girls, some of them won't."

"Which one will you spend the night with, Matt? Lorelei? Conchita? Or maybe with Charmaine?"

Matt tried to hold his anger in check because it mattered a great deal to him what Carrie thought. He didn't want to hurt her, but he would not yield to her on this. Business was business, and in the case of Big John Calhoun, business meant three, maybe four million dollars.

Calhoun had come to Cripple Creek with three of his employees a year ago. He and Matt had spent two days and two nights talking business and when it was all wrapped up, Calhoun had said, "Now that that's behind us, let's go get us some relaxation. You know a place?"

Matt had taken them to The Chateau. Charmaine introduced the girls, who served conversation and smiles along with the drinks. They had inch-thick steaks, potatoes and hot biscuits, and drank a couple of bottles of good Spanish wine. After that they'd played faro.

A little after midnight one of the men excused himself and went upstairs. Soon after that, the other two men followed.

"One more brandy and I'll call it a night," Calhoun had said. He'd patted the remaining two girls on their behinds and said, "You all run along up to bed."

"My girls don't please you?" Charmaine had asked. "You don't find them attractive?"

"They're all mighty fine looking," Calhoun said smiling. "But it's not a girl I'm looking for, Miss Charmaine. It's a woman."

She'd arched one eyebrow in question.

He counted out three thousand dollars and laid it on the table. "I'd be real honored if I could have the pleasure of your company for the next four or five days."

Charmaine looked him square in the eye. "I rarely entertain the men who come here," she said.

Big John Calhoun had looked right back at her. "I didn't hardly think you did," he said.

"Three thousand dollars is a lot of money."

"I've got a feeling you're worth every penny of it."

Her lips had twitched.

"Can this place get along without you for a few days?"

"Why?"

"I thought we'd go on to Denver or Colorado Springs. Stay in one of those fancy hotels, eat some fine food and dance to some fine music. How'd you like that."

"I think…" Charmaine had picked the money up off the table. "I think I'd like that just fine," she said.

Now John Calhoun was coming back. He wanted the meeting to be at The Chateau and that's where it was going to be. No matter what Carrie said.

"I told you before that just because I'm at The Chateau it doesn't mean that I'm with any of the girls."

"Doesn't it?"

Matt's eyes narrowed in anger. "No, it doesn't." He took a step toward her. "I also told you that there hasn't been anyone but you from the time we made love." His eyes were level with hers. "That's not because I had to, Carrie. Not because of any obligation or a piece of paper that said I should be faithful to you. It's because I wanted to be. I care a great deal for you, but I won't let you or anyone else tell me what I can or cannot do. Is that clear?"

"Quite clear," she said.

"I'll be at The Chateau this weekend. I don't know whether or not I will spend the nights there."

A pain unlike anything Carrie had ever known clutched at her insides. With a smothered gasp she folded her arms across her chest.

"But even if I do," Matt went on, "I won't be with anyone else."

Carrie looked at him. "I don't believe you," she managed to say.

His mouth tightened. He took a deep breath. "I can't help that," he said.

She wanted to strike out at him, to hurt him as he was hurting her. She wanted to cry for a smashed dream. She wanted to beg him not to do this to her.

"Don't do this," she said in a low voice. "Because if you do—"

"Don't threaten me, Carrie. I'm my own man. I do as I please."

She took a step toward him and stopped, her hands at her sides. The anger seeped out of her, leaving her empty, devoid of feeling.

"I can't plead with you," she said quietly. "I don't know how."

"Carrie..." He reached out for her, but she stepped back, away from him.

"No," she said. "No." And before he could stop her, she turned and ran out the door.

It was only a little after eleven, but Carrie didn't care that she was supposed to sing. She didn't care about anything. She grabbed her cloak, and, not waiting for Worthy Magee, left the Golden Nugget and hurried down Myers Avenue toward home.

A startled Effie opened the door. "You're home early," she said, surprised. "Is anything wrong? Aren't you feeling well?"

"I'm perfectly all right."

"Would you like a cup of tea?"

"No, I would not like a cup of tea."

Effie's chin trembled. "I only meant—"

"I'm sorry." Carrie put her arms around the girl. "I didn't mean to snap at you, Effie. I'm sorry. This hasn't anything to do with you."

"Did something happen at the Golden Nugget? Did some of the men say something bad to you? If they did, Mr. Matt'll fix 'em good."

"No, it isn't anything like that." Carrie forced a smile. "Look," she said, "you don't need to stay. If Sarah is sleeping, I'll walk you home."

But Effie shook her head. "No need to do that. It's just around the corner and it's not late." She hesitated. "Are you sure I can't do anything for you?"

"No, but thank you."

"You look awful upset."

"I guess I am, Effie. But I'll get over it."

Yes, she would get over it and she would get over Matt. It might take all eternity to do it, but she would. By God, she would!

She helped Effie into her coat. She walked her to the door and gave her a hug.

Then she went upstairs to start packing.

Chapter Eighteen

"You're running away!" Hands on her hips, Charmaine glared at Carrie.

"You bet I am." Carrie opened a dresser drawer and, taking underclothes out, began stacking them on the bed.

"Why?"

"I think you know why."

"Because Matt's going to be at The Chateau this weekend."

"That's right." Carrie opened the wardrobe and frowned at the clothes hanging there.

"It's business," Charmaine said.

"Sure it is."

"Dammit, Carrie, will you listen to me?"

"I'll listen, but it's not going to change anything."

"A lot of businessmen hold their meetings at my place. They can let their hair down there, drink and gamble and raise a little hell after the business part of it is through. It doesn't necessarily mean they take advantage of everything The Chateau has to offer."

"Really." Carrie started folding her petticoats.

"It doesn't mean they're going to hire a girl for the evening."

"Doesn't it?" Carrie turned and faced the other woman. "But they will, won't they?"

"Some of them."

"And you'll make a lot of money."

"I hope so." Charmaine frowned. "It's my business, Carrie. I run a parlor house. It's how my girls and I make our living."

"I'm sure you like what you do."

"Not always."

"But it's easy, isn't it? Easier than actually working for a living."

"Easy?" Charmaine shook her head. "No, Carrie, it isn't easy. My place is better than most because my girls are like family, maybe because we're the only family most of us have got. Sure there are times when the men are nice and we're having a party and there's drinking and dancing and we're all having fun. But there are other times, like Christmas Eve, when regular people are with their families gathered around under a Christmas tree, and Christmas morning, when their kids are sitting there in their nightshirts, opening presents."

Carrie paused from what she was doing and looked at Charmaine.

"Some of the time it's a hard and bitter life," Charmaine said. "Once in a while it's dangerous." She sat down on the bed and looped her arm around one of the bedposts. "Cripple Creek is a boomtown, Carrie, and we get all kinds here. I'm careful about my clientele, a hell of a lot more than any of the other madams on the street, but once in a while a real bad apple slips by me. A couple of years ago one of the miners started beating on Dorrie. Before Miss Binty and I could get to him he'd split her lip and broken her jaw. She was in bed for a week and it was two months before Doc Taylor let her go back to work.

"Carry Nation claims Cripple Creek is the most lawless and wicked city to be found anywhere and maybe she's right. Lord knows we've got our share of drunks and sharpshooters, swindlers and crooks. We've even got our share of opium dens.''

"Opium dens!'' For a moment Carrie was so startled she forgot to be angry.

"It's a hard life, Carrie, and I guess there're times when a girl wants to forget and go off into some kind of lovely dream. Last week a girl in one of the cribs died from taking an overdose of morphine. A couple of months ago one of the dance-hall girls sniffed up too much chloroform.'' Charmaine shook her head. "So no, it isn't an easy life. But it's the only life some of these girls know. I make it as easy as I can for the ones who work for me, but I'm a businesswoman. I have to make money.''

"Do you ever...?'' Carrie hesitated. She didn't want to ask the question that had been bothering her for a long time, but now she took a deep breath and made herself ask, "Do you take care of any of the customers?''

"When I want to. But if you're wondering if Matt has ever been a customer of mine, the answer is no. Matt comes to The Chateau to drink and play poker, but he takes his other pleasures somewhere else.'' She looked squarely at Carrie. "And I don't think there's been a somewhere else since the day he met you.''

Carrie wanted to believe it. But even if she did, it really didn't change anything. The real issue between them was that Matt wanted to be free, that the very thought of making a commitment sent him running for the hills.

That was not the way it was for her. She wanted to belong to him, to be heart and soul a part of him. She wanted to be his life's partner, his wife. If that wasn't what he wanted then they had no future together.

"Talk to him," Charmaine said.

"We've already talked."

"You're not going back to the Golden Nugget?"

"No."

"You're going home then? Back to Ohio?"

"Just as soon as I can make the arrangements." She looked at Charmaine. "I don't belong here," she said. "I never did."

"Maybe not. But for a while there you seemed to be fitting in. What with your singing at the Golden Nugget, half the men in Cripple Creek are in love with you." Charmaine looked thoughtful. "I've been wondering about that. I think maybe it's because you're different. You're the kind of woman men dream about, the kind they marry."

"Not all men," Carrie said bitterly. "Not Matt Craddock."

"Maybe he doesn't know what he wants. Maybe if you gave him a little more time—"

"I've run out of time," Carrie said. "I'm going home."

And there was nothing Charmaine could say to dissuade her.

There was nothing Effie could say, either.

"But you're my best friend," Effie wept when Carrie told her she was leaving. "What'll I do without you?"

"We'll always be friends, Effie. And you have Noah. You love each other and I can leave knowing you're going to have a happy life with him. I'll miss you, but this is something I have to do. I came to Cripple Creek because of Rosalinda, but Rosalinda is dead. This isn't my home, it can never be my home."

"But what about Mr. Matt? I thought you and him...I thought there was something real special between the two of you."

"There isn't."

And there never can be, Carrie thought. That's over. Finished. There was a train leaving Sunday afternoon and she and Sarah would be on it.

Sarah was another problem. When Carrie told her that they were leaving to go back to Ohio, Sarah stared up at her, puzzled, disbelieving.

"We're going away?" she asked.

"Yes, dear. This Sunday."

"But I don't want to go."

"I know, darling, but—"

"I won't go! I won't, and you can't make me!"

To Carrie's complete amazement, her sunny, adorable little niece suddenly turned into a three-foot ball of fury. She stamped her feet and howled like a banshee. She lay on the floor, her small face distorted with tears and anger, kicking, screeching at the top of her lungs, "I won't go! I won't go!"

With no idea how of how to handle the angry child, Carrie simply left the room and went to sit in the rocking chair by the fire in the kitchen.

The screeching stopped, the sobs subsided, and in a little while a silent Sarah came to stand in the kitchen doorway, her head down, her small body trembling with reaction.

"Come here," Carrie said.

Sarah sniffed, but slowly, reluctantly, she moved closer to Carrie.

Without a word Carrie picked the little girl up and drew her into her lap and began to rock her. "It's going to be all right," she said, as much to herself as to the child. "You'll like Ohio, Sarah. It's where your mother and I grew up. The town we lived in is a pretty place with lots of flowers and trees and nice houses. The home where Rosie and I were raised is gone, but you and I will buy another house. We'll settle in and pretty soon you'll go to school and make lots of new friends."

"What about Effie? Can she come with us?"

"No, darling. Effie will stay here with Noah. But one of these days, maybe even next summer, she and Noah will come for a visit."

"And Uncle Matt? Can he come, too?"

Carrie tightened her arms around Sarah. It was a moment before she was able to answer. "I don't think so, honey. Uncle Matt is busy with so many things. He has lots of businesses and the gold mine and—"

"Won't I ever see him again?"

"I don't know, Sarah."

"I love Uncle Matt."

"I know you do, baby."

"Aunt Carrie..." Sarah toyed with the buttons of Carrie's shirtwaist. "Would it be all right, I mean since my real mama's gone, would it be all right if sometimes I called you mama?"

For a moment Carrie couldn't speak. Then she kissed the top of Sarah's head, and, trying to hold back the threatening tears, whispered, "Yes, darling. Of course you can. I'd like that very much, Sarah. Very much."

Sarah snuggled closer while Carrie continued to rock her. And not until Sarah went to sleep did Carrie allow the tears to flow.

Carrie booked two seats on the train leaving Cripple Creek on Sunday afternoon.

Matt came to the house on Friday. When Sarah saw him, she flew into his arms, hugging his neck and crying, "We're going away, Uncle Matt. Did you know? We're going all the way to Ohio."

He looked over her shoulder at Carrie. "It's definite then?"

"Yes." She turned away, afraid to meet his eyes. "I thought you'd be at The Chateau today."

"Calhoun doesn't get in until tonight. I'll see him tomorrow." He put Sarah down. "You're making a mistake," he said to Carrie. "Just because we've had a little misunderstanding—"

"A little misunderstanding?" Carrie shook her head. "There isn't any misunderstanding, Matt. We're different people, that's all. You belong here. I never did and I never will. I'm going back where I belong. I'm going home."

Matt wanted to ask her to stay. He wanted to take her in his arms and keep her there. He wanted to ease the tight line of her mouth, the stubborn lift of her chin. He wanted to see her look at him the way she had the last time they had kissed.

But he knew that she wouldn't stay, not unless he became what she wanted him to be. And he wouldn't do that. He was a gambling man, a man who chose his own path. A man who had never let anyone, especially a woman, tell him what to do. As much as he wanted her to stay, he would not yield.

"I've come to say goodbye," he said.

"I'm glad you did." Her voice was coolly pleasant. "For Sarah's sake, I mean."

"I know what you mean." He looked down at Sarah. "How would you and your Aunt Carrie like to go for a ride in my rig?"

"I call her Mama now." Sarah reached for his hand, looked up at Carrie and asked, "Can we go for a ride with Uncle Matt, Mama? Can we, please?"

"I don't think we should, Sarah. We have a lot of things we need to do before Sunday."

Sunday. She was leaving on Sunday. Without thinking, Matt tightened his grip on Sarah's hand.

"Please," Sarah begged. Her chin trembled. "Please, Mama!"

Carrie looked at the child, then at Matt. This would be the last time she would see him. The thought of it cut into her like a knife, and a moment passed before she could find her voice.

"All right," she said. "Sarah, go get your hat and coat," and to Matt, she said, "I'll only be a minute."

But it took her more than a minute to try to regain her composure. She smoothed her hair, and, picking up the gray hat she'd first worn to Cripple Creek, she looked at herself in the mirror. Her eyes were more gray than blue, and her face seemed pallid and weary. A sob rose in her throat, but she held it back, and, taking the old gray cloak out of the wardrobe, went down to meet Matt.

Matt lifted Sarah up into the rig, then helped Carrie up, holding her hand a moment longer than necessary, reluctant to let it go.

The day was warm and though they might very well have another cold spell, for now at least it was a day to

enjoy. Without conscious thought Matt took the road
that led out to the mine, the road he and Carrie had
taken that other spring day.

The trees were more fully in bud than they had been
that day. The fresh new leaves of the quaking aspen
stirred in the gentle breeze. The fields were alive with
color, the blue and red of the columbine, the yellow of
daisies, the purple of thistles.

The Sangre de Cristo mountain peaks were still covered with snow, but the slopes of the nearer hills were
green with cedar and ponderosa pine. After the winter
snows the land had come alive again. It was a flower-
ing time, a new beginning.

But for Carrie it was an ending, a last goodbye to this
place that for a little while had been her home.

She stole a glance at Matt. He looked pensive. Sarah
linked her arm through his, and when she looked up at
him, he smiled. "I'm going to miss you, kitten," he
said.

"I'll miss you, too, Uncle Matt." She sniffled and
buried her face against his sleeve.

He slowed the rig. "Look," he whispered. "Sarah,
look."

A young doe hesitated just at the edge of the trees, its
soft tan face lifted, its dark liquid eyes frightened, yet
curious.

"Oh," Sarah said softly. "Oh, look at that. It's a little deer." She leaned forward and held her hand out.
"Here, deer," she called. "Here, little deer."

The animal's ears perked up. It took a step forward,
then with a start, turned and ran back into the trees.

Sarah, her eyes wide with wonder, leaned against
Matt's arm. "That's the prettiest thing I ever saw," she

whispered. Then she looked at Carrie and asked, "Do they have deers in Ohio?"

"Yes, of course."

"I bet they're not as nice as they are here." She cuddled closer to Matt and he put his arm around her.

"Sure they are," Matt said. "They've got all kinds of deer in Ohio." He flicked the reins across his horse's back. "It's a nice place, Sarah. I bet you're going to love it."

"But it won't be like here." She looked at Carrie, her bottom lip at half-mast. "I don't want to go," she said.

They rode for a way without speaking, each of them with their own troubled thoughts. Carrie wished she hadn't come. It was too difficult, being with Matt like this, knowing that their time together was almost over. On Sunday afternoon she and Sarah would board the train for Denver, and from there back to Ohio. She'd never see Matt again.

She looked away, out across the spring fields, her eyes blinded by tears. Oh, Matt, her heart cried. If only you were different, if only I could change the way I feel about things.

But she could not. She could not live in sin with Matt. Her father, although he had been a cruel and fanatical man, had been right about some things. When the Reverend Mr. Barnside married Effie and Noah, he had quoted the words, "And you shall cleave one to another for as long as ye both shall live."

As long as ye both shall live. That's what she believed in. She could not change.

Carrie was so preoccupied with her own thoughts that she was not aware that they had been climbing or that Matt had stopped the rig until Sarah asked, "How come we're stopping, Uncle Matt?"

"I just want to give the horse a rest, honey." He looked at Carrie. "And this is a special place."

Carrie looked up to where the ponderosa pines with their cathedrallike spires surrounded the field of columbine and yellow clover. This was where they had had the picnic, here under the trees. This was where they had made love. Matt had held her and touched her here. She had felt the warm earth beneath her back. And she had thought she would die with loving him.

Matt saw her tears. He wanted to take her hand, but he did not. He wasn't sure why he had brought her here, but he knew that once she left, he would never come to this place again. He looked at the tall trees and the meadow grass, and he remembered the touch of her skin against his as she lay beneath him. He remembered how she had lifted her body to his and cried his name in that final moment. He knew he would never again feel for a woman what he had felt for Carrie that afternoon.

She was going to leave, and though there was a part of him that wanted to get down on bended knee and beg her not to, there was that other part of him, the proud, go-to-hell part of him that would not bend or yield.

"Giddap," he said to the horse, and turning the rig, he headed back toward town.

Sarah was asleep by the time they reached Cripple Creek. Matt stopped in front of Carrie's house, and when he had jumped down, he reached up and took the child from Carrie. He carried Sarah inside and placed her gently on the sofa. "I won't wake her," he said.

"But she'd want to say goodbye to you."

He shook his head. "No, it's better this way. I'm afraid she'd cry and I don't think I could stand that."

He touched Sarah's cheek. "I'm going to miss her," he said.

"She loves you."

We both love you, she wanted to say. But didn't.

She went with him to the door. She held out her hand. "Thank you for taking us riding today, Matt. Thank you for so many things. For—"

Matt held up his hand, stopping her. "No!" he said harshly. "Don't thank me. I don't want your thanks. I want..." He clenched his fists so tightly his knuckles turned white. "Dammit," he exploded, "you know what I want."

"Matt, please."

He grasped her shoulders. "Why are you doing this? Just because I'm spending the weekend at The Chateau? I told you I wouldn't be with anybody else. There couldn't be anybody else for me. Don't you know that, Carrie?" He shook her. "Don't you know how I feel about you?"

"It isn't just because of The Chateau," she said, fighting for control. "There are other things, too. We're different people, Matt. We believe in different things."

"But if you care about me."

"I care," she said. "Oh, yes, I care." She rested her head against his chest. For a moment, only a moment. For one last time.

"Goodbye," she whispered. "Goodbye, Matt."

"I won't let you go."

"Yes, you will." She looked up at him. "Yes, you will, Matt."

"Carrie!" He drew her into his arms and kissed her, kissed her with all of his pent-up anger and longing, with frustration because he didn't understand, because he wanted her, and because he would not pay the price it would take to keep her here.

Her lips were cool and sweet under his, but the passion was gone and he knew that he had lost.

He let her go. "Do you want me to take you to the train?" he asked, his voice controlled, expressionless.

"No." She stepped away from him. "Effie and Noah will take us. Besides, you'll be busy at The Chateau."

He clenched his jaw and a muscle twitched under the pressure. "Yes, I forgot."

Carrie again held out her hand. "Goodbye, Matt. God bless."

He took a step toward her. "Carrie...?"

"No," she whispered.

For one moment more he looked at her, looked deeply into her gray-blue eyes, then, without a word, he turned away.

Carrie closed the door behind him and leaned against it, hands over her eyes, tears seeping through her fingers as she whispered his name in an agony of grief unlike any she had ever known.

Finally she went into the parlor and sat on the floor next to the sofa beside the sleeping child.

Chapter Nineteen

The sky was gray, the air cold. Carrie fastened Sarah's coat, then her own. Taking Sarah's hand, she went out the door and did not look back.

Noah, who had already put her trunk and suitcase into the carriage, waited at the curb.

"You all set?" he asked Carrie.

"Yes." She took his proffered hand to let him help her up. "Thank you, Noah," she said. "And thank you for taking us to the station."

"That's all right, Miss Carrie. I'm glad to do it." He lifted Sarah into her outstretched arms. "I mean I'm glad to help, but I sure wish you weren't leaving. The town's just not going to be the same without you."

"Nothing will be the same," Effie said sadly, holding a handkerchief to her eyes.

"You and Noah are coming to Ohio next summer," Carrie said quickly. If Effie started to cry, then Sarah would surely join in. She didn't think she could stand that.

The little girl had been unusually quiet this morning. She hadn't fidgeted like she usually did when Carrie dressed her, but had stood passive, her eyes lowered. Now, clutching Mary Agnes in her arms, her lower lip stuck out in a pout, she looked as though any moment she would burst into tears.

"I guess we're ready." Noah flicked the reins over the horses' backs. "Get along now," he said.

Carrie looked straight ahead all the way down Second Street. When they reached Bennett Avenue she didn't even glance at the bakeshop or the meat market, the One Price Shoes and Clothing House or the livery stable. But when they passed the general store, she turned her head for one last look.

Yesterday when she had stopped in to tell Mr. Davenport she was leaving, he had said, "I surely do hate to see you go, Miss McClennon. You and that little girl brighten up the store every time you come in. I'm going to miss you."

He'd taken half a dozen licorice sticks out of the candy case and put them in a paper bag. "Never did see a child so fond of licorice as she is," he said. "You give her these to eat on the train."

When she had left Mr. Davenport's store, Carrie had sent a messenger with a note to Charmaine, thanking her for her kindness in having taken Rosalinda and Sarah in, and for taking care of her when she was ill. "Say goodbye to the girls for me," she had written. "I'll always remember their kindness, and yours."

It was almost over. She had been here less than six months, yet so much in her life had changed. She was not the woman she had been when she left Ohio. Love had softened and tempered her, it had made her see so many things through different eyes. She had learned that everything was not just black and white, good or evil, that there were as many varied shadings of that concept as there were people. Her best friend had been a prostitute, she herself had been a saloon singer. And she had loved a gambling man.

She would never forget Matthew Craddock, for though she could not accept his kind of life, he would always and forever be a part of her.

"Something's burning," Effie said, breaking in on Carrie's thoughts.

"Some kids with a bonfire." Noah chucked to the horses. "Or maybe a farmer burning grass."

"Maybe." Effie sniffed. "Seems to me it's getting worse every minute."

"If it's more than a bonfire or burning grass the fire department fellas will put it out. They hardly ever get a call to do anything. Do 'em good to get routed out on a Sunday. They—"

Suddenly, the horses reared. Ears back, they tried to stop, jerking from side to side, whinnying, snorting, eyes wide and rolling.

"Whoa!" Noah tightened his hands on the reins. "Whoa, there!"

"What is it?" Effie asked. "What's the matter with them?"

"I don't know, hon. Dern horses got a mind of their own. Don't you worry, Carrie. We'll get you and Sarah to the station on time."

"I'm not worried," Carrie said. "I—"

A sudden clanging of the fire wagon bells interrupted her words, and Noah, still keeping a tight grip on the horses, looked back over his shoulder.

"Oh, Lord!" he cried. "Lord a'mighty. Look at that!"

"What? What is it?" Effie turned to look behind them at the same moment Carrie did.

"Oh, my God!" Carrie clutched at the seat in front of her. "It looks like the whole town is on fire!"

Noah snapped the reins across the horses' backs. "We'd best get you and Sarah to the station, Miss Carrie," he said nervously. "We might have some trouble getting back if those fire wagons are blocking the streets."

From the town, behind them, they could hear the clatter of the fire wagons. Then the bell of the First Methodist Church started to ring. People on the street turned to stare back at the town. Two men on horseback smacked their mounts and headed back toward Bennett Avenue.

Noah galloped the horses into the station. The conductors and the porters stood beside the train looking puzzled and curious.

"Train leaves in ten minutes." Noah hopped down out of the buggy. "You'd best get aboard, Miss Carrie. I'll just get your trunk down..." He stopped as a rig raced up beside him and a man jumped out. "You just come from town?" Noah asked.

"Yeah." The man took a handkerchief out of his pocket and wiped his face. "Damnedest thing I ever saw," he said, shaking his head.

"Fire bad?"

"Worse than bad, man. It's burning faster'n the fire boys can handle it."

"Where is it?"

"Myers Avenue mostly. Looks like every one of those houses are going to go."

The Chateau was on Myers Avenue. Matt was there with the Eastern businessmen. What if the Chateau...? "My God," Carrie said. "The Chateau!"

Noah's face paled. "I gotta get back there, Miss Carrie." He swung down from the carriage and started to take her trunk down, but she stopped him.

"Matt's there," she said. "And Charmaine and the girls."

"Yes'm, I know."

"I've got to go back."

"But the train's going to be leaving in a few minutes. You can't—"

"Noah, please!" She looked at Effie. "You'll take Sarah back home with you, won't you?"

"Of course I will." Effie's face went pale. She clutched the side of the rig. "But if the fire's bad I don't think either you or Noah ought to go anywhere near it."

Noah climbed back up into the carriage and Effie grabbed his arm. "Don't go," she implored him. "It might be dangerous."

"I gotta go. I gotta see how I can help." He gripped Effie's hand. "I'll get as close as I can to Myers Avenue. Then you can take the carriage and head for home as fast as you can."

Sarah began to cry. Hugging Mary Agnes, she wept, "I'm scared, Mama. I'm scared."

Carrie pulled her close. "It's going to be all right, sweetheart. I want you to be a good girl and go along with Effie."

"You come, too, Mama." The little girl clung to Carrie. "Don't leave me," she pleaded. "Don't leave me."

Carrie hugged her. "I have to," she said. "I have to find Uncle Matt."

The billowing smoke grew thicker. Bells clanged and church bells rang. Horse and buggies careened around corners. Townspeople, searching for loved ones called out to one another. A fire wagon, pulled by a six-horse team, raced down Bennett Avenue. A milk cart that had started to cross the street tried to get out of the way, but not in time. It overturned, milk cans flying in every direction as the driver jumped free, shaking his fist at the firemen as he scrambled for a foothold.

Noah reined the horses in. "I can't go any farther," he told Effie. "You take the reins now. The horses are real skittish so hold them firm." He shot a look at Carrie. "It's best you go on with Effie and Sarah," he said. "A fire's no place for a woman."

Carrie jumped down from the carriage. "I'm going," she told him. "With or without you." She reached for Sarah's hand. "Sit close to Effie and do whatever she tells you to do," she said. "I'll come back just as soon as I can."

"I'm afraid." Sarah coughed and covered her face with her hands. "Please don't go, Mama," she cried.

"I have to, baby. But I'll be back. I promise you, Sarah."

Noah jumped down beside her. "Get going," he told Effie. "Keep a tight rein and don't stop for nothing."

Effie bit down hard on her lower lip, then with a "Giddap!" she slapped the reins across the horses' backs.

Noah took Carrie's arm. "Come on," he said, and together they ran toward the tenderloin district.

The smoke grew thicker the closer they got to the fire. When they started down Myers Avenue they saw that the flimsy wooden structures that housed the cribs there were ablaze. The girls were on the street, huddled together, weeping, clutching shawls, or pillowcases filled with their belongings.

Farther down the street they saw the other houses burning.

"Lookit there." Noah stopped, his mouth agape. "It's Laura Bell's."

Flames shot up from the roof of the two-story wooden structure. A fire brigade tried in vain to aim water at the burning house, but as Carrie and Noah watched there was a terrible explosion. The fire crackled, and then, the roof caved in.

Women screamed. Somebody yelled, "Oh, my God, the girls! Were there girls still in there?"

Women lined the street, frantic, weeping, some wearing only kimonos or wrappers, some with shawls over their shoulders. The street was filled with smoke and confusion.

It was hard to breathe. Tears streamed down Carrie's face, partly from the smoke, partly from the shock of the scene around her.

Noah ripped off the kerchief from around his neck and handed it to her. "Cover your face," he yelled above the chaos.

Ahead of them they could see The Harem and Nelly Grady's. Both houses were on fire.

"You oughta go back," Noah said.

Carrie shook her head and followed him on down Myers Avenue toward The Chateau. They drew closer. "Oh, God!" she cried. "Noah, look!"

The house was ablaze, flames shooting out of the upstairs windows, curtains burning, sparks flying up to the roof.

"Lord a'mighty!" Noah ran forward, Carrie after him.

Firemen battled the blaze, their faces black from the smoke, cursing, sweating, shouting orders.

Frantic with fear for Matt, Carrie looked among the throng of people, trying to find him. She saw Dorrie and Conchita across the street on the grass, arms clasped around each other. She ran toward them just as Miss Binty, helped by a man Carrie had never seen before, came down the front steps of the house. Miss Binty's gray hair was singed, the bottom of her skirt was blackened.

"Get outta here," a fireman yelled at Noah. "You can't go no further."

But Noah pushed ahead, holding on to Carrie's arm, bringing her along with him as they hurried toward Miss Binty.

"Is she all right?" Carrie cried to the man helping her.

"Her legs are burned," the man said. "She needs help."

Noah picked the older woman up and carried her toward the place where Dorrie and Conchita were huddled together.

"She's bad burned," he told them. "If you see Doc Taylor, tell him. Do what you can for her."

Carrie took off her cloak and wrapped it around the older woman. "Have you seen Matt?" she asked. "Have any of you seen Matt?"

"We were upstairs when the fire started," Dorrie said. "He was down in the parlor playing cards." She wiped at the tears running down her soot-streaked face. "I don't know where he is, Miss Carrie." She buried her head in her hands, weeping. "It was awful! It was just awful."

Carrie rested a hand on her shoulder. "I'll be back," she said. "Take care of Miss Binty. She—"

"There's Charmaine!" Noah cried, and Carrie turned to see a man carrying her down the steps of the house. Another man came after them, his arm around Lorelei.

Noah and Carrie ran toward them. "Is she all right?" Noah called out to the man carrying Charmaine.

"She's unconscious." The big man shouldered past Noah and laid Charmaine on the grass. "She ran upstairs trying to get the girls out before we could stop her. She breathed in a lot of smoke." He knelt beside her. "Charmaine," he said. "Come on, honey, breathe for Big John."

"Matt Craddock." Carrie clutched at his arm. "Have you seen Matt Craddock?"

The big man looked up. His eyebrows were singed. Half of his handlebar mustache was burned off. "Last time I saw he was running up the stairs," he said. "Babette was still up there. He went after her—"

There was a thunderous crash behind them as part of the roof caved in. Above the terrible noise they heard a piercing scream.

"It's Babette!" Conchita jumped to her feet, pointing. "There, upstairs!"

Babette was half-out of the window, straddling the sill. The curtains were on fire, her hair was ablaze. Even from here they could see the whiteness of her skin, the frantic look of fear.

"She's going to jump!" Noah started forward, but it was too late. Screaming, Babette went out of the window, her arms flailing at the air.

Carrie looked up, her fist against her mouth. Her eyes went from the falling girl to the figure at the window that reached out for her. But it was too late. Flames engulfed him and Carrie screamed, "Matt! Matt!"

Before Noah or anyone else could stop her, she sprinted toward the house.

A fireman tried to block her way, but she pushed him aside, her only thought to get to Matt.

Carrie ran up the steps into the house, spurred on by her fear.

Half the stairway was engulfed with flames. She touched the banister and gasped in pain, her hand burned by the terrible heat. She went up the stairs, calling out above the crackle of the fire, "Matt! Matt, answer me! Where are you?"

Choking and coughing, her lungs on fire, she rounded the curve of the staircase. The figure of a man rushed down toward her. She reached out to him, crying his name.

He grasped her hands. But it wasn't Matt. It was Nathan LaRue.

She screamed and struggled to free herself. "Let me go!" she cried. "Matt's up there."

"He's dead." LaRue grasped her wrist and tried to pull her down the stairs after him.

"Liar!" Carrie struck out at him, trying to break free of his grasp, hysterical with fear and anger. "Let me go!" she screamed. "Let me go!"

He hit her across the face and she staggered back, stunned, hurt by the blow, almost suffocated by the smoke and the flames that came closer and ever closer.

"Let go of her!"

Matt stood at the top of the stairs, a derringer in his hand, smoke all around him.

"Matt!" Carrie struggled in a frenzy to break free from LaRue.

LaRue brought his gun up and leveled it at Matt's chest.

Carrie hit LaRue's arm with her hand and the gun spun out of his grasp.

"Bitch!" He reached for her. But his hand froze in midair and he looked up, stark terror on his face. Carrie saw, too late, the flaming beam falling toward them. She raised an arm to try to shield herself, as she was enveloped by an inferno of flame and smoke. As though in the distance, she heard LaRue's scream, Matt's cry, and then she was falling, down, down into the fire.

"Fire and brimstone," her father intoned. "Ye who have sinned will burn in eternal hell."

Burn. Oh, no! Oh, God, no! She opened her eyes and tried to cry out. She was surrounded by flames, choked by the terrible fire.

"Carrie!"

She saw Matt coming toward her through the flames. His coat was on fire. He beat it out with his hands, then he reached for her and pulled her into his arms.

"I've got you," he cried against her face. "Hang on, Carrie. Hang on."

He covered her with part of his coat and ran, head down, through one small path in the flames. Carrie fought for breath, but when she tried to breathe, smoke burned her lungs. God help us, she thought, as she slipped into unconsciousness.

Carrie felt the grass, wet beneath her back. A voice called out to her.

She wanted to open her eyes, but it was too much of an effort.

"Carrie, please. Oh, God, Carrie. Carrie-love, please."

Carrie-love. It was Matt. Her eyelids fluttered. She tried to speak, but when she did, she coughed. He held her up. He patted her back. "That's it, Carrie," he said. "Breathe for me, Carrie. Breathe for me because I love you."

I love you. She closed her eyes.

The next time she opened them, she was in bed in a room she had never seen before. It was a big room, twice as large as her bedroom in the house on Second Street. There were blue velvet drapes on the windows, and a thick Indian carpet covered the floor.

"Carrie?"

She turned her head and saw Matt sitting on the bed beside her. "You're here," she said in a voice that didn't sound like hers. Her chest hurt when she breathed, her throat was sore. "You're all right?"

Matt took her hand. "We're both all right, Carrie."

"LaRue?" She struggled to sit up. "He tried to kill you. He—"

"He's dead, Carrie. He died in the fire."

"Why was he there?"

"I'm not sure. John Calhoun saw him just after the fire broke out. He started after him, but then he heard Charmaine scream and went to help her."

"Charmaine? Is she all right?"

"She will be. John took her to Denver. She's in the hospital there and he's with her."

"The other girls? Miss Binty?"

"Doc Taylor's taking care of her. Dorrie's hands were burned, but she's going to be all right. Conchita and Lorelei are fine."

"Babette? What happened to...?" Then she remembered, the fire, the flaming window. Her eyes flooded with tears. "She's with her little boy," she said quietly. "She's with Timmie."

"Yes, dear."

"What happened, Matt? What started the fire?"

"Nobody really knows for sure, Carrie. Somebody said it started in one of the dance halls." He shook his head. "Over fifteen acres of the town have been leveled, people are without homes. Half of Bennett Avenue is gone."

"Sarah?" She struggled to sit up. "Is Sarah all right?"

"She's with Effie and Noah, Carrie. The street they live on was saved, none of the houses burned there. Neither did mine."

"That's where I am? At your house?"

"In my bed," Matt said with a grin. "And this is where you're going to stay until you're well enough to go downstairs for the wedding."

"The wedding?" Her eyes widened. "Who's getting married?"

"You are, Carrie-love. To me."

"Oh," she said.

"Any argument?"

She smiled. "No, Matthew."

He touched the side of her face and suddenly, unbidden, felt the sting of tears behind his eyelids. He thought of the terror of that moment when the beam that killed Nathan LaRue fell. He saw again the flames that had engulfed Carrie. He heard her piercing scream. He relived his own near madness when he raced through the flames to get to her.

He knew how close he had come to losing her.

With a smothered groan, ashamed of all that he was feeling, he covered his eyes with his hands.

"Matt?" she said. When she took his hand away, she saw the tears. "Darling," she whispered. "Oh, darling."

"I thought I'd lost you."

"I know, Matt."

"Don't ever leave me," he said.

"I won't."

He took a quivering breath and tried to smile. "How do you feel about marrying a gambling man, Miss Carrie?"

A gambling man. She put her arms around him. "I feel just fine about it," she said. "I feel just purely fine."

Epilogue

For the first time in its rambunctious history, the town of Cripple Creek, Colorado, was united. Before the ashes cooled, the folks there began to rebuild.

The homeless were sheltered in tent cities. Residents from the tenderloin, along with the hard-rock miners, saloon keepers, gamblers and two-fisted drinkers, all turned out to help rebuild the shops and homes on the other side of town. The more respectable folks worked right alongside of them, some even took in the unfortunate girls from the parlor houses.

Shacks were thrown up to serve the thirsty miners, and within a few weeks all the establishments along Myers Avenue were back in business.

On a sunny afternoon in May, Carrie McClennon and Matthew Artemius Craddock were united in marriage by the Reverend Hubert Barnside. A slightly pregnant Mrs. Noah Pierce was the matron of honor, and Miss Sarah Craddock, who had only a week before been legally adopted by Matt, acted as flower girl.

Lorelei Blue, Dorrie O'Keefe, and Conchita Sanchez were the attendants.

Charmaine, still recovering from the effects of the fire, sat in the front row between Big John Calhoun and

Miss Binty. With the possible exception of Mrs. Elvira Primrose, everybody in Cripple Creek attended the wedding.

"Do you take this woman for your wedded wife?" the Reverend Mr. Barnside asked the groom.

"I do," Matt said, looking into Carrie's eyes. "I do."

"And do you, Carrie, take this man unto your husband?"

"I do," she whispered, lost in his gaze.

"Then in the presence of God and these assembled I pronounce you man and wife."

Matt lifted her gossamer veil. "Carrie-love," he said.

And it was done.

*   *   *   *   *

Harlequin®
Historical

HISTORY IN THE MAKING!

Join Harlequin Historicals as we celebrate our 5th anniversary of exciting historical romance stories! Watch for our 5th anniversary promotion in July. And in addition, to mark this special occasion, we have another year full of great reading.

- A 1993 March Madness promotion with titles by promising newcomers Laurel Ames, Mary McBride, Susan Amarillas and Claire Delacroix.

- The July release of UNTAMED!—a Western Historical short story collection by award-winning authors Heather Graham Pozzessere, Joan Johnston and Patricia Potter.

- In-book series by Maura Seger, Julie Tetel, Margaret Moore and Suzanne Barclay.

- And in November, keep an eye out for next year's *Harlequin Historical Christmas Stories* collection, featuring Marianne Willman, Curtiss Ann Matlock and Victoria Pade.

Watch for details on our Anniversary events wherever Harlequin Historicals are sold.

HARLEQUIN HISTORICALS . . .
A touch of magic!

HH5TH

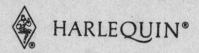 HARLEQUIN®

THE TAGGARTS OF TEXAS!

Harlequin's Ruth Jean Dale brings you
THE TAGGARTS OF TEXAS!

Those Taggart men—strong, sexy and hard to resist...

You've met Jesse James Taggart in FIREWORKS!
Harlequin Romance #3205 (July 1992)

And Trey Smith—he's THE RED-BLOODED YANKEE!
Harlequin Temptation #413 (October 1992)

Now meet Daniel Boone Taggart in SHOWDOWN!
Harlequin Romance #3242 (January 1993)

And finally the Taggarts who started it all—in LEGEND!
Harlequin Historical #168 (April 1993)

Read all the Taggart romances!
Meet all the Taggart men!

Available wherever Harlequin Books are sold.

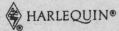

HARLEQUIN®

my Valentine

1993

The most romantic day of the year is here! Escape into the exquisite world of love with MY VALENTINE 1993. What better way to celebrate Valentine's Day than with this very romantic, sensuous collection of four original short stories, written by some of Harlequin's most popular authors.

**ANNE STUART
JUDITH ARNOLD
ANNE McALLISTER
LINDA RANDALL WISDOM**

**THIS VALENTINE'S DAY, DISCOVER ROMANCE
WITH MY VALENTINE 1993**

Available in February wherever Harlequin Books are sold.   VAL93

Harlequin
Historical

THREE
UNFORGETTABLE
KNIGHTS

First there was Ruarke, born leader and renowned warrior, who faced
an altogether different field of battle when he took a willful wife in
Knight Dreams (Harlequin Historicals #141, a September 1992 release).
Now, brooding widower and heir Gareth must choose between family
duty and the only true love he's ever known in *Knight's Lady* (Harlequin
Historicals #162, a February 1993 release). And coming later in 1993,
Alexander, bold adventurer and breaker of many a maiden's heart,
meets the one woman he can't lay claim to in *Knight's Honor,* the
dramatic conclusion of Suzanne Barclay's Sommerville Brothers trilogy.

If you're in need of a champion, let Harlequin Historicals take you back
to the days when a knight in shining armor wasn't just a fantasy. Sir
Ruarke, Sir Gareth and Sir Alex won't disappoint you!

IN FEBRUARY LOOK
FOR *KNIGHT'S LADY*
AVAILABLE WHEREVER
HARLEQUIN BOOKS ARE SOLD

ROMANCE IS A YEARLONG EVENT!

Celebrate the most romantic day of the year with MY VALENTINE! (February)

CRYSTAL CREEK
When you come for a visit Texas-style, you won't want to leave! (March)

Celebrate the joy, excitement and adjustment that comes with being JUST MARRIED! (April)

Go back in time and discover the West as it was meant to be . . . UNTAMED—Maverick Hearts! (July)

LINGERING SHADOWS
New York Times bestselling author Penny Jordan brings you her latest blockbuster. Don't miss it! (August)

BACK BY POPULAR DEMAND!!!
Calloway Corners, involving stories of four sisters coping with family, business and romance! (September)

FRIENDS, FAMILIES, LOVERS
Join us for these heartwarming love stories that evoke memories of family and friends. (October)

Capture the magic and romance of Christmas past with HARLEQUIN HISTORICAL CHRISTMAS STORIES! (November)

WATCH FOR FURTHER DETAILS IN ALL HARLEQUIN BOOKS!

CALEND